A
MURMURATION
OF STARLINGS

A
MURMURATION
OF STARLINGS

By
Mark Hobson

INSPIRED BY REAL EVENTS

PART 1

THE
WIDOWMAKER

1

TEMPLEPATRICK, NORTHERN IRELAND
1974

CROUCHING LOW BEHIND THE DRYSTONE wall, Liam Brennan, just turned seventeen a month earlier, gripped the Armalite semi-automatic tightly in his hands, its metal stock cold against his cheek.

He briefly closed his eyes and tried to control his breathing. He considered whether to utter a quiet prayer remembered from his childhood, but instead, images of his mother and his younger brothers and sisters crowded his mind. He wondered what they were doing right now and Liam found himself longing to be with them.

He stirred as his legs started to cramp from his uncomfortable posture, the cold seeping into his bones.

Liam opened his eyes. In the darkness, he caught a flash of white teeth as the man alongside him grinned and gave him a wink.

Liam tried to smile back, but his lips were dry and his throat parched and he turned his face away to hide his unease.

It was a mid-November evening at a little after seven. A dense fog clung to the damp earth of the field they waited in, its tendrils curling promiscuously through the bare branches of the lone tree by the roadside. The grey miasma provided them with the perfect cover.

The leader of their eight-man cell, Colm Lynch, had planned everything down to the smallest detail. Their target, a white Ford Transit van, should be coming by in just a few minutes. Inside were a bunch of local labourers, traitors all, who had been helping the Brits construct another of their fortified checkpoints on the outskirts of the village. It mattered not if they were Protestants or Catholics, Liam told himself. Their fate had already been decided by the Brigade Commander.

For nearly a week now, Liam and his companions had watched the workmen, learning their routines, their daily comings and goings. It was quickly decided that this spot was the best location to carry out the oppo, the ambush.

Each evening after knocking off at five, the gaffer would drive himself and his builder mates away from the steel checkpoint to the nearest pub in Templepatrick, The Store Bar. There, they would have two or three rounds of ale before setting off at seven in the evening, their route taking them south away from the village towards their homes in Armagh. Tonight, they wouldn't make it. Liam, armed with his Armalite, together with his small bunch of pals, would force them to a stop just the other side of the wall and while Liam stood guard, watching the roadway, the others would haul the builders out of the van and do the business. Then, when it was done, they would leave their bullet-riddled corpses lying in the road as a warning to others and dash over the field to where Danny O'Shea was waiting in a stolen Morris Marina. They would make good their escape by driving for the border, and all trace of them would disappear forever in the twisting, foggy lanes of Bandit Country.

Liam pulled back the sleeve of the boiler suit he was wearing and peered at his digital wristwatch. A present from his mother, its red numbers glowed brightly, so he quickly covered it up again, hoping nobody had noticed. Colm was a good leader, almost a father figure to Liam, but he had a crazy temper on him. He wouldn't hesitate to dish out a good thrashing should he think their ambush might be compromised.

Liam was the first to admit that he still had much to learn. Joining the Provisionals, much against his mother's wishes, had proven easy enough. Their recruiters were on the lookout for new volunteers to take up the cause, especially after the British Army had slaughtered those protesters in '72. The difficult part was adjusting to his new life: the constant indoctrination, his companions' hatred of the British drilled into him day and night, demanding more and more proof of his dedication. How far was he prepared to go? Would he follow orders without question? Was he prepared to die to see the dream of a reunited Ireland become a reality?

The first test had come just over a week ago.

Colm Lynch, who claimed that he could trace his Gaelic ancestry right back to Mael Sechnaill the Second, had wanted him to join a group of volunteers tasked with an important job. They were to pay a visit to a man thought to have loyalist leanings. In his naivety, Liam had assumed this meant calling around at the individual's house and perhaps setting him straight, maybe giving him a slap but nothing more.

But when they had arrived at the rundown terrace house in West Belfast, Lynch had instructed them all to place black balaclavas over their heads and to kick the door in. Then the older men had stormed inside so Liam, after a few seconds of hesitation, reluctantly followed.

He had been greeted with a scene of chaos. The man in question was grappling with the intruders whilst his wife and two young girls, interrupted from watching an episode of *It Ain't Half Hot Mum,* were screaming merry hell. But their hysterical pleadings fell on deaf ears. As his family watched, the husband was violently frogmarched from his home out onto the street.

The wife had run after them, her high-pitched cries echoing up and down the road.

Liam had expected the neighbours to come to their doorsteps to see what the racket was about and perhaps to intervene. Instead, he watched as curtains up and down the row of houses were hurriedly drawn shut. In the house next door, the volume button on a radio was turned up.

Standing on the pavement, Liam watched through the eye holes in his balaclava as the man was forced down onto the ground in the middle of the roadway. Then Colm Lynch had produced a gun from somewhere, an old revolver that looked like it dated from the War.

Liam learned later that what they did to him, the man's punishment for once sharing a cigarette at work with a Protestant, was called an IRA Six-Pack - kneecapping. Sometimes they used a Black & Decker power drill on a victim's knees, but outside in the open, that wasn't possible, so Colm Lynch carried out the punishment with his gun.

Two bullets to the elbows, two to the knees and two to the chest, the intent being not to kill him but to ensure that he spent the remainder of his miserable life in a wheelchair.

Witnessing the terrible sight of their victim twitching and blubbering on the road had palsied Liam's limbs so that when the others turned to flee, he'd found himself unable to follow. Someone had grabbed his arm and steered him away as gruff laughter rang out in the dark.

●　　　　　　●　　　　　　●

Waiting at the edge of the field on a cold and misty night, the memory made Liam's breath falter and threatened to derail his thoughts.

He needed to stay focused. If he became distracted or allowed the tiniest fraction of uncertainty to taint his commitment, then things could quickly unravel and go wrong. The very idea of letting the others down, especially their leader, was a prospect he would find more difficult to live with than any nightmares which might visit him in the dead of night. Loyalty was everything to them. These people with him tonight were just as much a family to him as his mam and brothers and sisters.

Just then, the faint rumble of an approaching engine reached them. A grinding of gears as the driver manoeuvered around the narrow country lanes.

Bang on time.

The van driver, together with his mates, would be bleary with beer, maybe cracking dirty jokes to each other. Completely unprepared for what was to come.

Liam raised himself ever so slightly on his haunches until his eyes were level with the top of the wall. He saw the headlights of the van light up the road where it came around a bend, then seconds later the Ford Transit came into view.

"Get down, you fucking idiot," Colm Lynch told him under his breath. "Wait for the signal."

Liam ducked back out of sight and checked the safety on his semi-automatic was turned off. He'd only ever fired it on a practice range at their leader's farm and if everything went as hoped, then he shouldn't have to fire a shot tonight. He licked his lips, his body stiff with tension.

Then they saw the signal. Two quick flashes from a flashlight in the next field over told them that it was indeed the correct van.

"Now!" shouted Colm Lynch, and, yanking down their balaclavas to hide their faces, they all leapt to their feet and scrambled over the wall, quickly fanning out over the road.

Suddenly facing a phalanx of gun barrels, the driver of the van rightly skidded to a halt on the slick tarmac. Two of the group blocked the road up ahead while their leader and several others dashed towards the back. Liam took up his position twenty yards away.

He looked on as Colm Lynch pressed the catch on the van's rear door and pushed it up.

A face stared out at them, a hard-featured man with a black moustache. Liam saw others clustered in the back, a whole group of them, and half a heartbeat later he noticed the helmet and green army uniforms, the guns, before a voice snarled, "Fucking Fenians!"

The night erupted with noise and flashing lights. There was an explosive ripping sound from a burst of automatic rifle fire that sprayed a hail of deadly bullets out from the back of the van directly into Colm Lynch and his companions. At such close range, they didn't have time to duck or dive clear and the hail of lead tore their bodies apart.

No! Liam's mind screamed in horror.

Two of his friends went down, bloodied and motionless. The others backed away as a group of British squaddies jumped from the rear of the Transit van. Another pair emerged from the driver's cabin, one wielding a wooden club, the other a long chain. They laid into the two Provos at the front who, like Liam, had frozen from the shock of the sudden turn of events. Their skulls were no match for the brutal weapons and in seconds they too were down on the ground.

Liam and the remaining ambushers fled.

In a mad frenzy, they pushed and shoved each other as more bursts of gunfire came from the British soldiers. Another of Liam's friends went down, he wasn't sure who and he didn't pause in his flight back over the wall.

He landed in the mud at the edge of the field and quickly scurried back to the shelter of the wall as bullets struck the other side. Seconds later, he saw somebody else come crashing down alongside him. Other than Danny O'Shea waiting way beyond the far end of the field in their getaway car, they were the only remaining members of their cell.

"Bloody bastards!" the man shouted over the din. "Someone must have sold us out and tipped them off!"

"Who?" Liam shouted back, his voice all tight.

There was a pause in the shooting, replaced by a voice barking orders, instructing the soldiers to outflank them. Another sound reached Liam and his companion. A car engine revving loudly beyond the hedgerow marking the trackway where O'Shea was waiting. It changed in pitch as it was driven at high speed before it faded away into the countryside.

"Traitor," the other man said, his voice muffled by his balaclava. "He's just signed his own death warrant. His family's too."

Liam rubbed the sweat from his eyes. The hand holding his Armalite was shaking and he thought he was going to puke up.

"Wh-what do we do now?" he stuttered. "Should we surrender?"

"Are you off your fucking rocker, boy? You're a Provo through and through, remember?"

Liam could hear soft footsteps approaching from the left and the right, of men closing in over the field.

"I know, but–"

"But nothing, you twat. Do you know who they are?" He jerked a thumb behind them. "They don't take prisoners, not the likes of us at any rate."

Surely they had to detain them, especially if they laid down their guns, Liam thought. His head was in a whirl. God, what was his mam going to say when she found out?

"They're soldiers, they have to stick to the rules," he uttered feebly.

The other man laughed humourlessly.

"Those aren't soldiers. Well, they are, but not your normal soldiers. They ain't the SAS, either. Those bastards are the Bogmonsters. Ruthless cunts, they are. Fucking covert special ops people, a rule to themselves. Like to kill us with baseball bats and hammers, they do. Smash our little Irish brains in."

"Oh, God."

His companion removed his balaclava and gave him a wry look.

So, this was it then? Cornered in a muddy field after a botched attack? People had warned him this was a dirty little war, but he'd shrugged their fears away, convincing himself that glory awaited their determined band of freedom fighters. What a joke that was, Liam realized now.

The man alongside him must have read his mind. He raised his firearm, saying, "We could go out in a blaze of glory, me and you, boy. Like Robert Redford and Paul Newman in that film. What do you say?"

Liam felt his mouth drop open.

"I'm pulling your leg, you gobshite. You, boy, get to fight another day. When I tell you to run, you run as fast as you can, understand? Keep running and don't stop, find somewhere to hide. Then contact our Brigade CO. He'll tell you what to do after that. You ready?"

Liam, his mouth too dry to form words, nodded. He felt his Adam's apple bob up and down.

"And don't you forget what happened here tonight, you hear what I'm saying? Our day will come."

Liam watched the man turn and disappear into the shadows with the parting words, "Now bloody run, boy."

Liam didn't hesitate. Keeping low, he sprinted away from the wall as fast as his strong, young legs would take him. Over the furrowed ground he went, no more a man grown but just a petrified teenage boy once again.

From behind he heard what he could only describe as a wild battle cry, "Long live the IRA!" followed by a long salvo of gunshots.

As he fled, the tune to an Irish rebel song came to mind, the sound of pipes playing like wind, but try as he might, he couldn't recall the words.

Something about a Provo company lying in the dark, fellow freedom fighters by his side.

The powerful images the tune conjured up no longer stirred his patriotic heart. Youthful vigour had blinded him against reality.

Instead, his stomach twisted into knots of dread.

2

HIS FIRST PRIORITY WAS TO find a spot to lie low. The whole village and surrounding countryside would soon be crawling with the RUC and soldiers on foot patrol, going house to house and kicking doors in.

Liam stumbled across field after field. His breath, restricted by the balaclava, came in harsh rasps. It was so loud that he was sure the sound would give him away, but to stop and rest until his heart slowed wasn't an option.

He clambered over a stile and jumped down into another field, this one a pasture full of sheep. The animals scattered out of his path, bleating noisily. He hurried through them, shooing the stupid animals aside.

A few minutes later and he came to a narrow trackway. He followed it as it filed through a small stand of trees and then came out onto a road. Liam paused momentarily, looking left and right. There was no traffic and just a single streetlight far away. Opposite him was a wrought iron gate.

Checking once more that the way was clear, he scurried over the road and, pushing open the gate, quietly slipped through the gap.

Ahead was a long and straight stone-flagged path running between an avenue of trees. To either side, just visible in the fog, he glimpsed a series of dark-coloured shapes, and it took him a second to realize that he was in a churchyard filled with gravestones.

Liam glanced towards the roadway, trying to decide what to do next, when the sound of a car approaching helped him make up his mind. So down the path he went, a small white stone church revealing itself through the mist. It was as good a place as any to hide, he decided.

Passing the bell tower, he jogged around the corner and up to the entrance. Shouldering his weapon, he grasped the round handle and pushed the wooden door open. Stepping inside, Liam heaved the door shut again and leaned his back against it, pausing to get his breath.

A flick of a light switch showed that he was in a small porch. On his left was a stand covered in leaflets and a village notice board with details of a Bring & Buy sale to raise funds for Oxfam. On the right was a low bench. To his front, another set of doors.

Liam guessed these would be locked, but he tested them just to be sure. So, he couldn't get into the church proper, therefore the porch would have to do. With a bit of luck, he could spend the night here and then in the early hours of the morning, in the pre-dawn gloom and after things had settled down, he would find a phone box and make a couple of calls.

Liam collapsed onto the bench and peeled off his balaclava. His face was slick with perspiration. He wiped it dry, then rested his head against the brick wall.

Boy, he was in a shitload of trouble. Everybody else in his team was dead, he was sure, including Colm Lynch. Now he was on the run, with the police and army no doubt setting up roadblocks and locking the village down. Maybe, he hoped, just maybe they hadn't seen him run away and didn't even know he existed. Perhaps they thought in the confusion and chaos of the firefight that all the IRA hit team was accounted for. It was a slim hope, but for now, it was the only possible advantage he had.

Holding his gun in his lap, Liam kept his eyes trained on the door, his ears straining for the sound of footsteps scraping on the path outside.

At some stage during the night, he must have drifted off to sleep for he woke with a start to find a middle-aged gentleman standing before him.

Liam felt a rush of panic course through his veins and he scrabbled for the gun, bringing it to bear on the stranger. The man, however, responded with a gentle smile and a calming gesture with his hand.

"Hello there, young chap. Don't be alarmed," he said. He had a slightly slurred voice, maybe from a stroke some years earlier, Liam thought. His hair was dark and curly and he had thick, grey sideburns.

The door behind him was ajar, emitting bright morning light. Liam craned his neck to look past him, trying to see outside.

Noticing this, the man eased the door shut. "There is nobody else with me," he assured Liam. "I come alone," he intoned with dark humour.

Liam glanced around, familiarizing himself with his whereabouts again, seeing that the inner doors leading into the church were still closed. With the newly arrived man blocking the exit, he was at a disadvantage.

"Who are you?" he asked warily.

"My name is Henry. I am the churchwarden here. I've come to open up and make the place all spic and span. Normally, at this time of the day, I am the only person out and about, but it seems you have been here for some time?"

Liam let the question hang in the air. With his dishevelled appearance and holding the gun, there seemed little need to explain things.

"Yes, well. Now, it looks like you are in a spot of bother. You must be cold and hungry."

The churchwarden delved into a pocket and produced a big set of keys, which he used to indicate the closed door.

"Shall I put the kettle on and make us a hot cup of tea? A sandwich perhaps?"

Liam saw him look towards his firearm, which he had instinctively kept pointing towards the churchwarden. After a moment's consideration, he lowered the barrel.

"Righto," the churchwarden announced, and with a flourish, he unlocked the door and gestured for Liam to step inside.

Henry the churchwarden led him past the font and into the nave, straightening knee cushions and prayer books as he went.

"I'm afraid that you can't stay here long," he explained as they walked towards the vestry. "We have a funeral service at ten. So, after you have had a hot drink, you will have to leave. I won't ask any questions as to the circumstances of your arrival, young chap, but with last night's drama – there are police stopping cars and carrying out enquiries – we just can't risk them finding you here. No matter what our political persuasions may be. You do understand?"

Liam nodded. He was still exhausted and his mind too befuddled to think straight. All that he really wanted to do was go home.

"Here we are. Sit down, won't you?"

Liam sat on a cheap plastic chair at a small table and waited while the churchwarden filled a red kettle with water from the corner sink. He plugged in the thick and frayed cord, then spooned tea leaves into a teapot. As the kettle heated up, he prepared Liam a ham and cheese sandwich, the vestry also serving as a little kitchen and storage space, it seemed.

Liam found that he was famished, so as soon as the sandwich was placed before him, he snatched it up with his free hand and started to eat. He regarded the churchwarden, studying his kindly face and relaxed manner. He seemed somewhat bemused with Liam, his head tilted to the side, eyes twinkling with merriment. Strange, considering how surprised he must have been to find a teenage gunman hiding in the church porch.

The churchwarden moved away to make the tea.

"A hot and strong brew, that should make you feel better," he told him as he put a cup on the table.

Liam propped his gun against the chair leg and drank, mumbling, "Thanks."

The churchwarden became quiet for a few moments. It allowed Liam a chance to consider his next move.

His options were limited. He needed to get in touch with his Brigade commander, who would possibly send people to pick him up, or, more likely, give Liam instructions on where to head for. Probably a safe house. Getting there wouldn't be easy. He would need to ditch the gun and get a change of clothes. He wondered if this man, Henry, might be willing to help even though he sounded initially reluctant. Plenty of people supported their cause, and up to now, the churchwarden hadn't shown any signs of anger or fear. The network of IRA sympathizers stretched far and wide, on both sides of the border. Could he be trusted?

Liam finished the sandwich and pushed the plate away. He sat back in his chair, peering up.

"I think," Henry said mildly, "that I should get Father O'Keefe and explain the situation to him. He will know what to do."

He moved across the vestry towards another door which, when it was opened, revealed a tiny cubbyhole with a desk and typewriter and, sitting on a cushion, a tabby cat. The animal stretched and yawned and came out to sniff around Liam's legs.

"Our chief mouser, a stray that found its way in here one day and decided it preferred the warm office to the churchyard. Father O'Keefe took a liking to it, so now the little thing has permanently moved in."

"Where is this O'Keefe?" Liam asked.

"In the rectory next door, preparing himself. I will call him and ask him to pop over."

He reached out for the green telephone. Liam quickly jumped up and grabbed his gun, bustling over to the office door.

Henry turned in alarm, phone receiver in one hand, index finger of his other poised in one of the numbers on the round dialer.

Liam moved closer, his senses on heightened alert. If the man were ringing the police, could he shoot him dead in cold blood? A churchwarden? God, he didn't know if he had it in him.

Luckily, he saw the finger was on the number 3, not 9.

"Sorry," he mumbled and sagged against the wall.

"No need to apologize."

Liam looked on as the churchwarden dialled a number and, when it was answered at the other end, listened as he bade somebody good morning. He explained that there was a small matter at the church that needed their attention, and could the

23

Father come straight over? Henry then replaced the large receiver.

"He will be along in five minutes," he said, smiling broadly.

•   •   •

Father O'Keefe was a tall man of advanced years with a large beard and a vigorous and thrusting posture, who bobbed up and down on the soles of his feet as he spoke. He was wearing a brown duffel coat with its wooden toggles fastened nearly to the top, but Liam could just make out the surplice and dog collar beneath.

The churchwarden briefly explained Liam's predicament. While the two men conversed just outside the vestry, Liam's eyes flicked back and forth between them both as he tried to gauge Father O'Keefe's reaction to this unexpected chain of events.

After a few moments, O'Keefe glanced in at Liam. Then he leaned close to his colleague, whispered something in his ear, and, after the churchwarden slipped away, stepped through the doorway.

"I must say," he said to Liam, pinning him with his intense blue eyes, "that under normal circumstances, I would be overjoyed to find a young man like yourself waiting in my church at such an hour, seeking solace and comfort. In these increasingly fractious and divisive times that we live in, it warms my heart to think that God still has meaning in the deliverance of hope. Alas, that is not the case here, is it? Indeed, your sudden appearance before us is not the work of Our Lord. Or perhaps it is."

He paused, as if offering Liam an opportunity to respond. Liam could think of nothing to say.

Perhaps he should just leave, he thought.

"Indeed," Father O'Keefe repeated to himself.

Liam wondered where the churchwarden had gone.

He subconsciously stroked his finger over the gun's trigger guard, a movement that caught Father O'Keefe's attention and caused a heavy frown to darken his brow.

"So, what are we to do with you?"

Liam watched him closely.

"The way I see it, we are presented with three different courses of action. Firstly, I could just boot you out into the cold and tell you to leave and not come back. That you have brought these problems upon yourself, and goodbye and good luck."

Liam narrowed his eyes.

"The fact that you are holding a gun, with which you seem well accustomed to using, would, it appears, rule out that approach. Which brings me to our second proposal. We could simply wash our hands of you and pass you over to the police. Let them deal with this silliness. In fact, Henry could, right this very minute, be explaining to them that we have an unwelcome guest, a lodger, in our midst."

"And leave you here alone, with me pointing this at you?" Liam raised the barrel of his gun a fraction. "I don't think so."

"Noted, young man. Very astute of you."

O'Keefe unbuttoned his coat and hung it on a hook on the back of the vestry door.

"I also don't think your fellow, how should I call them – freedom fighters? Yes? I don't think they would think too kindly of me and Henry if we were to hand you over. You are Catholic, I presume? A nasty business, sectarian violence. Everyone having to choose one side or the other with no room for the middle ground. As a religious man, alas, I too must decide where my loyalties lie. Which leads us to our third option."

O'Keefe strode over to where the teapot was and poured himself a cup, which he commenced to sip. The tabby cat wandered over and jumped up onto the counter. O'Keefe stroked it behind its ears. The cat purred loudly.

"We will take you as far as Ballyclare. There is somebody there who we can trust. He will allow you to use his telephone so that you can make whatever arrangements you need to continue with your journey, and, if necessary, to stay for a few hours. But you will have to be gone before his wife returns from work."

"Ballyclare? But that's in the wrong direction. I need to make for the border, or for Belfast."

O'Keefe drank from his cup, his face expressionless.

"That is our offer," he stated simply. "Take it or leave it."

Liam was thinking fast. Ballyclare was the next town over from Templepatrick, a small and nondescript place along the main road to the coast. Did the Republicans have people there, he wondered? Would he later be able to head south? More importantly, how were they to slip through the police and army cordon surrounding Templepatrick?

He looked up at O'Keefe and asked him directly about this last point.

"You leave that to us," Father O'Keefe replied.

At ten o'clock the mourners attending the funeral slowly filed in and took their places on the rows of pews. Father O'Keefe conducted the service. The deceased, a popular lady in the parish who worked at the local post office, had succumbed to cancer the week before. Her tearful friends and family, all dressed in sombre black, maintained a dignified and stony-faced silence throughout. Afterwards, as they went out to the churchyard for the burial, Father O'Keefe shook hands with each of them, offering words of comfort.

Liam watched proceedings through a narrow gap in the door from his sanctuary inside the vestry. While he waited for O'Keefe and the churchwarden to return, he went over their plan again, thinking it was the stupidest thing that he'd ever heard. So ridiculous in fact, that it might just work.

By eleven, everybody had left except Liam, O'Keefe, Henry the churchwarden and the undertaker, a ferrety little man called Fergal, who had been asked to stay behind.

Henry came to collect him, assuring him that the coast was clear. Liam crept out of the vestry just in time to see money change hands between Father O'Keefe and the undertaker, Fergal docking his cap and giving an exaggerated wink, which made Liam wonder if he wasn't a little drunk.

Henry led him down the central aisle of the church to where they stood in the nave. Lying on a brier alongside the font was a coffin with its lid already off.

Fergal was smoking a ciggie and drawing disapproving looks from Father O'Keefe, but the little man ignored him and smirked to himself as he pocketed his money.

"It was a little out of the blue, Mister O'Keefe, you ringing me up and asking me to bring along a spare coffin. I was just about to leave with the deceased. I had her all tucked up nice and neat in the back of the hearse with all the flowers arranged good and proper. Me and the lads had a right carry-on squeezing in the extra wooden box so that nobody would notice. But people can rely on me, everybody knows that,

Mister O'Keefe. Yes, if you ever find yourselves in a tight spot, then Fergal's your man."

"Yes, thank you kindly. Of course, the payment isn't just for your time and services, but also for your well-known discretion in these matters."

"In other words, keep my beak out, is that what you mean?" The undertaker laughed and blew smoke rings up towards the roof beams. "I'm not stupid, Mister O'Keefe. I knows what happens to blabbermouths in these parts. Ah, here is the young man in question," he turned as Liam approached.

The undertaker looked him up and down, his eyes squinting in concentration.

"He should fit, I reckons. I'll back the hearse up to the door." He turned and stepped outside.

Liam eyed the coffin, a tiny shiver passing up his spine as he contemplated what he was required to do.

"Is this the only way? There must be something else that we can try," he said to Father O'Keefe.

"Not at such short notice. It's only a matter of time before the soldiers arrive and search the church."

"Won't they want to check inside... there?" He nodded at the coffin. "When we reach the checkpoint?"

"Not unless they want a riot on their hands. Unscrewing a coffin lid and interfering with the dearly departed, even the English won't do that. Not in this part of the country."

"You're going to fasten the lid down?" Liam felt woozy.

"Of course."

"Won't I suffocate or something? I suffer from claustrophobia."

"Now, now, ten minutes of discomfort is surely preferable to spending twenty years in H Block?"

Father O'Keefe was of course referring to the Maze Prison in County Down.

"We'll even put some flowers on the top and drive slowly through the village. Now, chop chop, get yourself in there." Father O'Keefe clapped his hands together.

Liam placed his Armalite inside the coffin and then, with the two men's help, clambered in after it. He shuffled his feet to give himself more room, then lay back on the soft velvety interior. He heard a scraping sound as they lifted the lid off the stone floor and, just before they pressed it down and screwed it shut, Father O'Keefe's face appeared over the rim, looking in at him.

"Remember, wait until you hear the signal. Fergal will wheel you into the Chapel of Rest and check that his house is clear first before he lets you out. You can use his telephone and wait there until help arrives. Good luck and God bless, son."

The coffin lid came down, shutting out the light.

3

WEARING A BLACK DONKEY JACKET and bell-bottom trousers, a canvas duffel bag slung over his shoulder, Liam looked like any other man on his way to work the evening shift at Larne harbour. Still, he felt terribly exposed. He was sure people were looking at him out of the corners of their eyes, watching this stranger in their midst. So, feeling paranoid, he pulled his cap down to hide his features as he headed downhill towards the town.

Liam reached the foot of the slope and crossed over a muddy patch of waste ground. Just ahead of him were the choppy waters of Waterloo Bay and, further up the coast, the prominent landmark of Chaine Memorial Tower. That was his meeting spot. To get there, all he had to do was follow the railway tracks leading away from the bustling port.

As he walked, he cast his mind back, going over the events of the past few days.

It was a week since the foiled attack on the vanload of builders and his narrow escape. In that time, his life had irreversibly changed forever. Any illusions of living a normal existence had evaporated.

After safely reaching the Chapel of Rest in Ballyclare, Liam had gratefully climbed back out of the coffin, feeling like a walking corpse as he stretched his legs and massaged his neck.

The man called Fergal led him out of the mortuary, away from the unpleasant smell of embalming fluids, taking him into a wood-panelled hallway. On a stand was a telephone.

Liam had waited until the undertaker made himself scarce before dialling a number.

The man who answered had a gruff voice. He'd spoken little, had mostly listened to what Liam had to say, before telling him to wait for a call back. Three hours went by, with Liam and the undertaker sitting silently in the parlour, exchanging no more than a dozen words, their eyes watching the hands on a carriage clock slowly turn around to mid-afternoon.

Finally, the telephone had rung and Liam carefully listened to what was said down the line, this time by a different man. What he'd had to say and the instructions he'd passed on had left Liam scared and shocked, more confused and frightened than ever.

Simply put, he would not be going home for a very long time. His family was all under arrest and were currently being interrogated by the RUC. Their house was being searched top to bottom. Somehow – probably as a result of their getaway driver talking – he had been identified as one of the IRA men ambushed last night. A manhunt was underway north and south of the border.

To avoid being picked up, the best thing that he could do, the man ordered, was to get out of the country altogether. An escape route for similar fugitives on the run had been established over the past few years, one which entailed getting to the British mainland. Once there, he would remain hidden in plain sight by merging into normal society until it was thought safe for him to come home. He was warned that this could be several years from now.

Then the man on the phone had told him something which had rocked Liam even more. A bombshell revelation relating to his host, the undertaker.

He could not be trusted, the man told Liam.

There had been rumours, stories about him that called into question his loyalty, the man said.

He was a suspected informer, the man stated.

In an uncompromising voice that hissed with quiet venom, the man told Liam, "You deal with that streak of piss."

Then the phone went dead.

Liam had felt himself sway and he had to grab the wall to stop himself from going down in a heap. Closing his eyes until the dizzy spell passed, he'd gone back into the parlour on trembling knees, hoping the undertaker didn't notice his distress. Then Liam had sat back down.

He knew what needed to be done.

When given a direct order by the High Command of the IRA, you didn't dare disobey them. Not if you still wanted to be alive twenty-four hours later.

Liam watched Fergal as he'd slowly rolled another cigarette. After a moment, the undertaker had become aware of his scrutiny and he'd glanced up, that annoying smirk still on his face.

"Well?" he'd asked. "What's happening? The missus is back in a few hours and I want you gone before she arrives, you hear?"

"They're sending someone around to pick me up. They're moving me somewhere else."

"Oh, yeah. Where?"

Liam shrugged, never taking his eyes off the undertaker.

"Nah, makes no difference to me. As long as you are out of my hair, I don't give a tinker's damn."

He went back to licking the Rizla.

Liam pushed himself to his feet and stepped towards the parlour door.

"Where are you going?"

"To use the bathroom."

Out in the wood-panelled hallway, Liam paused by a picture frame hanging on the wall. It was a family photo showing the undertaker and his wife with two young children, probably their grandkids. They all looked happy and were smiling as they sat on a beach building sandcastles. Liam blinked slowly and turned away.

His gun was where he'd left it at the foot of the stairs by the coat rack. Liam picked up the Armalite and set the selector switch to semi-automatic, then walked back through to the parlour on stiff legs.

As he entered the room, the undertaker glanced up and, a moment later, his eyes dropped to the gun in Liam's hands. The barrel was pointing directly at his head. His mouth opened and the lit cigarette in his mouth fell into his lap, ash spilling down his sweater. Then he jumped to his feet and began to babble incoherently, but his words were cut off by the sudden report of the gun firing.

The single round hit him square on his pudgy nose and blew out from the back of his skull, splashing red droplets over the wallpaper behind him. The undertaker was flung back into his chair, legs and arms splayed outwards like he was doing star jumps. He didn't move after that. A dark patch appeared at the front of his trousers when his bladder emptied. There was a smell of excreta. A spiral of smoke from the burning cigarette coiled and swirled in the disturbed air currents.

Liam found it difficult to get his breath as though his lungs wouldn't fully inflate. He crashed through the doorway and stumbled over to the foot of the staircase, where he sat on the bottom step, shivering. He dropped the gun and noticed tiny little pinprick dots of red over his hands. He rubbed them on his thighs to wipe the blood away.

He did not know how long he stayed there, but some time later there was the sound of a car outside, its engine rumbling quietly. Liam heard footsteps on the gravel path and looked up to see the silhouette of a man through the front door's frosted glass. The doorbell chimed.

•   •   •

Leaving the body in the parlour, the driver of the car had led Liam outside and then driven him quickly through the back roads to a safe house close to Larne. It was a tiny, ramshackle cottage with good views in all directions and only one road in and out. But out back, there was a narrow walking track that headed towards a headland on the coastline and from there, wound down towards the edge of the town. This would be Liam's route once his transport across to the mainland had been arranged.

The driver remained with him at the safe house, to make sure that Liam stayed inside and out of sight. For five days, he'd bummed around the place, with too much time to think about what happened back at the Chapel of Rest. He ate little and barely slept. A scruffy stubble appeared on his jaw and rings developed around his eyes. He felt and looked much older than seventeen.

Finally, the driver, whose name he never learned, told Liam that it was time to go. He was given a set of old work clothes and a bag for his gun, as well as some sandwiches, a flask of soup and fifty quid in crumpled notes.

Liam had set off into a strong wind and driving rain.

Leaving the railway tracks, Liam's mind turned back to the here and now as he skirted around the sprawling port and ferry terminal and picked up the coastal road north of the town. On his left was a row of houses with tall gables, while beyond a white railing on the right was a rocky beach and the grey sea. White foam blew in the air.

Directly ahead, at the end of a short promontory, was the strange-looking Chaine Memorial Tower, a thin and tall obelisk that at one time was a lighthouse marking the safe channel into Larne.

Leaving the roadway, Liam crossed the grass and walked along a path running down the centre of the promontory towards the tower, then followed it around the stone obelisk. On the far side was a metal gate, then a flight of rough-hewn steps leading down to the rocky beach.

He glanced at his watch. He was ten minutes early. The fishing boat should be along at four, he'd been assured.

Liam found a rock to sit on, and while he waited, he contemplated what the future held for him.

Overhead, a murmuration of starlings swooped and whirled around the grey tower.

PART 2

THE LIFER

4

**Monster Mansion
HMP Wakefield
1984**

I T WAS ALWAYS THE SAME dream. Or, to be more precise, the final fragment of the same dream. Of the girl, sitting on a wooden bench with sunlight streaming through the window to shine through her blonde curls, creating a halo around her face. Smiling at him, but with a tinge of sadness in her blue eyes.

He wasn't sure if the dream was a true representation of the reality, for his memory of that brief moment was hazy after all these years. Perhaps his mind had altered the scene, moulded it into something less painful.

Lying on his narrow bunk bed, Francis Bailey held onto the image of her face imprinted on the back of his eyelids, reluctant to fully awaken. But, as consciousness swelled, the girl faded away.

He opened his eyes and looked up at the cream-coloured ceiling on what was his last day in prison.

The thought momentarily petrified him. He had hoped for this day for over a decade and had pinned everything on the belief that eventually, he would be going home. But now that it was really happening and the day had finally come around,

Francis found the idea of stepping outside, of reclaiming his life as a *free* man, to be a daunting prospect.

Pushing away these fears, he sat up and shoved the thin bedcovers back. Swinging his legs over the side, Francis came to his feet and dressed himself in the regulation dark trousers and blue shirt.

His small cell contained a bed, a closet fixed to the wall where he kept a few changes of clothes, a table and plastic chair plus a shelf on which was an assortment of personal items such as his toiletries, an electric kettle, sugar, teabags, several cartons of long-life milk and some packets of plain digestives, a few books, a Walkman with an assortment of cassette tapes, plus a shaving mirror. On the table was yesterday's newspaper opened to the crossword and a few pieces of correspondence from his solicitor. In another corner within view of the door's peephole was a tiny sink and steel toilet basin.

This was Francis' world. Had been for most of his time since the trial, except for the handful of occasions that he'd gone to the hospital wing. In a few hours, he would be leaving the safety and comfort of his cell and be swapping it for the outside world, with its wide-open spaces and its busy streets and shops, the healthy air and leafy parks, the thronging pavements and barking dogs and chirping birds.

God.

The enormity of this day threatened to overwhelm him. He had to take several deep breaths to steady his nerves, telling himself over and over that this would mark the passage from one life – a life of drudgery and misery – to another. The next chapter in his story.

Francis stepped over to the table and pulled out the chair and while he waited for the electronic slam locks on his cell door to pull back, he picked up one of the envelopes, the one with the Home Office stamp on the front. He withdrew the letter.

For the thousandth time, Francis ran his gaze over it, his eyes picking out a few keywords and sentences, phrases such as **overturned conviction, official exoneration, a questionable witness statement**. Further down was the brief explanation, **false confession due to duress coupled with a pre-existing medical condition that the jury was blocked from being told about** and **the Chief Investigating Officer had a history of previous cases found to be unsound**.

Finally, near the bottom and signed by Home Secretary Leon Brittan, the succinct summary from the Court of Appeal that the **conviction was quashed, with the recommendation that the prisoner be released as promptly as possible when arrangements for his safe rehabilitation into the community can be guaranteed**.

There it was, then, in black and white.

His murder conviction, for which he had been imprisoned for nearly twelve years, was deemed unsafe. Following the emergence of new evidence as well as serious question marks against the conduct of certain police officers and the insinuation that they had fabricated his guilt in order to *get someone* for the crime, the whole of the prosecution's case had been exposed as a sham, a set-up job. It had taken years of tireless work by his legal team and by his elderly mother who had pushed and pushed the Court of Appeal to look once again at the case. Finally, their faith had paid off. Because today, this day, Francis was going home.

He laid the letter on the table.

It was still early with the first light of dawn pushing weakly through the small window. Francis rose each morning before the prison came to life, as he slept little and spent most nights tossing and turning. Last night, he had lain in his bed unable to switch off his mind, thinking of his release. Finally, in the early hours, he had drifted off. As usual, though, his rest was disturbed by dreams and recollections, like a shadow hanging over him.

He doubted if that would change much on the outside. Not in the short term, anyway. His ordeal would be an ever-present companion that would follow him around forever, one life sentence replaced with another life sentence. Still, he would be a liberated man, unhindered by physical walls and rules. To go where he wanted and do as he pleased, with the weight of guilt removed from his shoulders.

Francis felt a small smile appear on his face.

First, he had the ordeal of one more breakfast to overcome.

When he'd first arrived here, like all new prisoners Francis had been required to take part in an induction course, designed to introduce him to his new life inside. His Personal Case Officer had treated him fairly enough, whatever his personal views on the crime that Francis was accused of and found guilty of. He'd offered him a few words of advice.

"It won't be easy for you, as a Lifer. Fifteen years is a hell of a long time, and this place has a reputation as being the toughest prison in England for good reason. My suggestion is to keep your head down and do your time. Don't create waves or cause any problems for the staff. Be a model prisoner. If you treat the screws right, then they'll do right by you. Give them problems and, I promise you, Bailey, they will make your time here a bloody nightmare."

Francis had sat there, listening and doing his best to follow what he was being told. All around him the prison building echoed to the sound of raised voices and guttural laughter, officers barking orders, catcalls from one cell to another, banging doors.

The Case Officer had noted his discomfort.

"If you behave yourself, then it might not be fifteen years at all. Everything you do, the people you mix with in the exercise yard and the canteen, the skills you pick up in the workshops, every minute of your life here will be observed by the likes of me and recorded and analysed. I will fill out weekly reports and observational assessments and file them away. They will all be studied by the gaffer, the Prison Governor, and he will make certain recommendations to his bosses on the Parole Board. If the Parole Board decides, at some stage in the future, that you have done your best to stay out of trouble, that will work in your favour, Bailey. They may decide, possibly, that you don't have to serve the whole of your sentence. It might be reduced by half. They might also think that the last year or two of your sentence could be served in an open prison, where you could perhaps be entitled to a day licence, a day release. Fifteen years sounds daunting to you right now, doesn't it? I can well imagine how that feels. I'd say that you are struggling to get your head around that, yes?"

Francis had simply nodded, too bewildered to reply.

"But if your sentence is reduced by half, fifteen years suddenly becomes seven or eight years, of which six or seven are done here at Wakefield, the remainder in a nice cushy prison with a nice cell and your very own TV and a games room and grounds to stroll in. Suddenly it doesn't sound so bad, does it, Bailey?"

He'd shaken his head, more alert now.

"Still, for a first-time prisoner residing here at Her Majesty's pleasure, your immediate future is bleak, make no mistake of that. Every day will feel like a year. The other prisoners will not go easy on you, considering the nature of your crime. There will be times when you find it all too much and want to end it all. To help you through it, you have lots of support. Prison isn't just to punish wrongdoers but is also to rehabilitate cons like yourself. We have a psychiatrist who you have access to anytime you like, or if you prefer, the prison chaplain. They are here to help you when things get too much."

The Case Officer had paused momentarily and leaned forward to speak with a softer, more confidential voice.

"But the best thing that you can do, Bailey, the best piece of advice that I offer to all new intakes, is simply this: get yourselves a couple of mates. People you can really trust. My old man told me that, when he fought in the War, the only thing that got him through it was having one or two real solid pals, lads that he knew would always be there through thick and thin. Pals that would help him during the darkest of times, and who he would help when they were struggling as well. Without them, he said he would never have made it through the War. It's no different in here. Don't try and do your time alone. Don't be the hard man who has no friends, who thinks he can get through his sentence as a loner. That's the worst thing you can do. It will break you."

Reaching into his desk, the PCO had brought out a thick manilla file, which he placed before him. Francis could see his name, date of birth and prisoner number on the front.

"So," the man said, "let's talk about your crime, shall we?"

•   •   •

"Fucking nonce!" Francis heard someone say as soon as he left his cell, then felt something hit his face with a splat.

The mouthful of spit ran down his cheek and he wiped it away with the back of his sleeve. Ducking his face and keeping his gaze on his feet, he scurried down the balcony, his overweight body giving him a waddling gait.

More prisoners were waiting, some just outside their cell doors and others leaning on the railing overlooking the suicide nets. He passed between them, feeling more spit fly at him until it was clinging to his eyes and hair. On the far side of the gangway, a pair of prison officers watched on impassively.

Running this daily gauntlet of taunts and abuse had become such a part of his life that Francis had grown immune to it. Rising to the bait was exactly what they wanted and he refused to react. Especially today. So he passed through the throng and headed towards the stairs leading down to the ground floor.

Part way down, another prisoner, this one with a small tattoo next to his eye and a leering grin splitting his face, fondled his own groin suggestively as Francis brushed by.

At the bottom, he threaded his way across the recreation hall of F-Wing. Stepping into the canteen, he joined the queue of inmates. While he waited to reach the serving counter, he endured more verbal jibes. He'd heard them all before. They weren't very imaginative to his mind. They showed the perpetrators up as dumb and thick, Francis told himself. Besides, he would have the last laugh when he walked out of here shortly.

When it was his turn, he passed over his plastic food tray. The man who was serving – a fellow inmate on canteen duty – glanced up and saw that it was Francis standing before him. Smirking, he scooped out a helping of something grey and sticky that might have been scrambled eggs and plopped it down onto the tray. Then, while Francis and those in the queue behind him watched, he made a show of hacking up a throatful of phlegm and slowly drooled it over Francis' breakfast, then passed it over, winking and blowing a kiss.

Francis moved away like an automaton as laughter and sniggers trailed after him. He spotted an empty table in the corner well away from the others and sat down. For a moment, he looked at the food, which was made even more inedible by the globule of green phlegm sitting on the top.

He became aware of the quiet that had descended on the canteen and when he looked up, he saw the faces all turned in his direction, watching him with hostile eyes.

Francis stared back dully.

Then he scooped up a spoonful of the food and, in a last defiant gesture, shovelled it into his mouth.

Despite his best efforts to heed his Personal Case Officer's advice, Francis had found it impossible to make friends during his twelve years of wrongful incarceration. Regardless of his continuous protestations of innocence throughout his sentence and his long legal battle to have his name cleared, once you were labelled a child killer, then that tag, that false characterization, was impossible to shake off. Even when the letter from the Home Office came, announcing his conviction was quashed and overturned, the hatred directed at him never ceased. Mud stuck.

So, contrary to what he was told during his induction, Francis spent most of his time on F-Wing, the prison's Exceptional Risk Unit, by himself. Nor did he crack or break down as had been predicted. He tried to spend his time productively, doing various courses and picking up skills in woodwork and art classes. He ticked all the boxes, was assessed by the quacks on a regular basis and, although he was the victim of regular physical assaults that had resulted in several stays in the hospital wing, he never started any trouble. He was the epitome of a model prisoner.

But the early release never happened. The transfer to an open prison never came about. He became convinced that somebody – possibly his PCO or the Prison Governor himself – had purposefully scuppered his chances. Because over the years, and despite doubts about his guilt being raised almost from right after the court case, the staff here treated him just as abysmally as the prisoners. The hatred directed at all child killers became a competition between staff and inmates, like they had a bet on who they could next push to the edge. After all, one more inmate lost to suicide was one less inmate for them to worry about and if it were a notorious murderer, then all the better.

But Francis refused to let them break him.

Just like he refused to react to the daily barrage of vilification and profanity such as he'd just experienced on his last morning at The Monster Mansion.

After breakfast, he was escorted to the Prisoner Release Management Office. It was the same room where he'd done his induction upon first arriving. As back then, his Personal Case Officer was there, sitting behind a plastic screen at the same desk. But whereas twelve years ago, the man had been firm but polite with Francis, now he struggled to hide his contempt for him. Francis watched as he slowly, reluctantly it seemed to him, filled out the Discharge Form, the PCO flicking his eyes up at Francis with barely suppressed malice. Francis showed no reaction. He drew comfort in the knowledge that the officer had not seen promotion during his twelve years as an inmate here.

After what seemed an age, the PCO finished and stared at Francis through the clear plastic separating them. He methodically folded the Discharge Form in two, then twisted around and glanced over to where his secretary was busy on her typewriter. Turning back, he held out the piece of paper.

Francis reached out for it, but the PCO drew his hand back a fraction so that Francis had to raise himself from his chair and stretch his arm further. Then the PCO did the same again, toying with Francis, forcing him to reach through the gap in the plastic until his fingers touched the edge of the paper.

"Stay on your side of the fucking plastic," the officer snarled under his breath with quiet menace, his hushed words nearly lost under the clack-clacking of the typewriter. "Or I'll put you on a charge. You're still a prisoner until you step out the door, Bailey."

Then he passed the form through the gap and Francis stepped back from the desk.

"Now clear out your cell and fuck off."

Francis returned to his cell. He started sorting through his things, deciding what to take – mostly his books and music tapes – and what to leave behind – the milk, biscuits and such. He put his few belongings into an Adidas bag.

He noticed on the bed a change of clothes: some trousers, a shirt, a sweater and a pair of cheap pumps. He removed his prisoner's clothes and put on the civilian ones. There was also a two-week bus and train ticket and an envelope with twenty quid inside, his gate money to tide him over.

As an afterthought, Francis lifted the newspaper off the table and folded it to the front page, catching a glimpse of his own image beneath the headline:

Innocent.

He shoved it into the bag.

He stood in the centre of his tiny cell for one last look around, strangely thinking that he might miss the place.

Then he shouldered the bag and turned towards the door.

Francis stopped dead.

Two figures were blocking the exit, inmates whom he recognized, the one with the small tattoo and the one from the canteen.

One of them was holding an electric kettle in his hand with steam billowing out of the top.

For a fraction of a second, Francis looked back at them, knowing what was about to happen but unable to do anything about it.

Then the kettle was thrust at him, and the boiling water was coming straight towards his face, and when the scalding mixture of water and sugar – designed to cling to his skin and melt his face, a home-made napalm – when it hit him, the agony was so intense that a whiteness blossomed in his mind.

Francis was screaming and rolling around on his cell floor and his face was afire with pain, the boiling substance seeming to eat down to the very bones.

5

FRANCIS' RELEASE FROM WAKEFIELD PRISON was delayed by a week. After the assault in his cell, a parting gift from the other Lifers on F-Wing, he'd been treated in the hospital wing for bad facial burns. The doctors told him bluntly that he would be scarred for life. However, with more treatment by specialists at Pinderfields General Hospital, these burns should be something he could live with.

"Count yourself lucky, you could have lost your eyesight," one of them told him. "At least you're alive."

Unlike the dead girl, they might well have said.

Eventually, on a sunny, if crisp morning, Francis was shown through the exit portal in the main gates and he stepped outside as a free man at last.

He stood there, bag in his hand and with his face tilted up to the sun, a cool wind blowing through his hair. He breathed in. There was a smell of freshly cut grass.

The gentle pipping of a car horn caught his attention and he looked to where a blue Astra was parked at the kerbside. The driver's window was wound down and a hand appeared, giving him a wave.

Francis walked over, recognizing his mum and sister in the front.

He crouched down and peered inside, a smile on his face.

"My boy," his mum said soothingly, "my boy, here you are at last." Then she saw the extent of his injury. "What have they done to you, dear?" She tenderly touched the gauze bandage covering his cheek.

"Those monsters," his sister, Pamela, said sternly.

His mum's face was a study of heartbroken concern, but Francis didn't want anything to spoil today. He took her wrinkled hand and kissed her palm.

"It's alright, the docs say it will fade."

"Get in the back, little brother. Let's go." Pamela said.

Francis opened the rear door and slung his bag on the seat, then climbed in behind his sister. She turned on the engine and pulled away. Francis watched the high walls and fences of the prison slip away.

His mum was looking at him over the back of her seat. He thought she looked much older than when he'd seen her during their last visit a month ago, and it struck Francis again just how much time they'd all lost as a family. Although life had frozen for him during the twelve years he'd spent behind bars, life outside had continued unabated. While he had been left to rot in the hell that was Britain's most notorious prison, the world had moved on. The lines on Mum's face and the blonde highlights in his sister's hair, with her large bangle earrings and confidence, spoke more of the passage of time into a new decade than his endless studying of the calendar on his cell wall.

He realized Pamela was saying something, her voice floating back to him on the breeze blowing through the window.

"What was that?" he asked.

"I was saying that we shouldn't just accept it. You were assaulted, Francis. They can't just brush it off as an everyday thing, part of prison life. Category A prisoners are supposed to be protected, shielded from violence."

Francis shrugged his shoulders.

51

"Besides, when it happened, you were an innocent man. With a clean slate. Under their care. It's just not right. Those bastards," her words had a venomous tinge that surprised him, "they made your life a misery right up to the last day."

"Please, dear, let's not—" their mother began.

"I'm sorry, Mum, but I don't think we should just drop it. For twelve years they - and I mean the prison staff as well as the other inmates - all did their best to destroy our Francis. All because those bloody useless, bent coppers messed up their investigation from the beginning and couldn't bring themselves to admit their mistake, even when it was blindingly obvious to everyone else. The things they did to you in that place, brother."

"I don't think Francis needs reminding of the things they did to him, Pamela."

In the back seat, his gaze locked on the trees and gardens passing by outside, Francis felt his face blush as he listened to their exchange.

"We should talk to Gordon, tell him to raise it at the hearing. Their offer to settle is pathetic. They're offering peanuts in return for a life ruined and Francis' reputation tainted forever. It's all a big effing joke, Mum!"

Francis watched the houses and shops slide away behind them as they left the town, the road soon passing between fields filled with sheep. In the distance, shadows from clouds moved languidly over the hills, rippling over folds in the ground. It was turning into a glorious spring day.

"What do you say, Francis?" his sister asked.

"About what?" he replied vaguely, thinking that it was soon time for the permitted one hour per day prison yard exercise and then remembered that, no it wasn't, at least not for him.

"About the assault, dummy! We should get one of those Polaroid cameras and take some photos of your face before the redness goes down. How's that sound?"

"Whatever," he mumbled and shrugged again.

Pamela sighed dramatically at his lack of response, his lack of motivation.

The inside of the car fell silent, with just the sound of the car tyres singing over the road. A beautiful sound, Francis mused.

Pamela reached forward and flicked on the car radio. Simon Bates' Golden Hour was on, playing a song by The Flying Pickets.

"We can talk about this tomorrow, after Francis has seen our GP. Did I tell you that Doctor Beechwood has had a baby, Francis? She's such a bonny lass."

"Yes, Mum."

"Let's get you settled in first. We've kept your bedroom just as it was, haven't we, Pamela?"

Francis let them drone on. He'd learned how to tune out voices during his spell inside and besides, now that he was back their living arrangements were a bit of a sore point. Pamela, divorced two years ago, had sold her home to raise money for her brother's substantial legal costs and was now living with Mother once again at their home in Calderdale. Things were strained, he'd come to understand from their monthly visits, and would probably only get worse before they got better.

Pamela eventually changed the subject.

"Have you thought about what you want to do, moving forward? We should think about getting you a job," she said.

Francis wasn't sure what he thought about that idea. Earning a living and doing something positive for the remainder of his life sounded good, on paper. Finding work might not prove as simple as that, though, and not just because of the high unemployment rates in the country. His sister spoke about a clean slate, of new beginnings, but some people would always wonder if he were truly innocent. People could be cruel and vindictive, no matter what the courts said. His treatment last week on the day he should have been released might be a reflection of the public's view. After all, that poor girl was still dead and the police's prime suspect at the time was now being released. With nobody else to direct their hatred at, Francis worried about what sort of reception he would receive from people.

Pamela, though, had a determined streak.

"I think I'll set up an appointment for you at the Benefits Office for next week. They can explain your options."

Soon after, they reached the tunnel passing beneath the motorway at Ainley Top, then began the slow descent down from the Pennine peaks.

They would be home shortly, Francis knew. He felt excited about that, but it also gave him the jitters, which was only to be expected, he fancied. Then a thought occurred to him, an idea.

He leaned forward so that his face was between his sister and his mum and he looked from one to the other.

"What is it, dear?" Mum asked.

"I want to go and see Dad," he told them quietly.

They walked through the wrought-iron gates and along the path that wound through the cemetery.

The burial ground was on a south-facing slope overlooking the small town. On a sunny spring day like today, the spot was a peaceful place to come and sit on one of the benches or wander amongst the graves. In the middle of winter, Francis remembered, it was a different matter, especially when an icy wind blew straight across from High Moor. It was also sometimes used by courting couples who would park up in the car park and even a spot where teenagers would hang out. In the adjoining Wainhouse Terrace, the Victorian promenade built by a local industrialist, junkies would shoot up and sleep in the damp shadows behind the stone pillars.

Dad's grave was marked by a simple granite headstone nearly hidden within the grander monolithic monuments. A low wall marked the edge of the cemetery just beyond. Francis stood quietly with his mum and sister, reading the short inscription, feeling strangely unmoved and detached.

His old man had died just a year after his conviction, succumbing to a series of strokes. His departure had left Mum and Pamela to carry the burden of fighting for justice between them. In an act of spiteful punishment, the prison authorities had refused Francis permission to attend the funeral service, claiming that he was a flight risk.

In the intervening years since, Francis had allowed memories of his dad to lose focus and move to the back of his mind. Trapped in prison, he had built a shell of protection about himself, a shield from the outside world that did not permit self-pity or sorrow to further poison his mind. It was the only way, he'd quickly learned, to contend with his bind, the rabbit hole into which he had suddenly, unwittingly tumbled.

So, as he contemplated his dad's final resting place, he felt a distinct lack of emotion, a blankness. The person buried here was not the same person he had known back then. Only the name on the headstone suggested a link with Francis' childhood, for his memories of Dad stopped on the day he was taken away from court in the back of a prison van. In Francis' mind, his father was still fit and healthy and full of humour, not a corpse turned to dust. It was easier that way. Going to prison was a good way to deal with grief, he thought grudgingly. The opportunity to mourn had been taken away from him.

Francis turned from Dad's grave.

"Let's go home," he said.

Home was a three-bedroomed semi in a pretty cul-de-sac edging onto the local park, with dense woodland at the back.

Pamela parked on the drive and switched off the engine, then removed the car radio as they climbed out.

Luckily, there was no fanfare to welcome him back, nor any unwelcome reporters loitering on his doorstep. The row of houses was quiet, although Francis thought he heard a door slam somewhere.

The three of them went up the steps and along the path across the front of the house. Pamela unlocked the front door, explaining how they would get a key cut for him soon.

"Welcome home," she added as they stepped inside.

Like Francis himself, the house seemed to be stuck in a time warp. Everything was just as he remembered, returned to how it looked before the police had ripped up the floorboards and ransacked the place. Brown and orange wallpaper in the living room, a floral-coloured suite, furry lampshades with tassels, a coffee table and magazine rack, plus shag-pile carpets throughout. Very 1970s, even though it was now in the eighties. In the kitchen, the same units and sink with the blue Formica surfaces and a beaded curtain separating off the walk-in larder. The only addition that he could see was a kitchen blind over the window, which, when he pulled it up, revealed the back garden to still be the same as well. Mum had kept Dad's tiny veggie patch going. She'd also kept the upholstered garden swing seat; Francis saw it against the bottom fence with a neighbour's cat sleeping upon it.

It was like a shrine to the previous decade. Francis wondered if Mum had kept it this way on purpose, to help ease his transition back into normal society. He wasn't sure if that was a good thing or a bad thing.

Upstairs was the same. The avocado bathroom with its pink fluffy toilet lid cover and toilet roll dolly on the cistern. Next, his bedroom, with posters of Marc Bolan and Steve McQueen on the walls and his collection of Weird Tales magazines. Back then, when he wasn't messing about in the woods behind their home he would spend most of his spare time up here, either recording the music charts on the radio onto his tape recorder or reading and although he was now turned thirty, Francis couldn't help a mistiness come into his eyes as the fond memories flooded back.

He strolled across to the wardrobe and looked inside. God, Mum had even kept his old kipper ties and the groovy shirts with the huge collars, as well as the flared jeans and tan brogues that he'd liked to wear on nights out with Jimmy Wade, his best mate. And there, at the back, was the famous purple waistcoat that he was sure channelled his inner Jimi Hendrix. What on earth had possessed him, he wondered now and laughed to himself.

He would have to have a serious cull of his old gear, Francis decided as he went back downstairs.

Later, they sat down at the kitchen table and ate homemade lasagne. Francis wasn't too keen on it, but he didn't like to upset Mum, who had gone to a lot of trouble. So he ate the lot, shovelling the food into his mouth. He caught himself with his arms protectively curled around the plate, a prison habit to stop other inmates from trying to pinch his food.

After their tea, the three of them sat watching TV. A new series called *Auf Wiedersehen, Pet* was starting, about a bunch of British builders working in West Germany, which they all enjoyed. Then the ten o'clock news came on, but when Arthur Scargill popped up talking about the striking miners, Mum quickly switched off.

"Can't stand that man," she exclaimed.

Francis lay on his old bed in his old bedroom, once more unable to sleep. Orange light from the streetlamp outside penetrated the thin curtains, lending the room an amber glow. His surroundings were at once familiar and unfamiliar to him. He cast his eyes about, seeing the vague shapes of furniture, bookcases, and the closed door.

The house was quiet, a silence that unsettled him. Francis was so used to the nighttime sounds of prison, with the snoring and coughing of other prisoners, the occasional sound of someone crying out in their sleep or low voices talking, that the nocturnal stillness of his old house made a restful night impossible for him. It felt like a void waiting to be filled. If the night had a face, that face would hold a vulpine grin, he decided.

During the countless sleepless nights in prison, Francis had learnt a technique that enabled him to 'escape' the confines of his cell. In an almost meditative state, he would close his mind down to the present and remove himself to another place or another time. He would mentally shift locations.

Sometimes these would be real places that he had visited during his childhood. Other times they might be places in the world that he one day, at some tantalizing point in the future, wished to visit. They might equally be places that didn't even exist, except in his head. They might be of events past or events future, aspirations and dreams. Sometimes, if he revisited a particularly dark memory, Francis would alter the narrative and recreate a history, so that it ended with a better outcome.

Inevitably he would return to that day.

When that happened, Francis would snap out of his daydreams and retreat to the sanctuary of his cell room. The cold sweats would return, leaving him shivering and clutching himself, his whimpers swirling about him like ghostly voices. Sometimes, like tonight as he lay in his old house, the girl would travel back with him.

He didn't believe in the supernatural. Francis had no time for ghostly visitations of the dead coming back from beyond the grave. He was lucid enough to recognize it was just a dream vision or a memory recall, call it whatever you wished. Still, when it happened, it felt real enough.

Tonight, the girl wasn't all smiles with sunlight shining like a holy halo around her beautiful face.

This visitation revealed the true nature of that tragic episode.

The girl was curled up on his bedroom floor but surrounded by fallen leaves and tree roots. She was wearing the pretty blue dress and white socks pulled up to just below her knees, with one shoe on and the other lying a few feet away.

Francis knew, in his half-dream state, that she was dead, and that the movement he saw was the movement of thousands of feeding worms and maggots burrowing holes where her eyes should be and scurrying into her open mouth.

59

They feasted on her, for the girl had lain undiscovered in the woods for over a week, her corrupted flesh nourishing the soil.

But if she was dead, why did her neck, broken by strong hands, twist about as she searched for Francis with her sightless gaze? Why did her hand lift from the ground, beckoning to him with bloated fingers?

Francis withdrew from the horror and the girl faded, sucking another piece of his soul with her.

For the remainder of the night, his first as a free man, Francis rested upon his bed, knowing that, very soon, he would have to revisit that terrible day all over again.

Only then would the dead girl leave him alone.

6

THE FOLLOWING MONDAY, FRANCIS CAUGHT the 279 bus to the Benefits Office. Like millions of other young men living in Thatcher's Britain, he now found himself among the ranks of the unemployed, although for reasons beyond his control.

He found a seat upstairs and as the bus trundled through the morning commute, he watched the crowds of pedestrians and lines of traffic pour into the town centre. When the female conductor came upstairs, he showed her his bus ticket. He waited while she stamped a hole in it, catching the look she gave him under the peak of her cap. She moved on to the next passenger, making a point of saying good morning to them in a loud and breezy voice.

Francis ignored the slight.

He alighted from the bus on the corner of Fairfax Street. Pulling his baseball cap down, he crossed over and pushed through the stream of people towards the new pedestrianized shopping complex, trying to remember the directions his sister had given him.

He was just passing by Chelsea Girl when he heard a loud voice call out his name, and he turned to see a man waving and hurrying across.

"Fuck me, man, I thought it was you," the man said, taking his hand and pumping it vigorously. "I heard you were out. Well, I saw it on the telly that you're in the clear and then it said on

Ceefax that you'd been released. How ya doing, ya dickhead? It looks like you've been in the wars." He indicated Francis' face, which even with the bandage now gone, was all red and inflamed.

It was his old school pal and best mate, Jimmy Wade. Or, at least, he thought it was. Since Francis had last clapped eyes on him, sitting at the back of the courtroom and lapping up all the media whirlwind generated by the murder case, Jimmy's hair had receded faster than Prince Edward's. His teeth, likewise, seemed to have decided to do a flit as well, probably as a result of smoking too much weed. But the eyes were still the same, they still had that shifty way of skidding off to the side to watch people passing by, checking faces for people he owed money to.

"It's good to see you," Jimmy went on. He prodded at Francis' tummy with a bony finger. "Looks like they've been feeding you too much as well, pal. Three square meals a day, a roof over your head and no bills to worry about, can't be bad, eh? I did a few weeks in Armley myself, for possession, so I know what you've been through. Me and you, we're like soul mates." He laughed loudly.

A couple of women walked by and Jimmy leered at them, giving one a wink. She turned away in disgust.

"I think she fancies me," he decided.

Francis stole a look at his watch. It was coming up to 9:30, the time for his appointment, and he still needed to find the Benefits Office. He opened his mouth to make his excuses but then felt a heavy hand clamp down on his shoulder.

"Right, pal," Jimmy said, but his attention was already drifting, more concerned with other things, places to go, people to see. "I think we should have a proper catch-up, don't you? A night out and a pint, grab some chips on the way home, whatcha say? Right then, that's settled. I'll give you a bell and I can pick you up in my motor. You still at home with your mum, aren't you?"

Francis nodded.

"Nice one. I'll sees you later, gotta dash."

Then he was gone, flitting through the throng of people, eyes glancing at shoppers' handbags and back pockets as he went.

Francis took a big breath and set off again.

A few minutes later and he spotted the big orange sign – JOB CENTRE – and he cut a path towards the door, noticing the job advertisements in the window.

Inside, there was a desultory mix of people but predominantly young men. Some were sitting on the rows of chairs waiting to be seen, while a few stood looking at the job boards. A long queue threaded back from a counter where others were signing on. A yellow fog of nicotine hung just below the ceiling.

Someone took his name and checked it against a list. They were running late, Francis was informed. Somebody called Maureen would call him when it was his turn.

Francis wandered over to look at the jobs. On the wall was a poster that said YOUTH PROGRAMME OPPORTUNITIES. Another stated GET PAID TO LEARN NEW SKILLS. Francis went past them and looked at today's latest jobs. Lathe Turner, Hotel and Catering, Shop Work.

On the next set of boards, he saw vacancies for Engineering, Seasonal Work, another for Clerical Duties and the request MUST LIVE AT HOME WITH PARENTS.

He went back to the one advertising for a lathe-turner. Perhaps it might suit him; after all, he'd shown quite an aptitude in the woodwork classes that he'd attended. But the pay was miserly, more aimed at a school leaver, plus they required references.

"Mr Bailey?" a loud voice caught his attention and he turned to see a middle-aged lady in brown buckled shoes and sporting a tight perm looking around the room. She glanced down at the clipboard that she was holding and frowned irritably. "Mr *Francis* Bailey!" she said louder for everyone to hear.

Francis shuffled over, trying to hunker down unobtrusively beneath his cap. A skinhead by the window elbowed his mate in the ribs and they both scowled in his direction.

He reached the lady, whom he presumed must be Maureen.

"Ah, there you are. I was beginning to wonder if it was someone's idea of a joke, but apparently not. Never mind." She stared for a moment at the burns on his face and then looked at the clock on the wall. "We'll have to keep this brief."

He was happy enough with that, Francis thought as he followed her over to a desk.

Collecting together her paperwork, she scribbled a few notes down and ticked a column of boxes as she asked a number of questions.

"Is this the first time that you have made a claim, Mr Bailey?"

"Yes."

"Are you claiming for yourself or a spouse?"

"Just myself."

She made more notes.

"Do you have an up-to-date copy of your CV?"

Francis reached into his pocket and withdrew a single sheet of paper that Pamela had typed up for him. He handed it over and watched whilst Maureen read it, which took all of ten seconds.

"There's not much on here, is there? I notice you have a twelve-year gap in your work record. I would normally ask why that is, but there doesn't seem much point in your case, does there?"

She looked up as though awaiting a response, so he shrugged and mumbled, "That's hardly my fault."

"What was that?"

"I said, it is hardly my fault that I've been unable to look for work, is it?" he repeated, louder this time.

"Indeed. But notwithstanding that, any potential employer would see that as a disadvantage. When they ask why, which they inevitably will if you are lucky to be given a job interview," she seemed to sniff at the idea of this happening, "and they find out what you have been doing with your time, well, frankly Mr Bailey, they will wonder if you are reliable and trustworthy. In the current climate, with this horrible recession that the country is going through, I would hazard to suggest that they would hesitate in offering you paid employment. After all, there are three and a half million other people for them to choose from."

She went back to studying his CV, even turning it over to see if she had missed anything written on the other side.

"It says your interests include reading and watercolour painting." She looked over towards the job boards, asking him, "Did you see anything suitable?"

Francis opened his mouth to respond but he never got the chance.

"I thought not. Have you considered enrolling in one of our adult education courses? There are plenty of night classes at the local Tech School."

She pulled open a drawer in her desk and drew out a bundle of leaflets and passed several of them across

"Take a look at this literature and give it some thought. It might be worth your while. In the meantime, I need you to fill out this form. Please do so at one of the counters over there and bring it back when you have finished. And don't forget to sign it, otherwise we can't process your claim. There are biro pens available if you need one"

Francis took the yellow form.

"How long is it likely to take, before the claim goes through?" he asked.

"About a week, if our checks are satisfactory. You not having any children will speed things up. You will then need to attend the Benefits Office on a fortnightly basis to sign on in order to claim unemployment benefits. Failure to attend will mean your claim will be cancelled and a new one will need to be made."

"How much is it? The dole money?" he inquired quietly.

"£28.45p per week, paid every two weeks. You will be sent a giro cheque through the post which you can cash at the post office. Now please kindly fill out the form."

Thus dismissed, Francis came to his feet and walked across to the line of counters near the door. He found a stool and pen and set to work filling out the form, starting with his name, address and date of birth.

He'd just flipped over onto page 2 when he sensed somebody at his shoulder and when he turned to look, he saw it was the two skinheads from before. One of them had a gold chain around his neck, dangling against the outside of his torn t-shirt. His mate, who was skinny and covered with acne, was grinning like a fool. They both watched him closely.

Francis stared back and silently sighed to himself.

"Go on, Kevin, ask him," the spotty one urged.

"Give me a fucking chance, you spaz."

Kevin, who looked around eighteen or nineteen but fidgeted like a ten-year-old, leaned in until his face was just inches away from Francis'.

"So, what was it like?" he asked, a smirk appearing on his features.

Francis shook his head and shrugged.

"You know, doing it?"

"Doing what?"

"Stabbing her, you knob. Using a knife on that kiddie. Sticking it in. It takes some balls, does that." He almost sounded like he admired him.

Francis closed his eyes and breathed out through his nostrils.

"I wish I knew how it felt. To use a blade on someone. To keep stabbing 'em," Kevin was saying whimsically

"You fucking idiot," his mate interjected loudly, "he didn't stab her, he strangled her. With his bare hands."

"I knew that, you spaz! I was just testing him to make sure he really was the sick fucker who killed her, wasn't I?"

Francis tried to ignore them and continued to fill out the form.

"So, then? What was it like? You put your hands around her skinny little neck and squeezed the life out of her, right? How long did it take? Did she fight back?"

Kevin lifted his hands and mimicked the act of throttling someone and his mate did a strange little jig like he was dancing on hot coals, and the two of them were nearly wetting themselves from laughter as they dashed out the door, banging on the window and leering through the glass as they ran off.

Francis saw several heads turn in his direction and he felt his face flush, reddening his burned cheeks even further. He felt a hot pricking in his eyes and he rubbed at them with his sleeve, keeping them cast down at the form. Someone chuckled, but it was just a group of women hurrying along the pavement. A caretaker unlocked a door, his bunch of keys rattling and reminding him of the prison guards jangling their keyrings in the evenings.

Francis heard a buzzing sound in his head. He could feel his breath coming in shallow gasps. He clicked the end cap of the biro with his thumb, faster and faster. A clock ticked, a dog barked over and over, a typewriter carriage clanged loudly.

With a strangled whimper, Francis swept the sheaf of papers off the counter onto the floor and fled out of the door.

7

WHEN HE ARRIVED HOME, FRANCIS scurried straight up to his bedroom. He wanted to compose himself before Mum saw his distressed state. He sat on the edge of his bed and rubbed at his face vigorously, ignoring the pain this caused to his scalded skin.

He felt humiliated and angry.

The woman in the Benefits Office had treated him like an object of derision, something she would scrape off her shoe, while the two yobs thought the whole thing one big laugh, a lark. They were no different from the inmates and prison staff. Being a free man, cleared of any wrongdoing over the murder of that poor child, made no difference. People like that would believe what they wanted to believe, no matter what the courts said.

Tomorrow, they had another hearing to attend as part of his application for financial recompense. The family solicitor would be there. Francis could raise this with him. Pamela, if she'd have gone with him this morning, would have raised merry hell there and then, threatening to put in an official complaint and maybe even to contact their local MP, who just happened to be one of their staunchest supporters.

Francis though was too timid and unsure. He admitted this. All his life, through his childhood and teenage years, he had been a quiet and nervous boy. Not a mummy's boy. Just shy and introverted. An easy target for bullies at school and after, in the big wide world. Even at work, when he had been a caretaker's assistant at his old primary school, Francis had found himself picked on, by the teachers and, worst of all, the kids. Children as young as eight or nine taunting him, for crying out loud! Calling him stupid and slow just because he liked to spend time by himself, reading books and comics, instead of hanging out and doing normal adult things. About the only person who had treated him okay back then, the only person who really understood him and who Francis thought of as a friend, was his school pal, Jimmy Wade. Even that seemed to change after his arrest and trial. Until their paths had crossed this morning, anyway.

So the upshot was that Francis would just let the incident in the Benefit's Office slide. As he always did. Turning the other cheek was his speciality, after all.

Francis stood up and looked out of the window.

A bank of clouds had slid in over the trees at the back of the house. It was starting to shower.

Leaving his room, he went back downstairs and quietly slipped out the back door. He pulled his coat hood up as rain blew into his face. With the cap on as well, he felt cocooned from the world.

Crossing the lawn and stepping around the veggie patch, he went past the garden swing seat (now protected from the weather with a plastic sheet) and opened the gate in the fence. With a glance over his shoulder, Francis went through and followed the dirt track into the woods.

During the summer months, this was a beautiful place. Lit by beams of sunlight filtering through the leaves, tinging this woodland world with varying shades of green, it had been his favourite place ever since first venturing in here with his dad. Through his youth and into young adulthood, he would come here to play or to seek solace from the world around him. Safe behind the wall he had erected about himself.

Memories of those days threatened to engulf him. Of the good times that he'd spent enjoying his own company, away from all of the cruelty.

On a wet day like today, it was gloomy beneath the canopy of branches. He didn't mind though. The rain meant there was less likelihood of dog walkers. Right now, he wanted to be alone.

Because as well as the reminders of the good times, this place also triggered bad thoughts for Francis. The woods revealed his darker memories and moods, the trees and footpaths acting as markers to a small cache of stygian imaginings that were tucked away in the shadows at the back of his mind.

He walked along the dirt track deeper and deeper into the trees until the sepulchral shadows lent the woods a nebulous, twilight feel.

Francis listened to the rustlings of animals in the undergrowth; of squirrels scampering up tree trunks at his approach, of birds flitting through branches. He knew these woods like the backs of his hands, with every hollow and slope of the ground, each twist and turn in the meandering track, cauterized into his brain and still as vivid now despite the passage of time.

After five minutes, he reached a fork in the dirt track. Here, a felled tree lay just a few metres away. Francis walked over and felt with his hands along the back of the mossy trunk until he came to a particular knot in the bark. Leaning over the dead tree, he looked for a small split in the trunk, a tiny hole just big enough to push his fingers inside.

At first, he couldn't find it, so he pushed the hood of his coat back and removed his cap so he could see easier, and a moment later he spotted the hole. Reaching in, his fingers touched cold metal and he drew out a small key.

Pocketing it in his jeans and replacing his cap and hood, he went back to the dirt track and took the left-hand path until he came to a long and twisty tree root that looped over the ground to the right.

Bending down, Francis cleared away moss and detritus to reveal a flat stone slab resting on the earth. Probing with his hands, he grabbed the edge and lifted it clear.

Buried underneath was an oblong-shaped metal strongbox, exactly where he had left it over twelve years ago. It was rusty and the hinges were clogged with dirt, but otherwise it looked pretty much the same. More importantly, the box hadn't been disturbed.

Nobody except Francis knew about the strongbox, nor what it contained. Not his mum or his dear departed dad, not Pamela, especially not the police.

He had buried it here and hidden the only key that day, before fleeing back home. Francis didn't know why, he just had. He hadn't told anyone of it even during the horrible police interrogations and the trial. Not even during the appeal case. It was Francis' little secret, hidden away in his private little world.

Taking hold of the handles at each end of the box, he hefted it out of the hole and lay it flat on the ground. Francis knelt in the dirt. Then, producing the key and hoping the lock hadn't rusted shut, he pushed the key in and twisted. After the slightest bit of resistance, the lock turned. Francis pulled the lid open.

Inside, there were three items.

Wrapped in an oily rag was a black SP50 Air Pistol. A present on his fourteenth birthday from his grandfather, it was the type where you pushed in the barrel and unscrewed a small plug at the back and loaded either a tiny lead pellet or a feathered dart. He'd used it for shooting at paper targets or tin cans and occasionally for rabbiting.

His parents had known nothing about the air pistol.

Beside the air pistol was a hunting knife. It had a wooden handle carved with the face of a deer. It came with a small leather sheath and its six-inch blade had a serrated edge. Francis had purchased the knife from a fishing tackle shop with his pocket money about the same time as he was given the gun.

His parents also knew nothing about the knife.

The last item lay at the bottom of the box and, to Francis, was the most precious of all. It was a piece of cloth folded up into a neat little square. He reached in and gingerly removed it, allowing it to unfurl to reveal it to be a small cotton handkerchief with initials embroidered into a corner.

S. R

The handkerchief had once been white, but age had turned it yellow and there were faint lines of dirt in the creases.

Francis brought it up to his face and sniffed the material, imagining that he caught a faint fragrance, a scent that made him gently breathe in, but in reality, the handkerchief was all musty and smelled unpleasant.

Closing and locking the strongbox again, Francis returned it to the hole and covered it over with the stone slab and scraped leaves over the spot. Then he continued along the dirt track, clutching the handkerchief carefully, almost reverently, in his hand.

Shortly, he left the track and cut a route up a slope at an oblique angle towards a particularly dense thicket of trees. Pushing his way through brambles, he emerged at the edge of a shallow hollow.

Francis hesitated as he contemplated the remote location. Looking at the leaves and twigs scattered about, his mind superimposed the image of a tiny body furled up at the bottom, a young girl with her arms and legs tucked in, one shoe on and one shoe off, her blonde curly hair fluttering in the breeze, blue dress radiant despite the gloom.

To the Francis of today, the girl looked like she had just laid down and fallen asleep. She seemed peaceful and calm.

He remembered the reality of that day to be different, though. He recalled the creepy crawlies carpeting her body, the swarm of flies hovering in the air. The smell. His scream. Then, after his initial shock, the feeling of fascination which overcame his revulsion and the strange compulsion to go down into the hollow and retrieve the handkerchief from a pocket in her dress. A keepsake, to remember her by.

Finally, he recalled finding a good hiding spot for the strongbox, because Francis knew the police would want to know exactly why he'd been in the woods with an air pistol and a hunting knife shortly before discovering the body of the missing schoolgirl.

Back in the present, Francis blinked slowly and then stepped down into the hollow. Carefully, he lowered himself to the ground and curled up beside his imagined vision of the sleeping girl. He wrapped one arm about her translucent shoulder as if to warm her and shelter her from the rain.

In his hand, Francis clasped the handkerchief.

•   •   •

Feeling chilled and weary and thoroughly dejected, Francis traipsed back to his house and, after hiding the handkerchief and key at the back of his sock drawer, he ran himself a hot bath. Peeling off his damp clothes, he lowered himself into the steaming water and lay back with a groan.

He cast his mind back over the last few days since his release from prison, the sly looks and whispered comments, the hurtful insinuations, and his mind boiled at the cruel injustice of it all.

While he'd been incarcerated, there had been very little he could do about his lot in life. The days and then the weeks and months, eventually the years, had blurred into one endless existence of mind-numbing boredom and routine, with nothing to mark the days apart. Although classed as a Lifer sentenced to a minimum of fifteen years, because of the nature of the crime he'd been found guilty of – the killing of a child, the worst kind of offence that even other cons found repulsive – his was an indeterminate sentence with no hope of parole unless he admitted his guilt. Francis had refused to do so, never wavering from his determination to always plead his innocence. Even through the darkest of days, he would not admit to something that he hadn't done. So, his misery went on and he'd existed in a kind of limbo, reconciled to the likelihood that he would never be released.

But, after twelve years of being locked away, things had dramatically changed. Their long legal battle to prove the conviction was unsound finally paid off. With the discovery of new, irrefutable evidence and a long-overdue admittance from the police that one of their detectives had willingly fabricated a web of lies and deceit designed to pin the blame on a gullible and shy local teenager, his circumstances altered. Cleared by the appeal courts, Francis was now back home with his family and finally in a position to do something about it.

Why should he hide away? Francis thought to himself as he bathed.

He'd done nothing wrong and he owed society nothing.

Society owed him.

Laying in the water, he briefly fantasized about taking revenge, of confronting the bent copper who had destroyed his life and paying him back. That wasn't going to happen, sadly. The detective in question had enjoyed a stellar career following Francis' conviction, promoted up the ranks and going on to be a prominent member of The Ripper Squad in the late seventies, before dropping dead at a New Year's Eve party two years ago.

Then there was the real killer.

The person responsible for the murder had never been found. Apart from Francis, there had been no other arrests. At the time, he was the only suspect the police had, and this had blinkered them to all other avenues of investigation, destroying his chance of a fair trial.

Which meant another avenue to vent his frustration had slipped through his fingers.

Francis felt truly vexed at his plight.

So, he decided as he climbed out of the bath and towelled himself dry, the only course left to him was to seek a full and complete apology, with no strings attached, to finally clear his name and absolve him of all blame for the murder. Tomorrow's hearing would begin this process when they would file a claim for court-awarded compensation, damages for the mental torture he and his family had endured.

Just then, he heard the telephone down in the hall ring and a moment later his mum was calling up to him.

It was his school pal, Jimmy Wade, she said. Something about going for a drink.

Mum thought it was a bad idea, but Francis determined more than ever that he'd had enough of people pointing the finger.

Sod them all!

8

THEIR SOLICITOR, GORDON DREYFUSS, MET them in the car park close to Bradford Crown Court at 9am sharp the following morning.

The hearing wouldn't be taking place in the court building. Instead, a room had been set aside just across Drake Street in the old St George's Hall.

Dreyfuss was a snazzily dressed man with dark tight curls smothered with hair gel and sporting a colourful bow tie. He smelled of strong cologne and walked with a cane walking stick. Considering how he dashed into the road and held the walking stick aloft to hold back the traffic, Francis surmised it was more for effect than because of any disability.

They entered through a side door to avoid a small gaggle of journalists waiting on the front steps. Inside, they were escorted by a member of staff to their meeting room on the second floor. Several people were already waiting, seated around a long table. Amongst them was a senior officer from West Yorkshire Police, his smart uniform and tie telling Francis he was the recently appointed Assistant Chief Constable. With him were a pair of lawyers from the Police Misconduct Service.

Polite introductions were made but no smiles were exchanged between the two groups. After they were served tea, the meeting soon got underway.

This was a preliminary meeting, the first of many sessions in the hearing, and was an opportunity for both sides to set out their stall and to establish whether there was any basis for a mutually satisfying outcome. It soon became apparent that this wouldn't be the case. The police had decided on the policy of closing ranks and protecting their reputation, still tarnished after the Ripper case. Another scandal was the last thing they needed right now. One bad apple did not mean the whole West Yorkshire Police Federation was rotten, although Francis wasn't sure how they came to that conclusion. A miscarriage of justice in such a high-profile case could not simply be swept under the carpet. Blaming it all on one bent copper wouldn't wash, surely?

Their solicitor, Dreyfuss, was also having none of that rubbish, Francis and his mum and sister were glad to hear.

"Even now," he was saying with a steely timbre in his voice, "my client is still waiting for an apology and an offer of recompense. Why can't West Yorkshire Police just do the right thing, say sorry, and tender a substantial offer for an ex-gratia payment of compensation?"

"The Police Federation has made a fair and balanced suggestion for financial damages which it believes truly reflects Mr Bailey's unfortunate dilemma," one of the police lawyers countered smoothly, "which we still insist was a case of mismanagement by the investigating officer in charge of the case. Who, unfortunately, isn't here to answer for his error of judgement."

"Error of judgement? A balanced offer? Twenty-five thousand pounds was the offer you made. Which equates to two thousand pounds for each year that my client was incarcerated, or roughly one hundred and seventy pounds per month, or, to put it another way, less than six pounds for each day that he was wrongly banged up!" He hit the table with his hand as if to emphasize his choice of phrase. "A punitive settlement doesn't even come close to describing it!"

"We were led to believe that Mr Bailey is of the mind this isn't just about the money, Mr Dreyfuss. The money is a side issue. Isn't that the case, Mr Bailey? May we call you Francis?" He smiled thinly, an effort that his face seemed to find difficulty in managing.

"Yes, no amount of proper compensation can restore my client's missing years, nor can it undo the original damage done, but it certainly helps," Dreyfuss came back. "People who are wrongly convicted should be compensated for all their losses on the same basis as other claims. The Court of Appeal clearly distinguished between Mr Bailey's innocence and guilt, and concluded he was the victim of a terrible injustice."

The police lawyer held up his hand to stay Dreyfuss and he quietly conversed with his partner. All the time this heated exchange was going on, Francis felt the glare of the Assistant Chief Constable burning into him across the table. Francis refused to look away and he looked straight back at him.

His mother must have noticed, for she put a restraining hand on his forearm.

"From a legal point of view, this is not a miscarriage of justice, Mr Dreyfuss. A miscarriage of justice, in legal parlance, is when a person is convicted of a crime but later their case is re-opened and their conviction found to be unsafe—"

"Precisely," his sister, Pamela, cut in.

"And only then when the actual guilty party is identified and convicted beyond reasonable doubt," the police lawyer went on with barely a pause. "Neither has happened in this case. There has been no trial or conviction of the person responsible for the murder of the young girl."

"Only because you never caught him, you fool!" Pamela blurted, unable to contain herself. "You announced that with no new leads, the case was being wound down. Where does that leave my brother?"

"Without a trial and successful conviction, there is no legal basis for your client to be officially characterized as the victim of a miscarriage of justice. Coupled with the fact that Mr Bailey made a full confession at the time also means—"

"This is a joke! Just like I said, Mum." Pamela was well known for having a low bullshit threshold.

"My client's confession, as you all well know, was made under extreme police duress, without the presence of a lawyer to advise him."

"Which, in the 1970s, was not a legal requirement. West Yorkshire Police were perfectly entitled to question Mr Bailey without legal representation. He was an adult, after all."

"My client also claimed that physical force was used to persuade him to make the confession and that the said confession – a fairy tale would be a more apt description – was written down later by the investigating officer."

"None of that was ever proven during his trial," the Assistant Chief Constable said, jabbing his finger across the table, the first time that he had spoken. "Therefore, it is irrelevant."

Dreyfuss sat back and slowly folded his arms.

"Was my client's medical condition at the time irrelevant as well, Assistant Chief Constable?" he asked quietly. "Amongst many things, this was not brought to the jury's attention."

"That was never established beyond doubt."

"Oh, come now," Dreyfuss replied to the police officer, and he reached into his thick file of papers. "I have the original medical report written by my client's GP. Here, take a look."

He leaned across the table with a sheet of paper in his hand, but the Deputy Chief Constable waved it away.

"As I understand it, our own experts came to a rather different assessment of his medical condition."

"Ah yes, increased testosterone that promoted violent tendencies, wasn't that what your experts said? The jury was given details of a completely different medical disorder, one that Mr Bailey has never suffered from. An open and shut case indeed," Dreyfuss sneered.

The meeting wasn't going how they had hoped, Francis decided.

"Please," said the police lawyer, "can we return to the main issues that we are here to—"

But the Assistant Chief Constable went on, cutting off his own man.

"You know, it was also never truly established just what your client was doing that day in the woods. To this day, he refuses to enlighten us."

Francis came more alert just then. Looking at the smarmy look on the police officer's face made his blood pressure go up.

"I still find it strange that not only was he the last person to see the young girl alive at the school, but he also just happened to be the person who found her body hidden in the woods just behind his home."

Dreyfuss shook his head. "Ancient history. Mr Bailey was the last person to see the girl, yes. He was the caretaker's assistant at her school and he came across her in the school changing rooms, in a very upset state. She came from a broken home and lived in a very chaotic environment, and was the victim of child neglect. She was crying and so Mr Bailey was simply trying to comfort her."

"Comfort her? That's one way of putting it!"

"What the hell does that mean?" Pamela demanded, and half came to her feet.

There was a moment of tense silence that swelled the air in the small room. Francis could feel another of his headaches coming on.

"You still can't help yourself, can you?" his sister said. "You're still trying to cover things up. You corrupt bastards!"

"Pamela, dear," Mum soothed.

After a few seconds, Pamela lowered herself back into her chair, but she looked like she was ready to launch herself across the table and grab the Assistant Chief Constable by the throat at any second.

"We are not here to conduct a retrial, are we not?" Gordon Dreyfuss informed everyone. "My client is innocent. That cannot be disputed. Today's hearing is to decide on a package of compensation appropriate to the wrongful imprisonment suffered by him. Twelve years were taken away from him because of a culture of incompetence and corruption in the police force. Twelve years of hell, of prison beatings, of injuries and punishments dished out to him by other prisoners and prison staff, of sexual assaults. Plus a lifetime of mental torture. In the meantime, while Mr Bailey was away, his family suffered in equal measures. They had to put up with vile gossip, harassment and criminal damage against their homes. His father died from the stress, his sister's marriage fell apart and she was forced to sell her home to pay for her brother's legal costs, and his mother was left having to live with the knowledge that her son, her child, was accused of the most heinous of crimes."

Dreyfuss paused and drummed his fingers on the tabletop as though deep in thought. It was a very good performance,

Francis acknowledged. Drama of the highest order that any actor would be proud of.

"All of this will be taken into consideration after we have studied the court papers and then submitted our claim, sometime in the next few weeks," he went on. "But I warn you, Assistant Chief Constable, that the sum we have in mind is significantly higher than your paltry offer."

"We'll see what the Home Office has to say about that. Leon Brittan has a reputation for being tough on law and order. Don't forget, the murder case has never officially been closed, just temporarily paused pending further developments," he finished, with a long stare at Francis.

The meeting broke up a few minutes later and the Assistant Chief Constable filed out with his legal team.

"Well, that went well," Francis mumbled under his breath when the four of them were alone.

"I thought that it did, actually," Dreyfuss quipped.

Francis, Pamela and their mother all stared at him.

Dreyfuss looked back, saying, "I've attended worse hearings, indeed I have. It's not unknown for violence to break out. Today's was a relatively quiet affair."

Francis shook his head as he shrugged on his coat.

"Besides, the Assistant Chief Constable is just in a bad mood because he is being seconded to South Yorkshire Police. Apparently, they need help cracking open a few striking miners' heads, which is just up that man's street."

"Champion," Francis replied.

They left the meeting room and Francis and his family waited in the hallway while their solicitor went to make a phone call. When he reappeared five minutes later, Francis asked what their next move should be.

"Now we pop over to the court building, young man."

They retraced their steps back down the staircase and out through the side entrance, once again avoiding the group of reporters from the local press who were still loitering at the front.

Entering the courthouse, they were quickly cleared through security and Dreyfuss signed them in.

"I took the liberty last week of ordering two full copies of the court records from both of Francis's original trial and retrial, as well as any associated documents," the solicitor explained as they followed him down a corridor. "I also asked for the transcripts of police interviews, doctors reports and the prison incident book – the latter should contain a complete catalogue of any injuries that you sustained while in prison."

"If they bothered recording them all," Pamela pointed out with a sceptical tone to her voice.

"I've thought of that, young miss, so I have also been granted access to witness statements from other prisoners, plus records of their disciplinary sanctions. If any of them saw your brother been assaulted or in fact were the ones responsible for attacking him, then we will find out, fear not."

"That must have taken some effort on your part," their mum said.

"The police and prison officials weren't exactly helpful, but in the end they had no choice but to hand them over. Democracy in action, Mrs Bailey. Ah, here we are."

He pushed open a door and stepped into a small room.

Inside, there were two desks and a stack of chairs. A cardboard box file rested on each desk, both bearing identical hand-written labels.

"One set for each of us. Everything we need to know is contained right here," Dreyfuss told them as he tapped one of the boxes. "From the information we glean, I think we should be able to present a very strong case for substantial financial redress. I will take this box, you take the other, and we can go over things in more comfortable settings over the coming weeks."

He smiled warmly at Francis.

"It will take some time. It will bring back lots of bad memories for you, sadly, but with a little patience and lots of hard work, we will get there in the end. Come along now, there's no time to waste."

•   •   •

They carried the boxes outside to their cars. Before they drove away, Dreyfuss told them he would be in touch in a few days after he'd looked at the files and come up with a proposal on how next to proceed. Then they bid farewell.

Pamela took them straight home.

As they turned onto their cul-de-sac half an hour later, she suddenly gasped and hit the brakes. Sitting in the back, Francis and Mum craned their necks to see what was wrong.

Daubed across their front door in red paint and big letters were the words

CHILD KILLER

They all stared opened mouthed at the graffiti. After a long moment of drawn-out silence, Pamela gave a little groan and slumped forward with her forehead resting on the car's steering wheel.

Francis climbed out of the car and walked over to the low wall near the edge of their flower garden, his brow furrowing. The paint had run so that it collected on the garden path like pools of blood.

He glanced around and caught the movement of a twitching curtain from two doors down. Further along the road, an elderly gent looked up from washing his car but when he caught Francis's eye, he quickly looked away and went back to his task.

Going back to the car, he tapped on the driver's window. Pamela wound it down. He thought that he saw a dampness in her eye. In the back, Mum was sniffling and dabbing her cheeks with a hanky.

"Take Mum inside," he told his sister. "I'll clean this up."

He found some old rags and turpentine in the garden shed and took them outside. Then he filled a plastic bucket with hot soapy water and grabbed a scrubbing brush from beneath the sink in the utility room.

Returning to the front garden, he was just in time to see a police patrol car slowly cruise by the house, its occupants glancing his way. Francis watched as it turned around in the turning circle at the end of the cul-de-sac, where the driver switched off his engine. They continued to watch him.

Francis returned their stares for several seconds, waiting to see if they would step out. Maybe one of the neighbours had called them, having seen the graffiti. The two coppers made no attempt to leave the comfort of their car, however.

Francis, of course, could report the vandalism and get the police to look into it, but something told him that this would be a waste of time. For all he knew, they could have done it themselves.

He turned away and set to work removing the offensive words from the door. Applying turpentine to the rags, he wiped at the painted lettering, which fortunately was still wet. He was able to remove most of it, then set about scrubbing the remainder off with the scrubbing brush. He would repaint the door tomorrow.

All the while, he was aware of the two coppers watching him from down the road. He could feel their eyes burning into the back of his skull. At one point, when Francis looked over his shoulder, he saw one of them making notes in his pocketbook.

Swearing under his breath, Francis turned around and flung the scrubbing brush into the bucket of soapy water and, with his hands on his hips, defiantly watched them right back.

The standoff lasted for around thirty seconds. Finally, the driver turned on the ignition and pulled away. He and his colleague made a deliberate show of looking his way again as they drove out of the cul-de-sac.

•　　　　　•　　　　　•

It was late in the evening when the second incident happened.

Mum and Pamela had gone to bed earlier than usual. The three of them had discussed the graffiti, wondering who might be responsible. Mum was certain that it wouldn't be any of the neighbours. She'd insisted that she got on well with them and most had been hugely sympathetic to their plight as it had become more and more clear that the quiet young man from next door was a victim of police bungling and corruption. On the news of his imminent release, some had even called around to offer their congratulations and best wishes, keen to mention how they'd known Francis was innocent all along.

Francis suspected that Mum was being a little naïve, was too gullible and trusting, and from Pamela's downcast eyes he guessed his sister shared this view.

He daresay that it was also a case of their mum wanting to move on, to not dwell on the nastiness. She had put up with this kind of harassment for too long and was weary of it. People would soon get bored and find something else to vent their spleen at, she told him before going up the stairs.

But then, after Pamela had followed her to bed and just as the time was approaching midnight, Francis, who was sitting in the living room with the TV switched off and just one weak lamp lighting the room, looked up from his ruminations as a movement caught his attention.

It was a shadow flitting across the closed curtains, the silhouette of someone hurrying along the garden path.

Then he heard the letterbox flap go and a second later the shadow went by in the opposite direction.

Francis leaped out of the armchair and rushed out into the hall and flicked on the light switch.

A horrible smell assailed his nostrils, seconds before he saw the steaming turd on the doormat.

He charged for the door in a fury and yanked it open and jumped over the offending matter.

Outside, he looked wildly in both directions up and down the cul-de-sac.

There was nobody around.

The neighbourhood was deserted. Most of the house lights were off. He thought that he heard running footsteps ringing in the distance but couldn't be sure. Somewhere, a fox was barking.

"You bastards!" Francis yelled into the night. "You bloody bastards. Come and show yourselves, you cowards! I'm not afraid of you!"

There was no reply. A cold wind was blowing down from the north, making the night cold, but Francis' blood was up.

He moved down the drive into the middle of the road.

"I've done nothing wrong! You won't force me to leave, do you hear? This is my home and I'm going nowhere!"

9

FRIDAY NIGHT AT EIGHT O'CLOCK and Francis was suited and booted for a night out with his old pal, Jimmy Wade. With help from Pamela, he had updated his wardrobe to something less 1970s. Tonight, he was wearing jeans with a matching denim shirt and brown desert boots. She had styled his hair with gel. He had ten quid in his wallet and was ready to go.

A car horn honking outside brought him dashing down the stairs. Mum was waiting in the hallway, looking all anxious and worried, still not convinced him going out was a good idea. The unsavoury incidents from a few days ago were fresh in her mind, no doubt, but Francis was having none of this cowering-away-in-their-home business. He wanted to make a point.

She hugged and kissed him and Francis squirmed away but told her that everything would be fine. Then he was stepping over the freshly-scrubbed doormat and through the freshly-painted front door and down the garden path, hoping the neighbours were watching.

He saw the lime-green Capri parked at the roadside and he walked towards it confidently, waving to Jimmy. Then he stopped dead when he saw the two women in the back.

Francis had assumed it would be just him and Jimmy, out for a few pints and a game of darts, like in the old days when they had first left school. Jimmy, it seemed, had other ideas.

He'd sprung a big surprise on him and going off the big grin on his face, he was enjoying the alarm he'd caused Francis.

Alarm it was because Francis had never been comfortable around girls. It wasn't because he didn't like them – he did, a lot! – but he'd never been one of the cool kids at school, was in fact the No 1 Geek who always became flustered and tongue-tied on the few rare occasions that girls or women had ever shown an interest in him. Now, after a forced hiatus of twelve years when it came to any romantic entanglements, he felt suddenly panicky and anxious at the prospect of going on a date, even if it was a foursome. He doubted his inability to woo a woman had changed.

If it was even a date. He didn't know what to think.

"Hi pal," Jimmy said. "You're looking cool, I like the get-up. I want you to meet Tracey and Mandy."

Jimmy pointed over his shoulder with his thumb at the girls sitting on the back seat.

Francis gave Jimmy a hard stare, before bending down and poking his head through the window, smiling.

"Hello," he mumbled.

"Hello Francis!" two voices sang out in unison.

One of them had dark hair and eye makeup like Cleopatra, the other a blonde bob and a Boy George hat on. They looked at each other and giggled.

"Well get in, why don't you?" Jimmy said.

Francis opened the passenger door but Jimmy held up a hand.

"You'll have to get in the back between the ladies. The front seat's knackered. Unless you want a spring up your arse, pal."

He patted the seat affectionately.

"This baby has seen lots of action," Jimmy added, eliciting more giggles from the back.

Jimmy pulled the front passenger seat forward to make way for Francis, who squirmed through the opening. Tracey and Mandy slid apart to give him some room in the middle.

"And keep your hands off Tracey, she's spoken for, pal."

Francis had no idea which was Tracey and which was Mandy.

He stared straight ahead. His throat felt dry and already his mind was blank and incapable of thinking of anything to say.

"Right, let's get this party started," Jimmy announced. He pushed a cassette into the tape deck and *Frankie Goes to Hollywood* burst into life. He pulled away from the kerb.

Francis resisted the urge to look out the passenger window because he knew Mum would be watching from the living room and anyway, he was distracted when Jimmy asked him, "Where do you want to go first, The Old Cock or The Royal Oak?"

"It's up to you, Jimmy," he answered quietly, trying his best to sound cool. "I'm easy."

"Alrighty, we'll try The Royal Oak first, the beer's better there. What do you say, ladies?"

"Yes!" they both chorused.

Jimmy was a fast driver. He also liked to brake hard in order to throw the girls about, as well as rev the engine whenever he stopped at a light. Francis was beginning to wish he'd stayed at home.

One of the girls – either Tracey or Mandy – slipped their arm through his, while the other – either Mandy or Tracey - twiddled her finger in his ear. Both snuggled up to him so that their cheeks were nearly pressed against his.

Jimmy must have noticed, for he altered his rearview mirror so he could see better into the back of his car. He gave Francis a wink and then lit a cigarette.

"So, what do you like to do, Francis?" asked the one in the Boy George hat.

"Oh, this and that, Tracey" he answered.

"I'm Mandy, that's Tracey. Do you like music?"

Francis nodded. His knowledge of music was out of date. Was David Cassidy still a thing, he wondered.

"Turn the music up, Jimmy!" Mandy called out.

"Are we there yet?" Tracey asked. "I'm dying for a Hawaiian!"

Francis wondered if she was talking about a man, thinking to himself, what kind of night was this going to be?

They pulled up outside the pub five minutes later and they all piled inside.

The Royal Oak hadn't changed much. From the outside, it appeared to be an olde-worlde drinking Inn of black and white oak beams and a pillared entrance porch that promised a tranquil interior of roaring fires and a jovial landlord. Inside, it was a dive.

Cheap tables and chairs were scattered about haphazardly, most occupied by a variety of patrons of different age groups and social classes, ranging from well-heeled yuppies out looking for a bit of rough to people on the dole nursing their pint. One elderly man standing at the bar looked like he was rooted to the floor, for although he swayed lazily from left to right, like all professional drinkers he refused to keel over. Maybe it was the sticky carpets that kept him upright.

The clink of pool balls came from the back room, while in the snug, a gaggle of pensioners squabbled over their game of dominoes. Cigarette and weed smoke rolled in dense waves beneath the low ceiling.

Mandy spotted a spare bench beneath one of the tiny windows and dragged Francis across. Tracey joined them while Jimmy ordered the first round.

When the drinks arrived, Jimmy snuggled up to Tracey and within a couple of minutes, they were having a game of tonsil tennis. Francis sipped at his beer while they canoodled.

Mandy leaned her head against his shoulder.

"Do you know, I think it's terrible the way they treated you, Francis," she said quietly.

He looked down at her, but with the Boy George hat on, he couldn't see much of her face.

"I read about it in the paper. About how they fitted you up and sent you to prison, then refused to believe your mum that you were with her at the time that little girl was... well, you know. I can't believe that sort of thing still happens, that the police can behave like that in this day and age. It's 1984, haven't we moved on at all after those riots in Brixton? I tell you, this country is going to the dogs."

Her voice was soft and she sounded genuinely sympathetic, he thought that he even detected a tremor in her words.

He didn't know how to respond. He wasn't used to people saying nice things to him, taking him at face value.

Then, to his surprise, Mandy tilted her head back and kissed him lightly on the cheek, which although it caused him to blush, also sent a warm glow melting through his body. He smiled back and drank from his glass. For the first time this evening, he was starting to relax. Perhaps the night would turn out to be okay after all.

Later, Mandy went with him to the bar for another set of drinks, and he felt confident enough to even go over to the jukebox and select a track – this one by *Duran Duran.* Mandy insisted that he have a little dance. He thought he might die from embarrassment but actually found himself having fun as they boogied away, with Tracey and Jimmy laughing along.

"Just like old times, pal, what did I tell ya?" Jimmy said and raised his glass.

Francis gave a thumbs up before Mandy moved in for a cuddle and another jive.

"I like you, Francis," she purred in his ear. "Do you like me, too?"

Francis nodded and pressed his hand against the small of her back.

"Will you be my boyfriend?"

"I guess so," he replied, trying to keep the stammer out of his voice.

"I bet you haven't had many girlfriends, have you?" she teased. "Even when you were younger."

"Only one or two," he lied because there hadn't been any.

"Oh, Francis, you little honeybuns." She stuck out her bottom lip and looked up at him with sad brown eyes. Then she smiled, saying brightly, "But you have one now. Me!"

They decided to move on to another pub. They skipped the Old Cock because it was full of rugby players celebrating a win, instead going to The Upper George. Frequented by Hells Angels and popular for its live bands, the pub was always busy with drinkers getting plastered before heading for a nightclub.

They walked along the short, covered alleyway towards the entrance, but at the last second, Mandy steered Francis away towards the Gents.

Before he knew what was happening, she had him pressed up against the wall and her lips were pressing against his own. Her tongue probed the inside of his mouth. He could taste peppermint on her breath.

For a couple of heartbeats, a sense of panic and uncertainty threatened to send him fleeing in confusion. This sort of thing didn't happen to him. Then he felt Mandy grab his hands and push them against her plump breasts.

"You can have a feel, babes," Mandy said breathlessly. "I don't mind."

Francis squeezed with his hands, moving them around in precise circular movements like he was kneading dough, and this made Mandy giggle. Her giggle quickly morphed into a moan and she kissed him passionately.

"Do you want to do it?" she asked him.

Francis wasn't sure. He'd never done it before. He cast his eyes towards the door, thinking to himself that the Gents' toilets weren't the most romantic place to *do it.*

"I bet you do, don't you? There's a Johnny machine on the wall there, have you got twenty pence?"

Francis fished in his pocket for a handful of change and picked out a twenty pence piece.

"Oh God, babes," Mandy groaned as she squirmed against him and then he felt her unfastening the front of his trousers. They fell to the floor and Mandy was pushing at his y-fronts and then she stepped back, leaving him standing there with them around his ankles.

Mandy looked at his limp penis and began to laugh. She pointed with one hand and the other covered her mouth as she had a fit of the giggles. Now, her laughter wasn't so pleasant or jolly. Gone was the merriment of moments ago. Instead, it had a coarseness to it, an earthiness that made Francis' tummy do a queasy backflip.

Suddenly the door to the alleyway flew open and Jimmy and Tracey were there and they were pointing at his penis and laughing as well, and Tracey was bent double and tears were pouring down her face.

"I told you," Jimmy was saying, "I told you it was tiny! Look at it! Look at his balls as well, they've fucking shrunk!"

Francis felt his face heat up and he caught sight of it in the mirror, all red and splotchy. He hurriedly hitched up his underpants and trousers, but somehow his tiny limp penis and testicles got caught up and he had to tuck them inside, which caused even more belly laughs.

"They showed a picture... of his dick... to the judge! They had a fucking doctor as well, telling him why he has a tiny prick! The jury weren't told, lucky bastards! It put me off me tea!" Jimmy guffawed. "Look at it, Mandy!"

Mandy looked and sniggered and snorted so much that she was close to sobbing.

Francis' vision wobbled and was tinged with red and although he wasn't aware of moving, he must have done so because now his hands were balled into fists and his knuckles were splashed with somebody's blood and instead of laughter, he could hear screams echoing off the tiled walls, and Jimmy Wade was on the floor and his face was like mashed beetroot.

10

THE POLICE CONSTABLE BUNGLED HIM along the covered alleyway towards the patrol car. A small crowd had gathered to watch, their faces lit up in various expressions of excitement at the free drama playing out before them. Further along the pavement there was an ambulance with its rear doors open, allowing Francis a brief glimpse of the medics patching up Jimmy's mangled face.

"Watch your head," the officer advised, before purposely banging Francis' head against the patrol car's doorframe. "Oops."

Francis slumped onto the backseat. His hands were cuffed behind his back, making his wrists and arms ache. The situation triggered all kinds of horrible memories, making him break out in a cold sweat. This couldn't be happening all over again, surely?

He watched as the police officer and his colleague went over to talk to Mandy and Tracey, taking notes and nodding sympathetically as they listened to their statements. He wondered if it was the same two constables he'd seen the other day, outside his house.

After a few minutes, they came back and climbed into the front of the car.

"Can you please get in touch with my mum?" Francis asked.

"Nope."

"Why not? She'll be worried sick when I don't come home?"

The two officers looked at each other and smirked. One of them mumbled something.

"Sorry, what did you say?"

"I said, shut your fucking trap."

Francis recoiled at the words, even though they were spoken very quietly.

"Wh- what?" he stammered.

"Don't you fucking understand English, you little shit?" the driver asked as he turned to scowl at Francis. "I told you to shut up."

"But… but…"

"But… but…" the other constable mimicked in a squeaky little voice, making his mate laugh.

The car engine came to life and they drew away from the pub, leaving the crowd of onlookers behind. Francis thought that he saw Mandy and Tracey smiling to themselves.

"Are you arresting me?" Francis asked, ignoring their suggestion to keep quiet.

There was no answer.

"I didn't do anything wrong," he pleaded, even though he knew that he'd assaulted Jimmy, leaving him lying in a pool of piss with a bloody nose and split lip. God, he was in trouble. Of all the idiotic things that could have happened, getting himself hauled off to the cop shop and charged with ABH just days after coming home from prison was the worst of them. He didn't even know whether the terms of his parole even applied anymore, after his conviction was overturned. Was he out on licence? Would he be back in Wakefield Prison before the night was over? He desperately wanted to speak to his mum.

"Please, you have to understand. I was provoked. I'm sorry that I hit Jimmy, but they were laughing at me and then before I knew it, he was…"

Francis's words trickled to a halt when he realized that they were having no impact on the two police officers.

He looked out of the side window, seeing the Kwik Save supermarket go by on the right, which made him twist in his seat and peer out of the car's rear window.

"Hey!" he called. "Why are we not going to the police station? It's the other way, near the swimming baths."

Again, there was no response from up the front and a horrible heavy feeling slowly sank into his stomach like a heavy stone. He licked his lips and swallowed, hoping, praying that he was wrong. They wouldn't, would they? Surely not. Jesus.

"Wh- where are we going, officer?" he asked meekly. "What are you going to do with me?"

They were still giving him the silent treatment, leaving him to conjure up all kinds of different scenarios as to what might happen. None of them were particularly pleasant.

Francis only had a few minutes to worry about this because they soon left the town behind and were then heading towards the industrial estate on Holmes Road.

Soon after and they turned onto an area of waste ground.

Maybe they were just trying to frighten him, give him the heebie-jeebies.

Yes, that was it. They wanted to scare the life out of him, make him cry and beg. Then they would let him go. Perhaps that's how they got their kicks, their Friday night jollies.

The driver turned off the engine and the two police officers stepped out of the car. Francis heard them conferring over the car roof but couldn't hear what they were discussing.

Then the rear door was opened and Francis was hauled out.

He cast a quick look around. It was very dark here, far away from the town lights. The place was probably deserted at this time of night, with all the premises locked up for the weekend. Unless there was a security guard and a guard dog somewhere, it was just Francis and the two police officers.

He was marched around to the back of the car, then he watched while the driver opened up the boot and shone a torch inside. In the back, Francis saw with dismay a collection of batons and baseball bats. A tremor passed through him as it struck home precisely what they had planned.

"Which do you want, Jacko?" one of the coppers asked.

"Give me the aluminium one. It's nice and short so I won't need to swing it much."

"Good choice, it packs a punch. I'll have the cricket bat tonight, I reckon."

They delved their hands inside and came up with their preferred weapons of choice.

"Okey-dokey," the driver said and turned to contemplate Francis.

Francis looked on as they both wielded their bats, smacking them into the palms of their hands and practicing their swings like they were about to hit the home run or go out into the middle at Lords.

"This is cr-crazy," Francis stammered. "Can't we ta-talk about wh-what happened—"

He never finished the sentence. A fist flashed out, smacking him hard on the nose and he fell flat onto the ground. He lay there stunned and with his eyes watering.

He felt something all sticky and gooey run down his chin. The cartilage in his nose crackled and a sharp pain brought a gasp to his lips. He tasted blood in the back of his throat.

Pushing himself into a sitting position, Francis squinted his eyes and searched for the two police officers. Through his blurred vision, he saw one of them bend over and lean towards him. He thought it was the driver.

"Fucking pervert," Francis heard. "You sick little bastard. It's time someone put a stop to you. What do you say, Jacko?"

"Way past time."

"People like you never change. First of all, you killed that little kiddie—"

"I never, I never did—"

"And because you thought you'd got away with it, because you pulled the wool over the judge's eyes, you thought you'd try it again, didn't you?"

"What?" Francis blurted in confusion.

"That lass back there. She said that you exposed yourself to her in the Gents' toilets."

"That's not what happened!"

"She told us that you pulled her into the Gents, pushed her up against the wall, then got your pecker out and made her touch it. Her friend backs up her account. Then, when Mr Wade rushed in to help her, you lamped him one. You dirty, disgusting sack of shit."

"Disgusting sack of shit," Jacko agreed.

Francis was shaking his head. "No, no, no."

He scrabbled around so that he was on his knees.

"Now, we could haul you into the station, charge you with being a pervy little weasel and drag you before the courts, but I'm sure that slick lawyer of yours, whatshisname? Dreyfuss. He would just pull some stunt, find some ancient loophole from God knows when, and have you back on the streets in no time at all. Where you'll soon be on the lookout for your next unsuspecting victim. Who might not be so lucky as that lass in the pub. In fact, they might end up dead just like—"

"No!"

"Or me and Jacko here could handle this ourselves. Tonight. In the good old-fashioned Yorkshire way of how the police deal with little scrotes like you."

The driver hefted his cricket bat. In the lights from the patrol car, Francis saw that it was dinted and speckled with old rusty-coloured stains.

"Luckily for you, Bailey, we can't actually kill you. Much as we'd like to. Getting rid of your body and covering our tracks is not worth the aggravation, not to mention our time. But we can do you some serious harm, can't we, Jacko."

"Oh aye," Jacko agreed. "Some serious harm."

"Teach you a lesson that you won't forget. So that you get the message. To keep your dirty hands to yourself. Capiche?"

Francis tried to get to his feet, but he was still handcuffed and a little dizzy from the blow to his nose. Still, after a few attempts, he struggled upright. He was about to say something, anything which might ward off what was about to come, when a vicious blow to his solar plexus had him doubled over in agony and retching up bile. A high-pitched whistle was squeezed out of his lungs and he keeled over sideways into the dirt.

He lay there gasping, his whole body wracked with agony.

There was nothing he could do as the two police officers set about doing him some serious harm.

•   •   •

When he was at Wakefield Prison, the Monster Mansion as it was dubbed by the tabloids, the dozens of psychopaths, rapists and murderers imprisoned with him there had singled Francis out for special treatment.

Prisoners, even nutters like Charles Bronson, Britain's most violent inmate, and Robert Maudsley, so dangerous that he was kept locked in a specially-made glass cell for 23 hours a day after eating the brain of one of his four victims, held a particular loathing for child killers. Regardless of their own sickening crimes, they considered the murder of a child beyond the pale.

Several times, Francis had been assaulted and hospitalized. On one occasion, he'd been left with bleeding on the brain after having his head repeatedly slammed with his cell door. These attacks, in conjunction with his wrongful conviction, formed the basis of his request for compensation. Or, at least, they had done, before tonight.

It all seemed a moot point now. That wasn't going to happen anymore.

As Francis lay curled up in a ball in the dirt, hearing the patrol car pull away after the beating, he came to a decision.

Through the excruciating pain of broken fingers and bruised ribs, of smashed cheekbones and a dislocated shoulder, as well as the humiliation of having his trousers pulled down and kicked repeatedly in the groin with boots and bludgeoned with bats, Francis realized that he only had one option left to him.

For a long time, he lay there unable to move. The torment and suffering pulsed through every inch of his overweight physique, throbbing along his nerve endings so that it felt like they were on fire.

After an age, during which the stars overhead swung towards the horizon, Francis reached down with his bloody, dirt-encrusted hands and pulled at the waistband of his jeans.

A loud moan was dredged up from the pit of his stomach as he somehow found his feet. He nearly tottered over again, just about managing to keep his balance on weak legs.

The police had removed the cuffs. Not because they wished to ease his suffering, he was sure, but to remove evidence that they were involved in the punishing beating. Francis bent over, hands on his busted knees.

He tried to straighten but his body protested as waves of pain enveloped him and he cried out. His breathing came in short little gasps and he was sure that some of his ribs must be broken. His nose and jaw were all knocked out of shape and his airways were clogged with blood. Francis spat onto the ground, ejecting a few of his teeth in the process.

Turning about as best he could, Francis started towards the edge of the waste ground in a sort of bent-over, shambling gait, his dislocated arm tucked into his side.

After five minutes, he emerged onto the access road that led away from the industrial estate. It was still dark. He guessed dawn was a few hours away yet. There wasn't a soul about.

Good, he thought.

He didn't want anyone seeing him, he didn't want any passing motorist to stop and offer help.

Francis just wanted to get home.

Through the fog of his delirious mind, he knew precisely what to do

•   •   •

Luckily, he saw no one during the long walk back. Francis eventually reached his house just as the first streaks of dawn smeared the eastern horizon. He had no idea how he managed it. Sheer willpower had driven him through the pain barrier as he'd plodded along the deserted streets, one agonizing step at a time.

Fishing with his broken fingers into his jeans pocket, he found his door key and let himself inside. He closed it behind him as quietly as possible.

Francis paused at the bottom of the steps to listen. The house was silent. Mum and Pam were still in bed.

He lurched along the downstairs hall into the kitchen. Next door's cat was watching him through the window. Francis ignored it and ran the cold tap, splashing water onto his face. The lacerations on his cheekbones and jaw stung like mad. He found a glass tumbler and filled it, then drank copiously, again ignoring the sharp sting inside his mangled mouth.

Francis turned around. Slung over the back of one of the dining chairs was a canvas shoulder bag. His Dad would use it to collect veg from the garden during the summer, but now Mum used it for shopping at the local Hillards mini market.

Francis took it and stepped through the beaded curtain to the walk-in larder. He filled it with tins of beans, soup and rice pudding, then shoved in a few apples and carrots. From the fridge, he added a carton of milk, a bottle of fizzy pop, a few eggs and a pack of sausage. Then from the kitchen drawer he found a few utensils plus a tin opener as well as a box of matches and candles.

Leaving the kitchen, he passed along the hall to the living room. On the coffee table was the box file containing their copy of the court papers. Pamela and Mum had made a start on going through them, sorting out the important stuff and making up a separate folder with relevant pages and police reports and so on. This separate folder rested on top of the box file.

Francis took the brown cardboard folder and shoved it into his bag with the food. From the mantelpiece, he took Mum's old Lipton's Tea tin where she kept the housekeeping money. There were around sixty pounds inside and he counted out about half the money and stuffed it into his wallet.

Going back into the hall, Francis quietly slipped up the stairs to his bedroom. Working as quietly as possible, he filled the prison Adidas sports bag with socks, underpants, a few shirts, sweaters and a spare pair of trousers, plus some plimsolls. He also retrieved the handkerchief embroidered with the girls' initials and the key to the strongbox. He zipped the hanky up in the bag's front pocket, while he added the strongbox key to the keyring holding his door key and clipped them onto his jeans belt loop. Then he slipped on a heavy duffel coat and slung the bags over his shoulders, wincing at the fiery agony from his injuries. Finally, he grabbed a few meds including some painkillers from the bathroom cabinet.

On the upstairs landing, Francis briefly closed his eyes and breathed in and out through his bloody nose, and slowly a calmness descended.

Silently, he opened one of the doors and looked in on Pamela. She was sleeping soundly. Her hair was a tangled-up mess on the pillow. Francis smiled at his sister fondly and then edged back out.

He went into Mum's room. She was snoring lightly, and her face was serene and relaxed.

Francis bent forward, stifling a wince from the sharp pain in his ribs.

He kissed his mum's cheek and then stepped away and left the room, closing the door.

"Goodbye, Mum," Francis whispered as he went down the stairs.

11

WHEN FRANCIS STEPPED OUT OF the back door, he had no destination in mind, no real plan even. The only thought that occupied him was to get away, to leave his family and home behind.

Stigmatized by society and branded a monster by his friends and neighbours, hounded by the police, he now realized that no matter what the courts said, it would never be enough to satisfy certain bigoted people. He — and by extension, his family — would face harassment and hatred daily. Remaining in the family home and further ruining Mum and Pamela's lives was no longer possible.

Francis wondered whether he should at least write a note for Mum. To tell her why he was doing this. That he wasn't so much running away but was, instead, going to put things right.

He decided it wasn't necessary. She would know why. He figured she knew her son better than he knew himself.

Before any doubts should further delay him, he set off into the pre-dawn grey, with birdsong swelling from the treetops.

Again, he followed the path into the woods.

His bad limp and tender and bruised body meant that he was reduced to a stumbling kind of jog, but after a few minutes, he reached the spot where the metal strongbox was buried. Quickly unearthing it, he opened the Adidas bag and pushed the strongbox in amongst his clothes.

Francis continued on through the woods. Leaving the dirt track, he headed downhill until he came to the treeline. Beyond the woods, a long and sloping field took him down to a fence. He followed the fence for several hundred yards until he reached a gate. Passing through, he descended a steep cobbled slope known by locals as The Kop, then ducked into a narrow ginnel with a cast-iron lamppost at the end.

Emerging from the passage, Francis looked left and right. There was a pub on the corner which, at this hour, was deserted. The beer garden was cluttered with bottles and glasses with dregs of beer in them. Next to the pub was a row of holiday cottages with their curtains all closed.

He crossed over the quiet roadway and squeezed through a gap in a wall. There was an old iron bridge here over the canal and Francis hurried across and then down the riveted steps to the towpath.

The water in the canal was dirty and scummy with pollution. He passed a large advertising board with a picture of a beautiful woman smiling, her teeth glinting as she held up a tube of toothpaste. Then the towpath ran up alongside a railway viaduct with a row of arches underneath and he briefly wondered whether to stop and rest here, maybe try and force a small amount of food down, but when he saw the sudden flare of a flame from within the shadows, Francis realized that it was already occupied by some junkies cooking up their heroin, and so he hastily moved on.

He followed the canal as it aimlessly meandered away from the suburbs. The railway tracks swung away before looping back around and over the water across a large viaduct. As he passed under the huge brick buttresses, a British Rail passenger train rattled across and its engine echoed down to him in a series of booms. Over on the right, Francis saw the cricket pitch and, next to it, the local rugby club function rooms. A groundsman was running a heavy roller over the wicket and he waved across. Francis lifted his good arm and waved back but kept his face low and his collar turned up.

Half a mile further on, he spotted some allotments. A few gardeners were at work, laying out some netting over their fruit plants, and it prompted Francis to glance at the time. Coming up to eight o'clock. Mum and Pamela would be up by now. Maybe they thought he was having a lie-in, or maybe they already realized that he'd gone, taking half the housekeeping with him.

He pushed on.

Soon after, an unpleasant smell reached his nostrils, and he remembered about the sewage works just around the next bend. The stench encouraged him to leave the towpath. Forcing his way through a hedge, Francis found himself near the loading yard of a Plant Hire business. Next to it was Winterburn Lane, which they had driven down on their way back from Wakefield Prison on his release day.

Two or three miles away, he could just see the cars and lorries trundling along the motorway that ran across the top of High Moor, their windscreens flickering in the morning sun.

Francis stopped dead.

The cemetery where Dad was buried was merely a ten-minute walk from where he was right now. Having no other place in mind where he could go, Francis found himself climbing the steep path and through the gates into the burial ground.

He did not search for Dad's headstone. He had no wish to dwell on his passing. He'd already processed that chapter in his life when they had visited here the other day.

Francis's thoughts were in a different place now. He had neither the time nor inclination to be distracted. Because over the last few hours, ever since the beating at the hands of those two rogue coppers, his mind had been recalibrating his priorities. He was now focused with laser-like intensity on just one goal.

To confront the past.

And seek out the truth.

Francis skirted around the perimeter of the cemetery and cut along the pathway that led to Wainhouse Terrace, the crumbling Victorian promenade.

Built as part of a folly in the 1870s, it was a grade II listed building, which, regardless of its historical significance to the area, had been allowed to fall into disrepair. The brickwork was crumbling, the walls sprayed with graffiti, wild brambles grew everywhere, and the ground was littered with discarded needles and used condoms.

To gain access meant crossing a stone walkway and then passing through an arched entrance on the upper level, before descending a spiral staircase to the lower tier.

At the bottom of the stairs was the interior arcade with a low roof, held aloft by a row of columns. Here, homeless people and drug addicts would gather to chew the fat or sleep off their daily fix. A few piles of charcoal and ashes together with an abandoned supermarket trolley indicated someone had recently used the place, but at the moment it seemed deserted.

Francis found a spot set back from the entrance so that he'd be out of the cold breeze but with enough of a view to alert him to anyone approaching. Hopefully, he would have the place to himself overnight.

A Murmuration of Starlings

Brushing away leaves and pieces of litter, he cleared an area and lowered the bags to the ground, then sat down and leaned back against the wall, moaning softly to himself.

He spent some time going over his injuries more carefully. The wounds to his face, nose and mouth, although painful, were fairly superficial. The cuts would heal and the nose would reset itself, although it would probably be bent to one side from now on. There was nothing he could do about the missing teeth. It would add to his charm, Francis told himself.

His dick also hurt where they had kicked him. He prayed that no permanent damage had been done, but was sure that he'd be peeing blood for several days.

Two of his fingers were crooked and twisted and certainly broken. He was also sure the same applied to some of his ribs. He had a shortness of breath and there were sharp, dagger-like stabs of pain with each intake of air.

One of his kneecaps throbbed like crazy, so he rolled up his trouser leg to take a look. It was all red and swollen but when he tested it by flexing the knee joint a few times, the discomfort neither increased nor decreased. He hoped that meant it was just badly bruised or twisted. A few days' rest should help. Perhaps he could find a branch and use it as a walking stick.

The worst injury was his dislocated shoulder. His arm was all limp and hung at a very odd angle, and the pain was so bad that it made him want to cry. All he could do for now was try and fashion some kind of sling and take lots of painkillers.

He popped a couple of ibuprofen and washed them down with a swallow of fizzy pop, then took a third for good measure.

Finding one of his t-shirts in the Adidas bag, Francis set to work making a rudimentary sling. He tied the ends around his neck and also threaded the material through his trouser's belt to stop the arm flopping about. He made sure that the whole arm from wrist to shoulder was fully supported and Francis immediately felt the pain ease: instead of it being unbearable it was now just agonizing.

He delved back into the bag and again went through the few medical supplies that he'd taken from the medicine cabinet. There was a roll of fabric first aid tape. He used his teeth to tear off two long strips and wrapped them around the two broken fingers, taping them together.

Finished, he settled back and waited for the meds to take the edge of his suffering. For the first time, he noticed how chilly it was now the sun was starting to dip towards the horizon. He reminded himself that it was still only Spring. The nights could be cold, especially if the skies were clear. He should have brought a couple of blankets or grabbed a sleeping bag and kicked himself for the oversight.

Francis also noticed how hungry he was. He hadn't eaten since the evening before.

Clambering to his feet, he poked around the lower promenade and started to gather some firewood, snapping off a few branches from the brambles and picking up discarded pieces of timber. Soon, he had enough to build a fire and, ten minutes later, he was sitting before a roaring blaze.

He dragged the canvas shoulder bag across.

He took out one of the candles and lit it and stood it on a brick jutting from the wall. Then he opened a tin of baked beans and stood it upright on the fire, where the contents quickly heated up. As an afterthought, he opened the pack of sausages. Finding a green twig, he fashioned a skewer by threading two sausages onto the pointy bit and poking the other end into the ground so that the sausages were angled over the flames. Finally, he opened the carton of milk.

Francis enjoyed his repast as the sky darkened and the first stars appeared.

Tomorrow, he would come up with a definite plan.

First, he needed to sleep.

•   •   •

He woke early, feeling cold and stiff.

His shoulder had frozen up overnight and was numb, so before he tried to manipulate it, Francis swallowed some more ibuprofen. Then he stirred the embers of the fire to life and warmed up the remnants of the baked beans, wolfing them down with his fingers.

Several miles away was the small town of Brighouse. There was a library there, which would be an ideal location for him to go through the folder containing the more important court case papers and police reports from his trial. It would also be somewhere to warm up, he decided.

Feeling more positive, he gathered his things together and set off.

He left Wainhouse Terrace and the cemetery behind. He would try and find somewhere better to spend his second night. There were lots of disused garages and garden sheds, it shouldn't be too difficult to find one and to break in.

Hobbling down Winterburn Lane from the cemetery gates, he cut across several fields to avoid the sewage works and picked up The Calder and Hebble Navigation Canal further along the valley. After five minutes, Francis spotted a pathway branching away from the towpath and a short time later he was on the long road that ran parallel to Freeman's Cut, a small freshwater lake popular with water skiers in the summer months.

Before long, his knee was throbbing from the constant pounding on the hard pavement. He again determined that, at the first opportunity, he would find a walking stick or manufacture one from a stout branch.

First things first though. The library.

A half-hour later, the town came into view and he paused to get his bearings. After a moment, he spotted the large, grey bulk of St Martin's Church. He knew the library was on the edge of the church grounds.

He picked up the pace, his dishevelled appearance drawing curious stares from the few people out and about. Francis ignored them. They could stare all they liked.

Turning the final corner, he stumbled the last few strides and pushed at the library door.

It didn't budge.

Francis tried again, twisting at the handles and then knocking loudly, but the large oak entrance was locked solid.

Then he remembered.

Today was a Sunday. The library would be shut. All day.

Damn!

He spun away in frustration and felt wearier than ever. He was exhausted, his leg was hurting abysmally, and he was cold. He'd planned on spending all day in the comfort of a nice, warm library, hugging one of the radiators and strategizing. Now, he was left to wander the streets aimlessly, like some homeless man on his uppers, carrying all his worldly possessions with him.

Then he felt the first spots of rain on his face, accompanied by a stiff breeze that heralded the approach of stormy weather.

He hobbled across the church grounds as the heavens opened. By the time he reached leafy Church Street, Francis was close to being soaked wet through.

Quietly cursing the world, he reached the bottom of the road and turned right past a branch of New Horizons Travel Agency, which had a notice in the window for a week in Torremolinos for seventy-five pounds.

Grumbling and mumbling at the injustice of his life, Francis hurried through the heavy rain towards the underpass below Briggate and ducked down the slippery stairs.

It was draughty down here and smelt of piss and vomit but at least he was out of the rain.

He walked towards the far end. His footsteps echoed off the tiled walls.

He saw someone coming towards him. A tall figure in a heavy coat.

Francis hesitated. He couldn't see the man's face because the hood was pulled up.

He made a beeline for Francis on unsteady legs, one hand against the wall for support and the other clutching a bottle. Francis could smell the booze on him from several feet away.

The last thing he wanted was any trouble, Francis thought bitterly. He wasn't in the mood for more nonsense.

Then the stranger came to a stumbling halt before him, swaying a little. He held out the bottle.

"Fancy a tipple, a tot of the old firewater?" he slurred in a strong Irish accent.

PART 3

<u>SUSAN ROSS</u>
<u>AGED 9½</u>

12

FRANCIS COULDN'T SEE MUCH OF the stranger's face for, as well as the hood, a straggly beard and a head of wild hair hid most of his features. The main things he noticed were the glassy, watery eyes and the broken blood vessels on the cheeks, which mapped out the story of a hard life.

Again, he pushed the half-empty bottle at Francis. He snarled, showing an uneven row of rotten teeth. Francis hoped it was meant to be a smile rather than a threatening grimace.

Francis politely shook his head and moved to step around the man.

"It'll help with the pain. I'm no doc, but that shoulder needs popping back in, by the looks of it."

The Irishman indicated Francis's arm, leaning forward for a closer look and nearly losing his balance. It seemed to cause him amusement, because he said, "Oops, steady as you go," to himself and sniggered.

"I'm good, thanks," Francis told him.

"Please yourself, matey."

He took a long swig and belched loudly. His breath, like the rest of him, smelled ripe.

It was hard to put an age to him, Francis mused. He could be anywhere between his mid-twenties and his late fifties, so lived-in were his features, so haunted his gaze. Francis looked around at their surroundings, at the litter-strewn underpass, the piss stains on the wall, the leaking roof and puddles on the ground. In the corner near the far stairs was a sleeping bag lying on top of several flat pieces of cardboard. Two tin cups stood neatly on the bottom step, as well as a flat cap with a few coins inside.

"You live down here?" he asked bleakly.

"Do I fuckers like!" the Irishman responded indignantly, head wobbling in horror at the idea.

"Oh, sorry."

"I have my own digs, I'll have you know. It ain't much, I'll grant you. Certainly not a palace. But it's my home. Grander than living on the streets, anyway."

Francis didn't know what to say, so he smiled weakly and hitched his bags higher up his shoulders as he prepared to push by.

"I just come into town to do me a bit of begging, that's all. This is one of my spots. Normally you can find me outside Woolworth's but this fucking rain, Jesus Christ Almighty! Do you know what I'm saying? I used to have a dog with me, people are always more generous when they see a dog, you know? They felt sorrier for the fucking mutt than for me, can you comprehend it? But the poor mite died last year, of cancer. Put a bloody dent in my takings, that did. Tight bastards won't part with their spare change now, not with a fucking recession on. Fucking Thatcher!"

"Can't be easy."

"That's stating the bleeding obvious, my friend. But it looks to me like you haven't exactly had an easy ride of it, either."

He looked Francis up and down and his wrinkled face crumpled up even further at what he saw.

"If I wasn't mistaken, I'd say you crossed paths with the wrong people. Either that or you're Barry McGuigan's sparring partner. I can empathise with you, my friend. Been there, done that, blah blah blah. Yours truly here has been jumped more times than a Dublin Doxie."

Francis shrugged, completely baffled by the man's quick-fire delivery. Drunk he may be, but like all Irishmen, he liked to spin a yarn.

"A brasser, you shite hawk? A Sally? A woman with loose morals? Good God, you English drive me nuts. But as I was saying, it seems like you've been in the wars. All the more reason to have a snifter."

He waggled the bottle about to try and tempt Francis, but then he lowered it when he realized he was wasting his time.

"So what's your story?"

"It's a long one," Francis mumbled under his breath.

"In that case, I couldn't give a rat's arse. But you know what they say, a life making mistakes is more useful than a life spent doing nothing at all."

He wiped his hand across the back of his mouth, then screwed on the bottle top and slid it into an overcoat pocket.

"Well, whoever did that to you did a proper job," he went on. "They really worked you over, didn't they? What do you plan on doing about it?"

"What do you mean?"

"Well, you can't just let it stand, can you? Otherwise, people will think you're fair game for a beating. You have your reputation to think about, or you won't last two minutes on the streets."

"It's not as simple as that."

"In my experience, it's always as simple as that. You have to set your stall out early days. Being homeless isn't just about finding somewhere warm to sleep every night and having some

123

food in your belly. It's a constant battle up here." He tapped a finger against his temple. "Every single day."

"What makes you think that I'm homeless?" Francis asked, trying to sound peeved.

The Irishman was having none of it, though. He bared his teeth again and shook his head in pity.

"Oh, come on. You left home or walked out on your family or are hiding from your past. Maybe you have huge debts to pay or are wanted by the police or have a drinking problem, like me. Everyone living on the streets has a similar story to tell. But it makes no difference to me what your sorry tale is. It doesn't change the fact that you need help, my friend. For instance, that arm and that leg aren't going to fix themselves, are they?"

Francis just looked away.

"Thought not."

He glanced towards the end of the underpass. The rain was easing off.

The man seemed to reach a decision.

"Right then. Let's go and get you patched up."

Francis watched as the stranger turned and walked away. For some reason, he felt suddenly panicky at the thought of being left by himself, even though he'd known this man for all of a few minutes. He quickly shuffled after him.

"Where are we going?"

"To my place. As I said, it's nothing special. But you're welcome to stay for a bit. Until you're feeling right. If you want to, that is."

Francis, aware that he had little alternative, asked, "Is it far?"

"A ten-minute walk. It's mostly uphill. You're carrying a bit of extra timber, with all that pie retention, if you don't mind me saying, so it might be a slog for you. I can carry one of your bags if you like?" He paused and held out a hand.

"I can manage," Francis replied quickly, holding his bags closer.

The Irishman laughed gently and resumed walking.

They reached the stairs. Francis waited while the scruffy man rolled up his sleeping bag and gathered up his tin cups and pocketed the loose change. He pulled the flat cap down over his head.

"Follow me, then"

They climbed the steps, emerging into the daylight. The sky looked brighter. Cars swished past them, throwing up water from the gutters.

It occurred to Francis that he didn't even know this stranger's name, this man offering to help him even though he knew nothing about Francis or his circumstances.

"What do they call you, by the way?" he asked.

The Irishman looked back over his shoulder.

"Liam," he responded. "Just Liam."

Liam's digs turned out to be a clapped-out caravan high on the hillside overlooking the town. Other than a copse of trees and a couple of wandering goats, it was the only thing for miles about.

The caravan was one of those tiny, two-person jobs that were all the rage in the 1970s for adventurous folk going on camping holidays to Germany and France, as an alternative to the package holidays to the Costa del Sol. All you needed was a cheap car to tow it and a few groceries, and you could have a good old time at virtually no expense.

The wooden sides were warped from age and peeling away from the frame, so Liam had at some time nailed them back into place. One of the windows was cracked. Instead of replacing it, it was covered over with CND stickers. The repairs had the look of a botched job to Francis. The roof was green with mould.

On the side was a homemade awning, sheltering a barbeque pit, a fold-up deck chair and a black leather seat ripped out of a car.

There were fine views looking down towards the small town, but Francis hazarded a guess that when the winter weather came on, with the wind rocking the caravan from side to side and whistling through the crack in the window, it would be a bleak and demoralizing existence.

"Are you allowed to, like, just pitch up and stay here?" he asked as he stumbled across the field in Liam's wake.

"It's common land this. I've been here for two years and nobody's yet to tell me to move out. Now where have my bastard keys gone?" he grumbled, searching through his pockets.

He found them and unlocked the door. When he pulled it open, it sagged on its hinges.

"I'll warn you now, it's a mess inside."

Francis went up the two steps and squeezed his bulky frame through the doorway.

It was more cramped inside than he thought imaginable.

Directly in front of him was a table strewn with empty beer cans and crisp wrappers. There was a pot noodle with something crawling over the lip and feasting on the jellified mess inside. Several plates with morsels of food encrusted on them and a cup nearly filled to the brim with cigarette butts completed the mess.

To the left was a squalid seating area. The couches had burst open in several spots so that yellow foam sprouted out of the openings like mushrooms. In the corner, balancing on a shelf made up of bricks and planks of wood, was a small portable telly with an aerial on the top. Next to it on the floor was a stack of VHS tapes. Francis read one or two of their titles, which left little doubt as to their contents. The TV screen was speckled with whitish spots and Francis quickly averted his eyes.

The kitchen consisted of the dilapidated guts of what might at one time have been a set of smart units and a sink. Now drawers were overflowing with carrier bags and plastic knives and forks, there was a grimy bucket piled high with washing up, a two-hob gas cooker and a short washing line draped with grey socks and crusty-looking undergarments. Beyond the kitchen was a heavy drape, behind which presumably was the bedroom and toilet. He decided not to explore further in that area.

"Nice," Francis mumbled.

"Bang on!" Liam seemed genuinely pleased with Francis's assessment of his living arrangements.

He bustled in behind Francis and prodded him towards the tiny table.

"Sit your arse down," he said, clearing one of the benches for him.

Francis unslung his bags and lowered himself down. The place was a cesspit, but it was better than being outside in the cold and the rain. He was grateful to take the weight off his poorly leg.

Liam closed the door and then went to the cupboards over the makeshift sink. Rummaging around, he brought down a clean cup and a bottle of Irish whiskey. Placing them on the table, he poured a good measure, then held up a finger to stay

Francis from taking a sip. He wasn't in the mood for a drink anyway.

Francis waited while Liam slid open a drawer and removed a plastic container, then encouraged the drawer shut again with a heavy thump to the front. He brought the container over to the table. Sitting down opposite Francis, he removed a small pill jar and shook out two white tablets. Using the bottom of the pill jar, he crushed them up into a fine powder, collected it in the palm of his hand and sprinkled it into the whiskey, giving it a shake to mix them in.

"Codeine," he explained.

"What the..?"

"Believe me, you'll need it when I pop that arm back in."

Francis gawped at him, asking, "Have you done that before?"

"A few times. Not for several years mind. I think I've refined my technique, though. It's all about timing and getting the angle right. If I twist too far then the ball socket will end up completely out of place, which isn't good. That means a life-long disability for you. So, drink up."

Francis scooped up the cup and took a long sip, the fiery liquid seeming to flush out his stomach.

"Right, off with that sling and lay your arm on the table. Palm up, elbow to the side. That's good."

Liam looked up and met his eye.

"Before we do this, aren't you going to tell me your name?"

"Francis."

"An unfortunate name, but that's mothers for you. Okay, Francis," he said, taking a firm grip of Francis's forearm, "when I say so, I want you to lean back and pull against my hold with all your strength. You understand?"

"I think soooo!" Francis finished with a scream of agony as Liam twisted and pulled unexpectedly. There was a horrendous crunch from his shoulder. Then he passed out.

13

HE MUST HAVE BEEN ASLEEP for several hours because when he awoke, the curtains were drawn shut and the lights inside the pokey caravan switched on.

He was pressed back into the corner with his face scrunched against the rear of the bench. As he sat upright, a sharp bolt of hot pain in his shoulder made Francis choke and gasp involuntarily and he waited until the torment passed. He looked at the injured arm. A new sling had replaced the old one, this more professionally made from a clean bandage held together with safety pins. His fingers had also been reset with a pair of wooden splints. His leg was strapped up as well.

The sound of the TV drew his attention. Liam was asleep on the tatty couch, his legs stretched out before him. In one hand, he held a can of lager, while in the other was a lit cigarette with an inch of ash threatening to fall onto the floor. A wisp of smoke coiled up to the ceiling.

On the TV, the theme tune to *Minder* was playing as the end credits went up.

Francis cast his mind back over the day's events, recalling his frustration at finding the library closed and then his opportune meeting with this strange Irishman and his offer of help.

It suddenly occurred to him that while he'd been sleeping, there'd been nothing to stop Liam from going through his things and finding the court file and the strongbox and working out who Francis was.

He quickly hauled up his two bags from the floor. Delving into them, he was relieved to find the folder was still in the canvas shoulder bag, while the metal strongbox was in the Adidas bag and the small handkerchief in the front zipper. His set of keyrings was still hanging on his hip, the money still in his wallet.

He relaxed a little. Liam may well have searched through his stuff, but at least he hadn't robbed him.

Francis saw the whiskey bottle was still on the table. Wondering whether to pour another shot to take the edge off the pain, Francis instead pushed it aside and came to his feet. He'd rather suffer than be drunk. Stumbling over to the kitchen, he checked there was water in the kettle and put it on the gas burner and fired up the cooker. After finding teabags and sugar, he went through to the seating area while he waited for the kettle to boil. Leaning forward as quietly as possible, he took the cigarette from between Liam's fingers and dropped it into the cup of old butts on the table, then placed the beer can on the windowsill. He turned the TV volume down but didn't switch it off.

Back in the kitchen area, he made himself a strong cup of tea with three sugars. There was half a bottle of milk on a shelf, but one sniff under the silver top had him hurriedly replacing it. He fished out the carton of milk from his shoulder bag, taking an apple too.

He glanced at his watch. Ten o'clock. Having just woken up, he was no longer tired, but for the first time since leaving home, he felt reasonably safe and secure. He was warm with a roof over his head, although that was probably only temporary for a night or two. This place might not be The Ritz, yet it was a thousand times preferable to sleeping rough, he reflected as he munched on his apple and drank his tea.

Opening the shoulder bag once again, Francis drew out the thick cardboard folder. Clearing a space amidst the clutter on the table, he set it down and rested a hand on top, delaying the moment when he would open it and go over the case afresh.

He knew most of the details by heart, anyway. They'd become a part of his life for twelve years now, dominating his every day.

So what was he hoping to accomplish by dredging it all up again?

Did he imagine himself as some sort of amateur sleuth?

That he could achieve what the best legal minds in the land had failed to do and crack the case?

Or was he seeking some kind of self-absolution, a cathartic scourging of his soul, unburdening himself so that he could move forward?

The answers to these questions eluded him. All he knew was that this was something he had to do.

He opened the file.

On top of the first page was a large, glossy colour photo of the girl. A school photo, he assumed, showing her smiling and dressed in her best clothes.

Susan Ross.

Francis had worked as the caretaker's assistant at his old Primary School and Susan was a young pupil there. He remembered her as a sad and lonely child who came from a broken home, one of three sisters to whom their mother showed little affection.

There had been rumours that Susan in particular bore the brunt of her mother's scolding tongue and violent temper. So much so that Social Services had decided to investigate and place Susan under close scrutiny. The mother, of course, pleaded her innocence, providing the Case Worker assigned to her daughter's welfare the usual sob story of a husband who had left the family home and was refusing to pay maintenance for the children, of how she worked three different jobs to make ends meet and life was a struggle bringing up three boisterous girls by herself. The resulting strain sometimes meant she might snap at her daughters and maybe, when they were especially badly behaved, she might even have to smack them or send them to bed early. No differently than millions of other parents did, the mother pointed out. But she would never, ever abuse them. Nor were they neglected. They were always well fed and smartly turned out. Susan loved her new blue dress, for example. She was polite and was doing well at school. Family life might be a little fraught at times, but she loved all of her daughters very much.

It was all a pack of lies of course, and Social Services were convinced Susan was the victim of an angry, spiteful woman unfit to be a mother. They would investigate and, if necessary, take interventive action.

That fateful day in autumn, not long after the school term started after the summer holidays, had become blurred over the years in Francis' memory. His recollection of events skewered with time, the details no longer precise. The statement that he'd given the police, a copy of which was in the file, likewise could not be relied upon because it was given under duress and written down days later by the main investigative officer. But Francis remembered the basics.

It was the end of the school day and most of the children had left with their parents or gone home by themselves. While the teachers gathered their things or chatted in the car park, it was the job of Francis and his superior, a cantankerous old man named Mr Pritchard, to do their rounds, mop the floors, check for repairs and make sure all the windows were locked and the buildings secure in preparation for the following day.

As the colder weather would soon be here, Pritchard had also instructed him to carry out a spot of maintenance on the boiler and make sure the coal cellar was well stocked. The boiler room was below the small gymnasium and changing rooms, and as he was firing up the boiler and checking the pressure valves, Francis had become aware of a child crying and sniffling nearby.

Putting down his toolbox, Francis, who was just eighteen at the time, went to investigate.

He'd found the girl sitting on one of the benches in the changing rooms, her hair aglow with sunlight streaming through a skylight, blue dress matching the colour of her eyes. He'd recognized her immediately as the school was small with barely one hundred and fifty pupils, most of whom he knew and was on first-name terms with, even the older boys who teased him.

So when he'd come across nine-year-old Susan Ross sitting alone and crying, he'd immediately asked her what was wrong. Finding Susan upset wasn't unusual, but today seemed especially worse than normal.

Dabbing her eyes with a small handkerchief, Susan explained in a trembling voice how some of the other girls had been picking on her again and stolen her PE pumps, and that her mum would be furious when she found out, and she daren't go home, and everything in her life was horrible.

Francis's heart had gone out to the girl and he'd been thinking about finding Susan's teacher when a thought occurred to him.

Never mind, he'd told Susan.

I'll have a look in the Lost Property box.

He was sure there were several pairs of pumps in there, probably left behind by children who had recently started at the big school.

Because he'd wanted to check what shoe size she was, Francis asked if she could remove her shoes. Susan did so, handing them over to him.

Returning them, he'd told her to sit tight while he went to look.

Going over to the caretakers' office, a tiny cubbyhole near the stairs to the boiler room, Francis had glanced back once and been rewarded with a sad little smile on Susan's face.

Rummaging about in the box of left-behind or lost items, Francis had spent a few minutes searching before he'd found a pair of almost-new PE pumps of the same size, and then hurriedly returned with them.

Only to find the changing rooms empty, with no sign of Susan Ross. He'd checked the showers, the gym, and even the boys changing room next door. There'd been no sign of her and so he'd shrugged and returned the pumps to Lost Property.

He wasn't to know it at the time, but Francis was the last person to see little Susan Ross alive, other than the person who would soon take her life.

Holding the glossy photo in his hands all these years later, Francis gave a tiny shake of his head.

"What happened to you, Susan?" he quietly asked himself.

•   •   •

Liam stirred, drawing Francis' attention away from the crime file. He placed it on the table but didn't hide it away as the Irishman staggered to his feet. Looking around for his drink, Liam slurped down the last dregs of beer and burped.

He noticed Francis sitting there and it took a moment for his brain to catch up with his eyes as he slowly remembered who he was.

"Right, time for some shuteye," he slurred.

On badly wobbling legs, he went over to the TV and turned it off, then came through to the kitchen.

"Blankets, you need blankets."

Liam went through the curtain to his bedroom and reappeared with two heavy rugs, neatly folded. He handed them over. He contemplated Francis through bleary eyes, swaying in small circular movements.

"I'm afraid that you'll have to manage on the couch, Francis. Space is at a premium. Don't stay up too late doing whatever it is you are doing." He pointed at the file on the table.

He turned to go.

"Help yourself to the whiskey," he added over his shoulder.

14

WITHIN TWO MINUTES, FRANCIS HEARD loud snoring drifting through the curtain. He turned back to the file, flicking over the pages one-handed until he found the police Crime Scene Report.

The paper form had faded to a yellow colour and was crumpled at the edges. Francis straightened it as best he could and, leaning forward, he studied it in the dim light from the bulb above his head.

At the top, it was signed and dated by the SOCO, the Scene of Crime Officer. The times when the search of the murder scene commenced and concluded had been carefully marked down. On this occasion, the search lasted exactly two hours and fifteen minutes.

Like all such forms, its purpose was to carefully record and detail as much information as possible during an initial study of the crime scene. Various boxes had been ticked and brief notes written by the SOCO, documenting things such as any contact traces left by the killer – in this case, some footprints on the approach to the shallow hollow where the body lay as well as around the corpse itself. Plaster casts of these were taken. It was also vitally important to not only preserve forensic evidence at the scene but also to prevent cross-contamination. Normally, to avoid this, the officers carrying out these early examinations would wear overalls and overboots, and they would lay down wooden duckboards to avoid treading on evidence such as blood splashes, but for reasons never fully explained during Francis' trial, this was not done, an oversight that would have serious consequences regarding the guilty verdict.

In addition to potential contact traces, the Crime Scene Report also recorded transfer evidence, that is items that might have been transferred from the crime scene to the murderer, things such as soil, leaves, the victim's blood or hair, and so on. Or it might be items passed on from the murderer to the scene or corpse, things like fibres from his clothing.

Everything was photographed or bagged up and labelled and sent away for analysis.

While all of this was going on, the dog handler had walked around the area with an Alsatian to see if it could pick up any scents of blood splashes, a murder weapon or even more human remains. Murder and then suicide was always a possible scenario – this was unlikely on this occasion, but it had to be ruled out.

Once an initial search was complete, the forensic scientist from the Home Office laboratory over in Harrogate and a Police Surgeon began a much more detailed study, concentrating on the deceased little girl. Swabs were taken from various orifices. The dead girl's body temperature was noted at regular intervals (every 30 minutes was recommended) although, in the case of Susan Ross, this revealed little, because even to the untrained eye it was obvious her body had been there for several days. The time of death would prove impossible to clarify from recording body temperature alone. A careful study of the fly larvae covering her body would perhaps help to more accurately pin this down.

The Police Surgeon looked for obvious injuries – he noted marks and bruises as well as small lacerations to Susan's neck, and abrasions to her face suggesting she had been dragged by her feet over the ground. One of her shoes had become dislodged and it was hoped fingerprints could be lifted and a culprit quickly identified.

Of course, it was inevitable that Francis' fingerprints would be found on them after he had checked her shoe size in the changing rooms, evidence that the main investigative officer was quick to jump on.

When the forensic scientist and Police Surgeon were done, Susan Ross' body was placed on a plastic sheet and her head, hands and feet carefully wrapped in plastic bags to preserve evidence. She was then zipped up in a PVC body bag, carried to where the police vehicles were parked in nearby fields, then ferried to the mortuary at Huddersfield General for the autopsy.

In the caravan, Francis clipped the Crime Scene Report and accompanying notes back into the file.

Reading them had left him feeling grubby and soiled. A sensation akin to an ice-cold hand squeezing his heart made him recoil. The report was a cold and calculated forensic analysis of the crime scene where Susan Ross was found dead, sharing none of the horrors that Francis felt at the time of his discovery and relived now, twelve years on.

Unlike his recollection of his brief meeting with Susan in the changing rooms, which was unclear and disjointed, made vague by the passage of time, Francis' memory of finding her body in the woods was indelibly seared into his brain.

•   •   •

He'd been in the woods with the air pistol and hunting knife, using some of the trees as target practice. Francis was considering whether to go down to the long field beyond the treeline to see if there were any rabbits. Mornings were the best time of day to catch them frolicking about in the meadows and he enjoyed taking potshots at them. Sometimes, if he was lucky, he might even hit one. When that happened, he would use the hunting knife to skin the animal, but because his parents would not approve – they didn't even know about the gun and knife – he always left the carcass lying in the grass.

But then Francis had glanced at the time and realized he should get home. It was a Saturday and he and Dad had tickets to see Leeds play against Wolves at Elland Road. He was looking forward to the game, the new season was underway and Don Revie and the lads were hoping for a bit of payback because the last time the two teams met, Wolves had won, denying Leeds the league and cup double.

Going to the match would also take his mind off what had been a stressful week.

Young Susan Ross was missing. She'd vanished just over a week ago and Francis was the last person to see her, that afternoon in the changing rooms. A huge search for her was underway but so far no trace of the girl's whereabouts had been found. The police had questioned him twice, the first time at his home with his parents present, not as a suspect but merely as a witness. A few days later they had come to speak with him again, this time at the school in the Headmaster's office. The second talk had felt more aggressive, their questions franker. After one hour, the police had departed but had warned him that they would probably need to speak with him yet again and that he should remain within easy reach at all times. It left him feeling that the police weren't altogether happy about some of his answers to their questions.

Vexed by what the implications of this meant, Francis had struggled to get much sleep for the rest of the week.

So watching his beloved Leeds Utd would be a welcome distraction from the whole sorry situation.

Shooting rabbits and answering police questions would have to wait.

Francis had turned about and set off back. Deciding to take a shortcut, he squeezed his slim form through the densely packed trees and headed to where the woods sloped down towards the dirt track.

Suddenly, he'd become aware of loud squawking noises. Hesitating, Francis tried to pinpoint where it was coming from. Then he noticed lots of rustling movement emanating from a dense stand of trees just up ahead.

Altering course, he went over and forced his way into the thicket. There was a pungent, unpleasant smell hanging in the still air.

Emerging on the other side, he was just in time to see a pair of carrion crows pecking at a dead animal laying on the ground. They flapped away at his approach, squawking in protest. Then he'd looked at the carcass more closely and when the realization of what he was looking at hit him, an involuntary scream burst from his throat.

The shallow hollow contained the body of a young girl. In an instant, he knew her identity. The blue dress and blonde hair were unmistakable.

She was in a foetal position, her repose that of a child who had lain on the ground and merely fallen asleep. The hollow and much of the corpse were teeming with maggots. There was a swarm of flies and midges buzzing in a dense cloud a few feet above the ghastly remains. Through the carpet of larvae, Francis saw numerous yellow patches on Susan's bare arms and a face turned black from putrefaction.

Waves of nausea very nearly overcame him but after a moment, they passed, along with the fluttering panic that gripped his heart. Instead of running away, Francis found his young mind pricked with a bizarre and morbid curiosity, prompting him to stumble down the sides of the hollow.

Later, having removed the small handkerchief from Susan's dress pocket, Francis had returned home to raise the alarm. After first hiding the gun and knife and keepsake.

•   •   •

Francis pushed up his sleeve to check the time. It was well after midnight. He'd been looking through the file for more than two hours.

He stretched his body and felt a yawn coming on.

From the bedroom came Liam's steady snoring.

Reaching for the blankets, he lumbered over to the couch and made up a bed, grabbing one of the seat cushions for a pillow.

He stripped down to his smallclothes and, dousing the lights, slid beneath the covers.

Francis quickly drifted off to sleep.

15

THE SOUNDS OF SIZZLING BACON and the mouth-watering aroma of a full English breakfast roused him shortly after nine o'clock the following morning.

Francis had slept soundly, his night for once undisturbed by dreams. His arm felt slightly better. The stiffness and pain had reduced significantly and the joint was more supple. Likewise, the swelling in his knee had diminished, the sharp pain having contracted to just a dull ache. He could now support his weight on it without too much discomfort. It was amazing what a good night's sleep could do, he thought.

The weather outside was inclement: raindrops *pitter-pattered* loudly on the caravan roof and a blustery wind buffeted the walls.

Liam was at the two-hob gas cooker holding a frying pan and sprinkling pepper over a pair of fried eggs. A radio was playing quietly somewhere.

He noticed Francis.

"Make yourself comfortable, I'm just about to serve up the food."

Francis resumed his place at the tiny table, which was cleared of yesterday's mess and laid out with two sets of plates and cutlery as well as two steaming mugs of coffee. There was brown and tomato sauce and toast on the toast rack. It seemed Liam managed alright for himself, despite his miserable state of affairs.

Francis felt a little guilty. He should try and repay his new friend for his hospitality by perhaps tidying up the rest of the caravan, but on looking around, he saw it too was spruced up. Liam must have been up early and trying to make a good impression for his guest, even though he was surely hungover.

A plate crammed with food was placed before Francis. Liam sat down across the table with his own plate and began to eat. Francis tucked into breakfast.

"You know," Liam said around a mouthful of streaky bacon, "that stuff you were reading last night, it must be awfully important to you."

Francis glanced up from his plate, then looked away again.

"You saw me? I thought you were asleep."

"Most of the time. But someone like me, having lived this crazy existence for years, tends to always sleep with one eye open. I notice things. I observe people, even though mostly they don't pay me much attention back. Homeless folk are like ghosts; we blend in so much that it's like we don't exist."

"You're not homeless."

Liam wafted the comment away.

"So, we learn to never drop our guard. We always remain alert, day and night."

Francis raised an eyebrow. He wondered just how alert Liam could be when he was blind drunk, which seemed to be for a large percentage of his life. He kept this thought to himself.

"Things are different for me," he said instead. "I have a home, family. I could go back any time I like. This is only a temporary thing."

"That's what I thought, way back in 1974 when I first found myself driftless and uprooted from my old life. Here I still am all these years later. A drunk, an eejit, bumming about. You don't want to end up like me. I'm a prime example of how to completely fuck up your life." He slurped at his coffee and then shovelled in a mouthful of greasy egg.

"So what is your story?" Francis asked.

Liam shook his head and looked at him steadily with his steely eyes.

"You're changing the subject, my friend."

"No, I'm not—" Francis began.

"I was watching you last night, concentrating like fuck on that file you carry around in that bag of yours, guarding it like it's the most important thing in your life. So I'm laying on the couch pretending to be asleep and thinking to myself, what could be so terribly bad that caused you to run away from home, from this family you just mentioned, a nice middle-class lad, to end up wandering the streets and sticking out from all the other homeless people like a big sore thumb? As soon as I clapped my eyes on you yesterday, I knew there was something different about you. If I hadn't stepped in to help, you wouldn't have lasted two minutes. The streets would have eaten you alive, a soft, chubby boy like you."

"I was managing alright by myself—"

"Go and shite, why don't you? So this morning, while you were away in the land of Nod, I woke early as normal. Daylight comes through the drunk's roof the fastest, they say, and never a truer word was spoken. So I was up with the lark and standing right there, looking at you fast asleep and then noticing that file there," he pointed with his fork at the manila folder by Francis' elbow, "seeing that she was still on the table where you left her last night. So I'm like, here you are, a guest under my roof, so my house my rules, why not take a little peek inside?"

"You bastard! You shouldn't have, that's private," Francis cried, a feeling of panic passing through him.

"Shut your gob, you little jip. And stop getting your knickers in a twist. I had a good look inside that folder of yours, just to put my mind at rest. Bloody glad I did too. It was a real eye-opener, I tell you. Some of it was very interesting indeed. Made me rethink my first impressions of you because you aren't the sweet little cherub I had you down as, are you? Not by a long fucking shot. Jesus, Mary, Joseph and the wee donkey, you have one hell of a story to tell, don't you? Your past is nearly as dodgy as my own."

Liam picked up a piece of toast and crunched down on the corner, waggling his head and smiling appreciatively.

"It actually makes me feel better to know your life is even shittier than mine. Don't you fret, this is just a wee bit of craic on your behalf, my friend. There's no need to poop your pants, your secret is safe with me."

Francis watched Liam carefully as he tried to gauge the mood.

"So now you know all about me I guess you'll be wanting me to leave?" he asked. "Give me ten minutes and I'll be away." He started to push himself out of his seat.

"Fuck off, you shitehawk. I'm not kicking you out. You're famous around here, for all the wrong reasons, but still a local celeb. As long as you hang around, it makes me feel like Saint Bob Geldoff."

Francis dropped back onto the seat and stared at his half-eaten breakfast. He was no longer hungry.

"How much of it did you read?" he asked quietly.

"Enough to get a general gist of your predicament. As soon as I saw what was in there, I put two and two together. There can't be many people around here called Francis recently released for a murder they didn't do, can there?"

Francis shrugged.

146

"And now here you are, living rough having walked out on your family, leaving your dear old ma to pick up the pieces and not knowing whether her only son is dead or alive. For all she knows, you might have topped yourself. After everything that she's been through, as well. You're one cruel bastard, Mr Bailey. I guess that's what prison does to you, eh?"

"As I said, it's only temporary. I'll go back home when all of this is done."

"When all of what is done?"

"This," Francis snapped, taking the file and shoving it into the shoulder bag angrily. He turned and stared out the window at the rain and the goats in the field.

A long and drawn-out silence developed. On the radio was a news report about a policewoman shot dead outside the Libyan Embassy in London. Liam leaned across and switched it off.

"Are you eating that?" he asked, nodding at Francis' abandoned breakfast.

Francis shook his head, so Liam grabbed the plate and scrapped everything onto his own.

"Tell me, what is it you're trying to accomplish exactly?"

"I don't know," Francis admitted.

"Because, take it from me, going over the past and putting yourself through the wringer never gets a man anywhere. Do you think I haven't tried? Do you think I haven't confronted my own demons? Raking over what's been and gone didn't work for me, all it did was turn me to drink. Are you looking for closure? Forget it, you won't get any. Is it revenge that you are after, revenge against the men who sent you down, or the bastard who really killed that wee kiddie? What if you achieve some kind of vengeance or payback or whatever you want to call it? What then? Do you think it'll make you feel any better?

147

Oh, you might get the gobshites off your back, the eejits convinced you did it, like the people who beat the crap out of you. It might make them crawl back under the rock they came from."

Liam cut into his egg and dipped his toast into the yolk. Just before cramming his mouth with food, he leaned forward, saying, "It won't alter the past. You'll still be haunted by the shit deal that life dealt you."

"Is this meant to be a pep talk or something?" Francis asked bitterly. Outside, the goats were pulling up a wild turnip from the ground.

"Just telling you a few hard truths and giving you some sagacious advice."

"And just what is that advice?"

"To leave it. To let it go. Because it's just not worth the grief. You still have most of your life ahead of you, so you should move on. Enjoy yourself. Do something positive. You can't get the last twelve years back, those bastards took those from you forever, but don't let them take your future as well."

Francis felt his face grow strained and tense. His eyes were moist and he rubbed them harshly with the back of his hand. If only he could do that, he bemoaned, knowing that for him, it was impossible.

"But you have to decide for yourself. You have to do what you have to do," Liam concluded, then gathered up the plates.

•   •   •

Later, the rain fizzled out.

In the afternoon Liam announced that they needed to stock up on food. They would go to the supermarket, he told Francis.

Together, they went back down the hill to the town. As they walked, Francis pretended his leg was still giving him some bother and hung back a little, and while Liam strode on ahead, he slipped out his wallet. Removing a couple of notes, he pushed them into his trouser pocket. Even after their earlier disagreement, Francis still wished to show his gratitude by paying for their food. He just thought it best Liam didn't see the rest of his cash.

Soon they were turning onto Wharf Street beside Mill Royd. Just ahead of them was Fine Fare Supermarket.

They crossed the road towards the entrance and the lines of shopping trolleys but Liam kept walking until he disappeared around the far corner. Francis hobbled to catch him up.

He was in time to see Liam stop before a chain-link fence. There was a gate, on the other side of which was a delivery entrance and two large metal bins. The gate was locked with a padlock and chain.

"Keep an eye out will you, pal?"

"What are we doing back here?"

"Shopping, what d'ya think we're doing?" Liam said with a shake of his head. "There's tonnes of perfectly good food in those bins there, canned food, meats, bread, milk, vegetables, everything you can imagine and all thrown out by the imbeciles that run this place just because it's past its best. It's a crying shame. So we might as well help ourselves."

"But we can't just take it."

"Of course we can. They don't care less what happens to it. I come here two or three times a week, I'm practically on first-name terms with the security guard who comes around the back for a smoke."

Liam stepped back and looked up at the top of the fence.

"Now stop acting the maggot and give me a leg up. I'll just take a quick gander inside."

With help from Francis (who used his good arm to support his friend's weight, still wishing to nurse his injured one) Liam was soon over the top. He opened the lid on the first bin, releasing a pungent odour of rotting foodstuffs. Francis wrinkled his nose.

"It's the plastic packaged items that keep the longest, and the tinned things of course, such as soups, tinned potatoes, tinned tomatoes. Bread is okay for a week past the date because even when it goes stale you can still toast it. Potatoes keep forever. But the powers that be insist everything gets thrown away. What a waste. Good for the likes of us, though."

Liam leaned his upper body into the bin and rummaged around.

On the other side of the fence, Francis kept a nervous watch. The street was empty other than a few pigeons pecking at the ground.

Looking back over his shoulder, he saw Liam emerge with several items and stack them neatly on the ground. Amongst them, Francis saw a bag of sugar, Yorkshire pudding mixture and a can of hotdog sausages.

Liam moved across to the next bin.

From this one, he scavenged some ready salted crisps, a jar of pickled onions and three glass bottles of lemonade.

"We can get 5p for each bottle if we take them back afterwards," Liam declared proudly.

He produced some plastic bags from somewhere and started to pack up his shopping. He passed them over the fence to Francis, who despite his trepidation, was starting to buzz with the thrill of what they were doing. Liam clambered over.

"A piece of piss," he bragged, winking at Francis.

Francis grinned back.

"Right, next stop is the off-licence near the park."

The day had brightened considerably with blue skies and fluffy white clouds skimming over the surrounding hills, promising a fine evening.

They went by the canal basin with its brightly coloured barges and hurried past the MOT Centre, ignoring the shouts of derision cast their way by the mechanics. Liam must be a familiar figure around these parts, Francis presumed.

After five minutes, they arrived at the off-licence. It was a small, tatty-looking shop with wire grills over the windows. Liam pushed open the door and the two of them went inside.

A young woman with hair like Farrah Fawcett and bangle earrings was seated behind the counter. She looked bored as she flicked through a copy of Smash Hits. She barely glanced up as they walked past.

At the back of the shop, Liam checked the round security mirror near the ceiling to make sure that she wasn't looking, and then grabbed a bottle of Napoleon Brandy. He handed it to Francis.

"Shove this inside your sling," he whispered.

"What?"

"Keep your voice down, stupid. Jesus, do you want to get caught? Now hide it in your sling, will you?"

"But—"

Sighing loudly, Liam opened Francis' coat and pushed the bottle into his arm sling, nestling it snuggly by his injured arm. Liam fastened the duffel coat up again.

"Come on."

"I don't think—"

Ignoring his protests, Liam cajoled him to the front of the shop and past the counter, wishing the woman a good day as they left through the door. She didn't even notice them going.

"Just keep walking, nice and casual like," he urged once they were outside again.

"For Pete's sake, Liam. When you said we were going shopping, I didn't think that it would entail doing this."

"Ah, away with you. Stop being a wuss. Anyway, getting nicked for shoplifting would be the least of your worries."

They hustled along the pavement, paying little attention to the few curious stares they drew from other pedestrians. Skirting around a small car park, they nipped over a busy road and then through some gates and into a park.

Strolling between the flower beds, they picked up a cinder path and followed it around the bowling green. At the tennis courts, they found a bench close to the toilet block.

Liam retrieved the brandy bottle, broke the seal and took a long drink, sighing with satisfaction. He held it out for Francis.

Francis looked at it. Then, unlike the previous day in the underpass, he accepted the bottle and took a gulp. The liquid, smooth and tasting of cinnamon, pleasantly warmed his stomach, so he took another swallow.

"Go easy, that's strong stuff if you're not used to it." Liam had a twinkle in his eye.

Handing the bottle back, Francis sat back on the bench. A gentle breeze stirred the leaves on the trees. The quiet hum of a bumble bee lent the park a tranquil ambience.

"We did well today. A good haul. They normally empty the bins on Wednesdays and Fridays, so Monday is a good day to come and see what they've thrown away over the weekend."

He patted Francis on the shoulder.

"You need to work on blending in more, however," he added, "but after a while that comes naturally. Once your clothes grow shabby and threadbare, nobody will pay you the least bit of attention. Mostly, that's how we like it."

Liam held out his hand.

"We make a good team."

Francis shook it gladly.

Liam looked over to the toilet block. Francis followed his gaze. A man in a suit was just disappearing into the Gents.

Liam took another drink from the bottle, glugging away at the liquid. He wiped a hand across the back of his mouth. His beard was speckled with droplets.

He came unsteadily to his feet. Passing the bottle over, he said, "I'll be back soon. Don't move from this spot, okay?"

Then he went across to the toilets and followed the man inside.

Francis waited. After five minutes, he was starting to grow a little concerned.

Then the man in the suit reappeared, looking all rumpled and flustered as he scurried away.

Moments later, Liam came out.

Francis saw his friend pocketing a five-pound note and he quickly averted his gaze, feeling his cheeks flush.

16

NEITHER OF THEM SAID MUCH on the way back to the caravan. Francis wasn't sure who was the most embarrassed over the incident in the park. He wondered what chain of events had brought Liam to a point in life where he was reduced to clandestine meetings in public toilets with strangers to earn a few paltry pounds?

It certainly put his own problems into perspective, and he cast his mind back to their conversation at breakfast and Liam's urging that he should try and move on. Francis drew no comfort from the knowledge that everyone, whatever their status or background, had bad things to deal with. It wasn't a competition: nobody had a monopoly over life's challenges.

He might ask Liam about it when the time was right.

For now, he had enough on his plate, harsh though that sounded.

By the time they reached the field and the caravan, Liam had polished off half the brandy.

"I'm starving. Let's get some food going," he slurred, pointing at the barbeque pit.

Stumbling over to a log pile beside the caravan, he searched for a few dry pieces of wood.

"I'll start the fire. See what you can rustle up to eat. Oh, and get a couple of cans of lager from the fridge, will you."

Still winded from the long uphill walk, Francis went inside. From his bags, he took the half-eaten pack of sausages left over from yesterday and a large tin of baked beans (when it came to cooking, he wasn't very imaginative). Finding a pan, he put the sausages inside, opened the tin and poured the beans over the top. Grabbing some beers, he went back outside.

Liam had a good fire going. He was sitting in the old car seat, staring at the flames. Francis placed the pan on the grill, tossed a beer over to him, and pulled up the folding deckchair.

The evening sun cast a soft orange glow under the awning. They basked in its warmth, eating their meal, drinking beer and admiring the views across the Pennine peaks.

The goats wandered over. Francis went back inside to retrieve his shoulder bag and fed them some carrots by hand.

Eventually, the inquisitive animals wandered off, content to chew on the grass. Soon after, Liam was snoozing.

Francis dragged the file out from the bag and leafed through it until he found Susan Ross' autopsy report.

The forensic pathologist who conducted the autopsy on Susan Ross, Professor Reuben Mortimer, preferred to keep extensive longhand notes on his post-mortem examinations. The reasons were simple. Writing out a hard copy of his findings by hand had the advantage of slowing him down and allowing him more time to think on what he was doing. The more carefully he conducted his examinations, the better the results would be. It was also routine during criminal cases for these notes to be used as evidence in court. Pathologists had to expect rigorous cross-examination by defence lawyers, who would try and find holes in their testimony. Often, pathologists were asked to produce their original notes. Accurate records could make all the difference to the outcome of a trial.

He also liked to produce body charts to back up his findings. Showing gruesome photographs of wounds and injuries to a jury could naturally provoke strong, emotional reactions which may cloud their judgement and prejudice their verdict. Having charts explaining such things as multiple stab wound tracks, body temperature or internal examinations meant they could be more calmly displayed during a court case in a clinical, and therefore less emotionally charged manner.

Autopsies always followed a set pattern to ensure that nothing was missed. Upon arrival at Huddersfield General, Susan Ross had been wheeled into the mortuary and placed on a stainless steel table. A description of her body was made and her height, weight, apparent age and general condition recorded. Samples of fly eggs and maggots were taken, which would be sent off to Manchester University to determine the precise time it took for the fly eggs to become full maggots. This would help establish a time of death and whether she was killed in the woods or elsewhere and the body moved later.

Next, her clothing was removed and bagged up.

A full external examination then commenced, starting at the head and neck, followed by the chest, abdomen, upper limbs, lower limbs and genitalia. More swabs were carried out and fingernail scrapings and clippings were taken.

The head revealed no obvious wounds other than small abrasions to Susan's face, backing up the crime scene techs' suggestion that she'd been dragged over rough terrain. Bruising on the neck hinted at throttling and when Professor Mortimer manipulated her neck, he quickly deduced that her hyoid bone was snapped, either with a ligature or considering the bruises, a powerful person's bare hands.

More bruising on the child's shoulders and arms might indicate a beating or that she'd been held down, but the onset of decomposition made it hard to be sure if these were older, more historic marks as a result of long-term abuse.

The body showed some signs of Livor Mortis at the front. Not to be confused with Rigor Mortis, Livor Mortis was a reddish discolouration at the lower parts of a corpse where the blood congealed after death. If Livor Mortis were present, it indicated that a body had been moved – in this case from lying on her front to being found in the woods and lying on her side. It might also suggest the victim was transported from one location – the location where the murder took place – to a second site: the woods behind Francis' house.

Moving onto the chest and abdomen, Mortimer found no injuries, although the skin of her upper chest was revealed to have cyanosis, a deep blue mottling effect that was evidence of asphyxiation.

There were no injuries to the victim's genitals, hips or legs. There were no signs of sexual assault. The soles of her feet had tiny pinprick punctures, perhaps from walking on stony ground or glass shards. As she was wearing socks and shoes, these must have been caused elsewhere and at another time.

Professor Mortimer then started on his internal examination.

Beginning with an opening incision behind one of Susan's ears, he cut downwards in a curve to the breastbone and back up to the opposite ear. Taking a bigger scalpel, the pathologist continued directly down from the sternum in a straight line, dissecting her body in two, all the way to her pelvic bone.

Carefully, he sliced and cut the skin away from the muscle and bone of the victim's chest and peeled apart the two flaps of skin, laying them on the steel table. He then checked for under-the-skin bruising, the presence of which might indicate internal bleeding and injury.

Next, he turned his attention to the organs. To reach them meant removing a rectangular section of the breastbone. Normally he would use a small electric saw to do this, but for a child of Susan's age, whose bones were thin and not fully developed, he could crack through them using bone-cutting forceps.

With the organs now accessible, Mortimer first studied them within the body cavity and then, with help from his assistant, removed them one at a time. They were weighed and thin slices cut off and applied to microscope slides. The pathologist would study these later for signs of illness and disease. Samples from her stomach and lower bowels would reveal her last meal. If the contents corroborated with what the child's school said she had eaten for lunch the day she went missing, this would further enable them to determine the approximate time of death. If the contents differed, it would suggest she had eaten elsewhere, perhaps given a meal by her kidnapper.

Returning to the skull, Mortimer shaved away Susan's hair and then made an incision over the crown of her head just above her ears. Peeling the front and back portions apart, he used a tiny hand-held circular saw to cut away the dome of the skull, then prised it open using a tiny chisel and hammer.

Mortimer closely examined the membrane around the brain to see if he could spot damage from old skull fractures or bleeding on the brain. Satisfied that she had suffered no blunt instrument trauma, he then used a pair of skull traction tongs to remove the brain.

Once samples were taken for closer study, the brain was bagged up and placed in a vacuum-sealed container and placed in the refrigeration unit.

On early observation, the pathologist spotted no obvious injuries or signs of illness other than the injury to the child's neck. He decided to take a closer look there to confirm his suspicions that she had died from strangulation.

Strangulation, or throttling, was one of the most common forms of murder. It is up close and personal, a nasty way to kill another person, as unlike using a gun or a crunching blow to the skull, it takes three or four minutes to accomplish and involves lots of brute strength. Most of the time, the victim is much weaker and smaller than the killer. It is regarded, therefore, as the bully's way of murdering a person.

Sometimes, a murderer might use a ligature and these leave very specific 'signatures', such as abrasions and burn marks on the neck. If a rope is used, they might even be patterns left in the skin which perfectly match the patterns on the murder weapon.

Throttling, when a murderer uses his or her bare hands to strangle their victim, tends to leave clearly identifiable bruising; fingermarks and indents from fingernails, just like the ones that Professor Mortimer identified during his autopsy of Susan Ross. These, he would later put into his longhand notes, appeared mostly at the sides and rear of Susan's neck. Other indications of strangling apart from cyanosis on the skin were Tardieu's spots, specks of blood from burst blood vessels on the heart. Mortimer went back to where the organs were. Yes, he could see this was the case. He instructed his assistant to photograph and record his discovery.

To be absolutely sure that Susan Ross was strangled to death by a person, presumably a man, with large and powerful hands, he decided to surgically open up her neck. Cutting down either side of the neck, he pulled back both sections of soft tissue and quickly observed that, although the hyoid bone was

159

snapped as he'd noticed earlier, there was no separation of the vertebrae and no burst blood vessels. That ruled out death by hanging. Nor was the vagus nerve damaged. Too much manual pressure on the vagus nerve would overload the heart and induce death by heart attack, which was called vagal inhibition. He also ruled out smothering, such as with a pillow over the face, as he found no fibres in the mouth or throat. Finally, he saw no blockages in the windpipe such as small pieces of food, so he was able to rule out accidental choking.

Professor Mortimer was confident in his conclusions.

Susan Ross was manually strangled to death from the front, in an as yet unknown location, her corpse later being dumped in the woods. Analysis of the food samples from her stomach, later backed up by the results on the fly eggs and maggots from Manchester University, indicated that she had been held captive for at least 48 hours before she was killed.

Francis finished going over the autopsy report and accompanying charts.

He'd found nothing yet that stood out in the file, nothing that set off alarm bells in his head. The scene of crime officer and the pathologist had done thorough jobs, it seemed. They had gathered and preserved forensic evidence professionally and laid out their conclusions precisely.

So why, Francis wondered, did the police choose to misinterpret those conclusions? Why had they conducted their investigation in such a ham-fisted way? Was it a case of one bent copper as the Assistant Chief Constable insisted at the hearing in Bradford, or had there been a bigger conspiracy, a decision to ignore the facts because the murder squad found themselves under intolerable pressure from above to get results and close the case quickly? How high up did it go?

Why were they so determined to send an innocent man to prison?

Francis glanced around. Liam was drifting in and out of sleep (or at least, he seemed to be, Francis told himself).

The setting sun hung just above the horizon like some huge fiery eyeball, watching the world.

From the file, Francis plucked out the transcript of his third police interview back in 1972, the pivotal one which still chilled him to this day.

He relived the whole frightening experience over again.

It was two days after Francis had stumbled over the body in the woods. Now, early one evening, Francis, together with his parents, was in the living room watching *On The Buses.* It was one of his favourite sitcoms and he was trying to get his mind off the horrible incident. His older sister, Pamela, had recently moved out to live with her boyfriend, who would soon become her fiancé and then her husband.

A loud and insistent knock on the front door made them all jump.

Dad looked at the wall clock, mumbling something about silly buggers disturbing them on a weeknight as he pushed himself out of his armchair.

Francis, who still liked to sit on the rug with his legs crossed even though he was eighteen years old, continued watching the TV, half-listening as his dad answered the door. In the hallway came mumbled voices, the words indistinct. Then there were footsteps and the living room door swung open.

Francis and his mum looked up and were alarmed to see a tall man in a suit walk in, followed by a pair of uniformed policemen.

"What are you doing—" Mum started to protest but was cut off by the man's gruff, no-nonsense voice.

"Francis Bailey? Are you Francis Bailey?"

Francis, startled, just nodded dumbly.

"I'm Detective Sergeant Wolfe. We'd like to have a chat with you, about Susan Ross."

Francis looked from the man to his mother. Behind the policemen, Dad was standing in the doorway looking confused.

"What's going on?" Mum asked, getting to her feet.

"There's nothing to be alarmed about, Mrs Bailey. We just wish to ask your son a few extra questions about the missing schoolgirl."

He tried to smile reassuringly, but to Francis it looked like a cruel little slash across the man's jaw. His eyes turned back to Francis and fixed him with a hard and penetrating stare.

"But you've already spoken to him twice about that. He's told you everything that he knows."

"Yes, I'm aware that some of my colleagues have chatted to Francis regarding this. We just have a few follow-up queries, that's all. Just to clear a few things up about dates and times, simple matters like that. It would be very helpful. It won't take long, I promise."

"I don't see that it should be a problem," Francis' dad said placatingly as he pushed into the living room. "If it helps the police to find that poor girl."

"Precisely," the detective sergeant replied, nodding, that grin still stitched to his face.

"I suppose so," Mum agreed quietly, rubbing Francis on the back.

Francis stood there feeling alarmed and a little scared. He remembered the second time the police had spoken with him at the school. That had been an unpleasant experience, and something told him this would be even worse. He swallowed the lump in his throat.

"Right, we'll have him back home as soon as we can. We'll leave you watching your TV programme."

"Wait, I thought you meant you'd talk to him here," Dad blurted. "In his home."

"Oh no, it will have to be down at the police station, Mr Bailey. We have to follow protocol, you know how it is?"

"Well, no I don't actually. If you only need our Francis to help clear up a few things, like you just said, then why on earth can't you just—"

"I don't make up the rules, sir. I've been given my instructions to bring your son in to help us with our inquiries. So that's how it is going to be. If everything goes alright, your lad should be home by bedtime."

Ignoring the gobsmacked look on his parents' faces, DS Wolfe turned to his men. He scowled because one of them was watching the telly and laughing quietly at something. The policeman soon snapped back into alertness at the sound of his boss barking out instructions.

"Escort the young gentleman to the car, would you constables?"

They moved in on either side of Francis and placed firm grips on his forearms.

"Mum?" he said pitifully as they led him from the room. "Mum, Dad?"

They took him down the hall and out the front door and Francis glanced back in time to see both his parents watching from the doorway as he was escorted down the drive of their home. Dad had his arm around Mum's shoulder, who looked close to tears.

A police panda car was parked at the curb.

"In you go, there's a good chap," DS Wolfe said, his voice all pleasant and modulated, and he even turned to wave goodbye to Francis' parents before climbing into the back of the car after him. The two uniformed officers got in the front.

"Where to, Boss?" the driver asked, removing his hat. "To Millgarth?"

He was referring to the brand-new purpose-built police HQ in Leeds.

DS Wolfe bristled, saying, "Sod that, we're not letting those flash bastards take the credit for this. Nah, get us down to Halifax nick, pronto."

"Right you are, Boss."

Francis could feel DS Wolfe looking at him and when he turned his face he saw that the pleasant if fake smile had vanished. Instead, it was replaced with something that oscillated between a smirk and a sneer. The detective seemed to have gone through some bizarre metamorphosis. The polite and dedicated copper was no more. Now a hateful, stonyhearted person was sitting beside him, with his cold and baleful eyes drilling into Francis.

With a flourish, the detective produced a set of handcuffs.

Francis looked at them and then back up at DS Wolfe. The look the detective gave him left little doubt about what would happen if he didn't comply. Francis held out his hands.

"Behind your back, lad," Wolfe said very quietly. "You know the procedure."

Francis put his hands behind him and shuffled into a sideways position and felt his wrists being painfully twisted upwards and the cuffs snapped into position.

When he sat back, Wolfe was leaning into him and had his mouth very close to Francis' ear.

"Now we're going to have a proper talk about that kiddie, me and you, lad," he whispered. "I'll get the fucking truth out of you, one way or another."

Francis had no idea what the time was because the tiny interview room had no clock on the wall. It felt like he had been here forever.

On arriving at the police station on Harrison Road, DS Wolfe and his two uniformed officers had marched him through the main entrance. The desk sergeant had glanced up briefly to see who was being brought in and then he'd gone back to filling out some paperwork. On the desk next to him was a steaming mug of coffee. He looked set for the night shift.

They led Francis down some steps to the basement level and past a door marked CELLS 1b to 8b. They walked along a corridor and stepped through a doorway near the far end.

One of the constables left and Francis was brusquely ordered to sit at a small table. Wolfe took the seat opposite. Apart from another chair in the corner, there was no other furniture in the grey-walled room. A fluorescent bulb in the ceiling flooded the small space with very bright, harsh light.

They waited in silence. Francis kept his gaze fixed firmly on the tabletop, unable to meet Wolfe's stare. The other constable guarded the doorway.

After a few minutes, he heard footsteps approaching. A WPC entered. She sat on the spare chair, crossed her legs, then took out a pen and pocket notebook.

"Right, Pickford," Wolfe addressed the male constable, "shut the door and remove Mr Bailey's handcuffs."

Once the cuffs were off, Francis rubbed some life back into his wrists.

He still tried to avoid looking at Wolfe because he had the feeling the policeman was enjoying making him feel intimidated. Francis' discomfort seemed to amuse the other, who dipped his head to intrude into Francis' eye line. Pickford, on the other hand, didn't find it funny at all. Francis felt a hand grab hold of the back of his shirt collar and pull back, forcing his head up.

Now he was face to face with the Detective Sergeant.

Wolfe started talking, with the WPC hurriedly taking notes.

"We need to go back to what you told my colleagues when they came to talk to you, Bailey. I'm not satisfied with your account of that day in the school."

"How do you mean?"

"I don't think you've been completely honest with us about—"

"I have, I told them—"

"Don't interrupt DS Wolfe, do you hear?" Pickford, who was still standing behind Francis, growled.

Francis turned his head to look at the constable, but his head had barely moved before it was roughly twisted to the front again, the policeman nearly pulling his long hair out by the roots. Francis yelped in pain and surprise.

"Eyes front. When an officer of the law is asking you questions, you don't turn your back on them. Didn't your parents teach you anything?"

"Why do you insist on lying, Bailey?" Wolfe asked him. "About that time you saw Susan Ross in the school changing rooms?"

"I wasn't lying."

"That's not what we've been told, by another witness."

"What? Who?"

"Your boss, the head caretaker. Mr Pritchard. He's been very helpful, in contrast to yourself, by providing us with lots of very useful pieces of information. First of all, he explained that there are strict rules against male members of staff from entering the girls' changing rooms whenever a pupil is in there. The girls' safety is the number one priority, he insists. So I want to know what exactly you were doing in there, creeping around while Susan was present."

"I told the police," Francis said hurriedly, his voice coming out as a squeak. "I was turning on the boiler when I heard her crying. I went upstairs and she was upset. Because some of the girls had taken her pumps. I said I'd try and find a pair of replacements."

"Yes, yes, we've heard all of this before. Something about it doesn't feel right to me or Constable Pickford here. Isn't that right, officer?"

"Yes, Boss. An eighteen-year-old man, loitering in the girls' changing rooms when everybody has gone home. Everybody except little Susan Ross, that is?"

"Does that ring alarm bells to you, Pickford?"

"It sounds like a big effin' klaxon going off to me, Boss. I get a horrible feeling in my stomach every time I ponder on it."

"Do you often do that, Bailey?" Wolfe said, addressing Francis again. "Lurk around the school, hoping to find girls by themselves?

"No, I—"

"You see, your boss, Mr Pritchard also told us that your account of what happened that day is wrong. He tells us that he saw the two of you, yourself and Susan, leaving the school together."

"What?"

"He has told us that he saw you leading Susan away from the school grounds. 'Enticing the poor lassie away' was how he put it."

"That's not true. Why would he say that? He wasn't even there!"

"Well, you tell me, Bailey. Why would he say that? Are you saying that he's fibbing? He offered that information freely, he came to us today with this vital piece of information. Pritchard tells us that he didn't wish to make unfounded aspersions about your questionable conduct and general behaviour, because believe it or not he likes you. Yet when he heard that you were the person who 'found' Susan's body, in the woods just behind your house, he felt that it was his civic duty to come forward and tell us what he saw."

"He's talking nonsense, I tell you! I never left with her! When I came back with the replacement pumps, she'd already gone!" He wiped at his eyes and his fingers came away damp with tears.

"Don't shout at the Detective Sergeant. And keep your hands on the table." Constable Pickford snatched Francis' hands and banged them down onto the tabletop.

"Have you done that kind of thing before? Leaving the school with pupils? Do you have an unhealthy interest in children, Bailey?"

"No, absolutely not. That's a sick thing to say."

"Does anything trigger these bouts of unsavoury behaviour?"

"Nothing."

"So the urge just comes over you, then? Like a spur-of-the-moment thing, when the opportunity arises? Is that what you're saying?" Wolfe asked, leaning back in his chair.

"This is ridiculous. Can I see my mum and dad? I think they should be here"

"Sorry, that's not going to happen, Mummy's Boy," Pickford snarled. "You're a man now, so start acting like one and tell us the truth. Unburden yourself, it will make you feel much better, trust me."

"When you took her," Wolfe went on, "was it in your mind at that time to do Susan any harm?"

"Are you deaf? I never took Susan! I just went home like normal!" Francis shouted as his anger spilled over.

A hard blow to the back of his head from a closed fist whipped his head to the side. Instinctively, Francis reached up with one hand to rub at the stinging pain, only for his hand to be slapped onto the table once again. This time, to keep it there, Constable Pickford gripped Francis' fingers, twisting at them until they went red. The officer's wedding ring gouged into the skin of the hand. Francis felt his tears start to flow freely.

"I don't think my colleague believes you. I can't blame him. Stop lying through your teeth, lad, and tell us what fucking happened. Where did you take her?"

Francis said nothing. He was too frightened to reply.

"Alright, well I'll tell you what I think happened, shall I? You approached Susan Ross in the school changing rooms for some repellent reason. You probably gave her some fabricated story to persuade her to leave with you. Then, when you had enticed her to some quiet location, maybe even to your house while your parents were still at work, you committed some filthy crime."

The WPC glanced up just then, catching DS Wolfe's eye, who looked back at her coldly until she resumed her notetaking.

"Then you murdered her to keep her quiet and dumped her body in that bit of woodland close to where you live. That's about the tall and short of it, isn't it?"

Wolfe nodded to himself, satisfied with his summary.

"Oh, and our forensic boffins have found irrefutable evidence to support my view, reinforced by Mr Pritchard's witness statement. Am I fucking awesome, or what, Constable Pickford?"

"You're a legend, Boss."

"That I am. You see, Bailey, I'm a copper known for getting results. Even when under huge pressure from Fleet Street, The Chief Constable and Ted bloody Heath, I nearly always come up trumps. I have a near-perfect record and a little runt like you isn't about to spoil that."

"I – did – not – kill – her," Francis managed to blubber, stressing each word.

"Do you know what they call us county coppers, those flash bastards in Leeds? They call us Ghurkas. Because we take no prisoners. We never make any arrests, they say. The twats also think we're a bunch of donkey wallopers, a bunch of thick hicks. Now I don't take kindly to being labelled that way. What police officer would, after all? Especially from that Reginald Gregory, the Chief Constable, who is the most useless knob the world has ever known. So all I can do is prove them wrong, show those twats at Millgarth how we do real police work over here."

Wolfe was quiet for a moment while he let the implications of that sink in.

"We already have enough on you to charge you, lad. Your blood and sweat are all over the crime scene. We have your fingerprints on her shoes, for crying out loud. Right this very minute, I have officers going over your gaff and tearing the place apart looking for more clues, more proof. Your parents are distraught. So be a good lad and save them from any more upset and tell us what happened, eh?"

Francis just shook his head.

"We know you throttled her and that she fought like mad to stop you. We can tell from her fingernails that she scratched you, but I can't see any marks on your face."

"I think I should talk to a solicitor," Francis said desperately.

"A solicitor? Fuck me, this kid is thicker than we thought, Pickford! Are you dim-witted or something? Was your brain starved of oxygen at birth?"

Wolfe and Pickford both laughed. The WPC went on writing.

"You've been watching too many cop shows on the telly. Do I look like Kojak, and does Constable Pickford here look like Jason King? Fuck off with this shite about solicitors. Right, constable, get his bloody clothes off, will you?"

"Do I have to? Can't we get Jean here to do it instead?"

"As tempting as that is, I don't think Jean will oblige us."

The WPC over in the corner demurely uncrossed her legs. Her face was going bright red.

"We need to find out where he was scratched, don't we?" Wolfe told his officer.

"I suppose so, Boss."

Francis was dragged to his feet.

"Take your shirt off," Pickford ordered.

Slowly, with shaky hands, Francis unbuttoned his shirt and peeled it off.

"And your vest, you fat slob."

He did as he was told, placing his clothes on the chair. He was shivering uncontrollably with fear, so he hugged himself.

171

DS Wolfe stood upright and came around the table. First looking into Francis's eyes for any hint of disobedience – there was none - he carefully inspected Francis' chest and back for any tell-tale scratches.

"Hold your arms out to the side."

Francis did so.

"Nothing. Very well, remove your trousers and underpants. Pickford, put his shoes in an evidence bag. We'll compare their soles to the footprints we found at the crime scene."

Francis slowly stripped down to his y-fronts. He was snivelling and had streams of snot coming from his nostrils. He wanted to pee.

"Well, what are you waiting for? Get them off," Pickford said, pointing at his baggy underpants.

Francis pushed them down over his trembling knees and deposited them on the pile of clothes. Quickly, he covered his privates with both hands.

"No, you fucking don't," Pickford warned. "We need to check every inch of you for marks. Move your hands, or I swear to God I'll beat your bollocks flat with my truncheon."

Francis glanced nervously across the room to where the WPC was sitting. Thankfully, she had averted her gaze. He removed his hands from shielding his privates.

"Fuck me!" Pickford exclaimed. "Would you take a look at that, Boss?"

"God in hell."

"That's one heck of a small todger you have there. Do you see his balls? They haven't even dropped, Boss."

Wolfe was leaning forward with his hands on his knees to get as close a look at the spectacle as he dared. His mouth was stretched wide in a huge grin and he shook his head in wonder.

"Come and look at this, Jean!" he called back over his shoulder. "I bet you haven't seen one like this before."

But the WPC was shaking her head, her face a picture of mortification.

"There's nothing to fear, believe me. I doubt even my Aunt Nellie would be frightened by this thing, and she hasn't been rogered since my Uncle Herbert was killed by the Japs. Would you effin' credit it?"

Wolfe pushed himself upright.

"Are you sure you're eighteen, lad?" he asked.

"The bloody retard hasn't even got a boner. You must be losing your touch, Jean," said Pickford, before laughing loudly.

Wolfe tried to keep a straight face, pretending to be genuinely concerned. "Have you sought help for this? There must be a proper medical reason for somebody who has an underdeveloped penis. Poor sod."

After a minute, both policemen got over their amusement and went back to inspecting Francis for any scratches on his skin. They found nothing.

"What next, Boss? Do you want me to start twisting his testicles and give him 240 volts?"

"You'd best wait until after the doctor has checked him over in the morning, Pickford. Get him dressed. We'll give him a bit of time to ponder on things overnight and see how smart-alecky he is after a night in the cells."

"Do… do you mean… I can't go home?" Francis stuttered.

Wolfe didn't answer. He headed for the door and then turned back.

"There's one more thing. Did you take anything from the girl's body? A trophy or something? Because the girl's mum, when she went to identify her before the post-mortem, she told us something was missing. A small handkerchief that Susan always kept in the pocket of her dress. Now it seems to have disappeared. Have you got it hidden somewhere, Bailey?"

Francis shook his head, his mind a complete mess of paranoia and panic as he thought about the metal strongbox buried in the woods. Why, oh why had he taken that handkerchief?

"Because if we find it at your place, you are well and truly screwed. Now get some clothes on."

•   •   •

It was later that night, and Francis lay underneath his blanket on the lumpy couch. He was too wired up to switch his mind off, so getting some sleep was an impossibility for now.

Thinking back to that infamous night in the interrogation room stirred a variety of different emotions. He was angry, he was disgruntled, and he was foolishly ashamed. But most of all Francis was overwhelmed by a flood of despair.

The police interview and subsequent forced confession and murder charge resulted in the double tragedy of a life ruined and Susan Ross and her family denied the justice they deserved.

The trial that followed was the polar opposite of fairness and impartiality. It was a one-sided affair with the outcome telegraphed to the world by an indifferent media. Only later did the Fleet Street tabloids call it a farce and a satire, a travesty of justice. At the time, they lapped up the scandalous details laid out to the jury by the police and the prosecution lawyers by filling their newspapers with sensational headlines and rabble-rousing claims.

It was, in short, a grotesque pantomime.

In spite of every rule regarding Francis' detention and police interview being blatantly broken, in spite of his forced confession being quickly retracted, in spite of the late disclosure of evidence to the defence team, the trial judge allowed the case to proceed.

The false witness statement from Mr Pritchard saying Francis and Susan had left the school together was never challenged as the caretaker was not cross-examined by an inadequate defence lawyer. At one stage, it was discovered a conversation between DS Wolfe and a junior prosecution counsel was overheard by a juror during which they decided to change the medical condition that Francis suffered from. The condition – Hypogonadism, where a male experienced diminished function of his testes and low production of sex hormones, making them incapable of intimate relationships – was altered to one where increased testosterone occasioned violent outbursts. The judge failed to discharge the juror and the real facts of Francis' health and growth issues were never brought to the jury's notice.

It was also never made clear that, in the pathologist's view, there were no signs of sexual assault nor indeed of a sexual motive for the crime. They had no forensic evidence to support this claim, regardless of what DS Wolfe had told Francis during the interrogation. This was just one of many police lies. Lying to a suspect like this was against the law.

DS Wolfe's past record, which wasn't as impeccable as he liked people to think, was waved away by the prosecution as irrelevant. He was actually commended by the judge for his work on investigating the murder of Susan Ross. The words *professional, determined,* and *driven* were used in the trial judge's one-sided summing up.

The end result, when the jury foreman announced the jury's verdict, was inevitable.

17

SOMETIME BEFORE DAWN, WHEN THE ascendancy of night surrendered to the birth of the new day and the audience of stars yielded to the coming of the sun, the sound of the caravan door closing roused Francis for a moment.

He blinked his eyes, hearing footsteps fading away. His dreamy brain pondered on where Liam might be going at this hour. Then sleep drifted back, like a naked woman slipping beneath the blanket with her lover. Francis closed his eyes.

The next time he awoke it was fully light. Warm sun rays pushed through the dusty windows and curtains. Glancing at the clock, Francis was surprised to see that it was mid-morning. He had overslept.

The caravan was quiet. He could hear birdsong and, further off, the goats bleating.

Francis dragged himself out of bed and rolled up the blankets, shoving them under the couch. Then he remembered hearing Liam leaving in the early hours.

He called his name and stepped across the tiny kitchen and slipped through the curtain. The toilet was empty. There was no sign of Liam in his bedroom either; the bed and floor were a mess, strewn with unwashed clothes, paperback books and scrunched-up tissues. Francis wrinkled his nose at the odour of stale sweat and retreated into the main living area.

Opening the door, Francis went outside. Blinking at the brightness of the morning, he took a quick look around. The chairs were still in the same place as the night before and there were beer cans strewn about in the grass. The firepit glowed with orange embers.

He couldn't see Liam anywhere.

Strolling over to the copse of trees, he peered into the gloom beneath the leafy canopy and again called out his friend's name, louder this time. There was still no reply.

Shrugging his shoulders, Francis went to rustle up some breakfast.

He got the barbeque going again with a few pieces of kindling and some logs, then put a kettle of water on the grill and brewed a mug of strong coffee. There were some Frosties at the back of one of the cupboards. The milk was starting to turn, but he used it anyway.

Sitting in the deckchair, munching on his cereal and drinking the hot coffee, Francis contemplated the day ahead. Since meeting Liam, he'd spent much of his time reading about the court case. Yesterday, his new friend asked what his ultimate goal was and now Francis was beginning to wonder the same thing. He'd been hoping for some sort of inspiration. That by looking again at the minute details of the case, a path forward would be revealed to him. All that had happened was old memories had triggered new pain, like some sick souvenir for a man doomed to be haunted forever by his past.

Maybe Liam had been right.

Maybe he should just leave it and do something positive with his life.

Where was Liam, by the way?

He'd been gone for five or six hours now with no explanation or note telling Francis when he would be back.

Had he gone bin raiding again?

Or begging for money outside Woolworths?

Was he at the park, meeting more men in the toilets like yesterday?

Francis didn't wish to dwell on that any more than he had the previous day, but it was a reminder that he knew nothing about his new friend. In contrast to Liam, who knew all about Francis and his past.

For a panicky moment, Francis wondered if Liam had slipped away while he slept to inform the police of his whereabouts.

Then he thought, so what if he had? He'd done nothing wrong.

Francis didn't really believe Liam would do that anyway.

Still, he was curious about him. Enough to have Francis going back inside the caravan and once again slipping through the curtain to the bedroom.

He contemplated the clutter. He wondered where to start. What was he even looking for anyway? Some insight into Liam's history? There must be a chain of events that led him to this lifestyle, this existence on the fringes of society. As Liam said himself, everyone living on the streets had a similar story to tell.

Was it even his business? Francis asked himself.

No, probably not. That hadn't stopped Liam from snooping through his things and prying into his life.

He stepped into the small room.

First of all, he checked the cluttered bedside table for any family photos or letters, an old address book maybe. There was nothing obvious, just the usual things people kept near their beds, like a plastic bottle of spring water, a cheap travel alarm clock and some reading glasses. He flicked through a few of the paperbacks that lay scattered about just in case any names were written inside, turning them upside down in case Liam had slipped anything between the pages. All he discovered was a crumpled Polaroid photo of a dog, now being used as a bookmark.

In the narrow wardrobe, Francis found mouldy, moth-eaten clothing on the hangers and dirt-encrusted labouring boots on the floor. He searched through the pockets. Again, there was nothing. On a shelf near the top was a stack of girlie magazines. He found a large black bin liner pushed into the back of the wardrobe, but a quick glimpse inside revealed more old clothes that looked like they hadn't been worn for years. He thought it unlikely they would contain anything of note, so he closed the wardrobe door and stepped away. His gaze shifted around the bedroom one more time.

Crouching down, he looked under the bed. The floor and underside of the bedsprings were clogged with dust. There was a plate with the remnants of some pasta, which must be at least a month old, Francis reckoned. There were several smelly socks all scrunched up into balls and a single glove and nothing else.

He walked over to the tiny window. CND stickers covered the plastic pane and a row of blue Smurfs stood on the sill, no doubt collected from petrol stations at some point. Outside, its face nearly pressed up against the pane, one of the goats watched him silently, its bug eyes rolling in their sockets.

Francis turned away, frustrated with the pointless exercise of poking about like some nosey busybody, then stopped dead.

Near the base of the wall on this side of the bed, he saw one of the square wall panels wasn't quite fitted right. The edge didn't sit flush with the others and the two screws that would hold it in place were missing.

Having another peek through the window to check there was no sign of Liam – the goat was now licking moisture from the plastic pane – Francis went down onto one knee and ran his fingers around the bottom edge of the wall panel. He tugged at it. It flexed outwards and then sprung back with a vibrating hum.

He tried again, using his poorly arm as well this time and tugging with more force, and the panel came away in his hands.

Behind it, there was a dark cavity. A good place to hide something, Francis decided.

Leaning the panel against the bed, he reached into the opening with one hand.

Feeling around, his fingers touched something big and bulky and made of coarse material. Gripping it, he dragged whatever it was out from the cavity.

It was a brown duffel bag with drawstrings and two leather handles on the top. Quite long, it was the sort of bag in which a workman might keep a spirit level and his other tools.

He lifted it onto the bed and unfastened the drawstrings.

Inside, was a musty old donkey jacket with leather shoulder patches. He pulled it out and, after checking the pockets, placed it over the bedknob. Next, he found a pair of bell-bottomed jeans and a flat cap. Again, they revealed nothing.

Francis stood looking at the assortment of clothes. He was baffled. Why would Liam hide them in the wall cavity?

Obviously, he didn't want anyone stumbling across them. Not that he had many visitors, Francis speculated.

At a guess, Francis fancied his friend to be involved in various chancy, probably illegal, activities. Maybe he was a burglar or a thief and this was his breaking and entering gear.

But then, there were no tools in the bag, things such as a crowbar to jemmy open windows or a Slim Jim to break into cars.

Hang on though. There was something else in the bag. Something wrapped up in an oily and smelly towel.

Francis lifted it out. Whatever it was, it was heavy, and he needed both hands to carry its weight.

He unfolded the towel.

Shit, he figured as he gawped open-mouthed at the object.

Francis wished now that he'd minded his own business, because on the bed before him was a firearm, a machine gun. He knew next to nothing about guns, other than his air pistol, which compared to this one was like a child's cap gun. This was the real thing.

It was well maintained, too. The gun barrel was well-oiled and the plastic stock was polished and smelled of wax.

Francis sat down on the bedcover and ran his fingers through his hair.

What kind of trouble had he got himself wrapped up in? Just who the heck was Liam? Was that even his real name?

Then he thought about the country of his friend's birth and came to only one conclusion.

"Christ, bloody hell," he breathed.

All kinds of things flashed through Francis' mind and every one of them left a sour taste in his mouth.

If his friend were on the run, then it explained a lot. It also raised many new questions. Questions such as: just what had Liam been involved in back home in Ireland? Why did he still have the firearm? (and keep it in good condition). Also, most importantly, did he intend to use it again?

Francis didn't know an awful lot about The Troubles in Ulster, but he did know that at times in the seventies, while he had been serving out his prison sentence at The Monster Mansion in Wakefield, Northern Ireland was virtually in a state of full-scale civil war, an armed struggle that had soon spread to the British mainland. Why, just two years after his imprisonment in 1972, the IRA had blown up a coach load of British soldiers and their families on the M62 motorway, just a few miles from where he was right now.

Was Liam involved in that atrocity?

That was impossible to know.

One thing Francis did know for sure was that whatever dark secrets lurked in Liam's past, it had set him on a downward spiral of homelessness and alcoholism, forever cut off from friends and family. His life was a bleak one spent raiding bins to find food and pulling tricks with men in the park toilets for five quid a time.

Francis carefully picked up the gun.

It was hefty but compact and it fit snuggly into his arms. Briefly, it gave him a feeling of power. Then he thought about the things it might have been used for and that sentiment was replaced with revulsion.

What should he do?

Putting the gun and clothes back into the duffel bag and returning the bag to the wall cavity would be the obvious thing to do. Then what? Report Liam to the authorities? Or carry on as normal and pretend that he'd never found the thing?

Whatever he decided, he had to make up his mind quickly. Liam would surely be back soon.

Sitting at the kitchen table, he waited for Liam to return.

Francis had decided, probably unwisely he conceded to himself, that the best thing was to confront his friend about his discovery. He wanted to give him the benefit of the doubt. Not that there was any acceptable excuse for having the gun. Yet, after all the help Liam had given him, he couldn't just rat him out or walk out on him. They were both in dire straits, two men from different backgrounds, and in the few days that they'd known each other, a bond had developed between them.

He owed Liam that much, at least.

And Liam owed him an explanation.

So Francis waited with the gun held loosely in his lap and his eyes fixed firmly on the door and, after a half-hour, he heard footsteps approach the caravan.

Liam came stumbling through the door and it was obvious that he was steaming drunk even though it wasn't yet midday. He looked even worse for wear than usual. His hair and beard were a straggly mess and his heavy coat was weighed down with a bottle in each pocket. There were grazes on his knuckles as though he'd been fighting.

As he came in, he nearly toppled over. Grabbing the doorframe, he heaved himself into the kitchen and when he saw Francis at the table, he laughed coarsely and wiped a hand over his wet lips. Then he did a comic double-take when he saw the gun Francis had a hold of and his eyes refocussed, becoming immediately alert. His slack jaw went all tense.

"You found it, then?" he growled through his teeth. It was a redundant question.

Francis nodded, waiting for his friend's further reaction.

"Whoopy-do, big fucking deal," Liam said, his voice a drunken drawl. Then he staggered through to the living area and collapsed onto the couch.

Francis stood up. He was taken aback by Liam's response to his discovery, or lack of response would be more accurate. Of all the reactions he'd expected, ranging from flat-out denial that the gun belonged to him to a violent confrontation, this wasn't what he had banked on.

He followed Liam, taking the gun with him.

"We need to discuss *this*," Francis stated, hefting the firearm.

"What's to discuss? You found the bloody thing, so that's the end of it. Serves you right for poking around."

Francis ignored the rank hypocrisy. He shrugged his shoulders with frustration and gave a shake of his head, saying, "But... but...."

"Don't start, you hear? I'm too bloody tired. So I have a little secret, a murky past. I never claimed to be a saint."

"A little secret? You have a machine gun hidden in your bedroom, for Pete's sake."

Liam, who was sitting on the edge of the couch, suddenly slumped forward and buried his face in his hands. He stretched back the skin on either side of his eyes, then swept his fingers over his unkempt hair. He seemed close to falling asleep.

"Are you a terrorist? Are you, I don't know, some kind of IRA sleeper?"

"Ah, don't exaggerate, you shitehawk."

"A hitman?"

"Christ on a pogo stick! Will you wind your fecking neck in, man?"

Liam looked up then and Francis saw his eyes were bloodshot once again, all watery and maudlin.

"You don't know what you are talking about, my friend. Trust me, you don't want to know. I got mixed up with the wrong crowd when I was young, many, many moons ago, and now I'm paying the price for being an eejit. I'm not some kind of romantic freedom fighter, that's all a load of bullshit they tell you to get people to join. They show you pictures of attractive women holding a gun and shooting at British squaddies and say come and be a part of us, you'll be a hero to your people, when what they really mean is, do as you're told or we'll burn your house down. Then they put a gun in your hands and send you out into the night and they don't give a rat's arse if you get yourself shot up. It's all bullshit!"

Francis, who was still fuming, carefully placed the gun on the table.

"It's not loaded," Liam told him.

"I wouldn't know," Francis snapped back.

There was a conversational void during which the tension between them stretched the atmosphere until it was drum-tight.

Liam reached into his pocket and brought out one of the bottles.

"You think that's going to help?" Francis remarked.

"Do you know what?" Liam said back, his eyes relighting like the embers in the barbeque pit just outside the open door, "I think it might do me the world of good. Anything to drown out your lecturing shite. Now drop it, boy."

"Don't call me boy. I'm older than you."

"Then stop acting like one," Liam shot back and took a long gulp, his eyes fixed on Francis as though defying him to snatch the bottle away.

"Are you still involved in that kind of thing?"

"If I were, you wouldn't still be breathing, *boy*."

"Then why have you kept the gun?"

"I don't know, I just have. What the hell am I supposed to do with it? Hand it in to the police?"

But Francis wasn't fooled that easily. "You could have got rid of it somehow, I'm sure. Ditched it somewhere. Just how long have you had it?"

Liam rolled over onto his side, waving his hands vaguely and saying, "I don't know. Ever since I came to England. A few years."

"How many?"

"Nine or ten, I think."

"Jesus! You've had it hidden all of this time? What the hell did you do? What are you on the run from?"

"I told you to drop it."

"Did you kill someone?" Francis demanded, ignoring Liam's warning. "You did, didn't you? Why else would you go on the run and then hide out for years in this grotty little hovel? Drinking yourself to death?"

Liam gave a slow, sarcastic handclap and actually laughed out loud.

"Way to go. You hit the nail right on the head there, Sherlock," he told Francis. "A pity you can't solve the mystery of who killed that girl, isn't it. Bloody hilarious, that is."

Francis ignored the jibe. "Who was it that you murdered? A soldier or a civilian?"

"Neither. He was an informer, a scumbag passing on information to the English and the RUC. A weedy little undertaker by trade. I was given orders to shoot the man, so that's what I did. Are you happy now?"

"What, and that makes it alright because he was a grass?"

"It did back then. Besides, orders are orders and you don't mess with those people."

"You sound like you're still a part of their movement," Francis hinted.

Liam said nothing back. He just stared up at the ceiling.

"If they gave you more orders to carry out another operation, would you still obey them?"

"I told you, I'm out of that game."

"But do *they* know that? It isn't something from which you can just quit, is it? You don't simply wake up one day and decide you no longer want any part of their fight? Not with all the secrets you know, the information you carry around about their activities. They'd sooner track you down and put a bullet through your head."

Francis found himself glancing towards the windows as though expecting to see balaclava-clad terrorists coming charging across the field. All he saw out there was the goat, which was rubbing its arse against the corner of the caravan.

"That's why you're living this kind of life, isn't it? Why you are keeping below the radar, living off-grid? To avoid drawing attention to yourself and them finding out where you are. It's all coming together now."

"My own life sentence," Liam mumbled.

"Will they find you? One day?"

"They haven't so far. I've been very careful."

"But you keep the gun just in case."

It was a statement, not a question.

"If I walked out of here right this minute and went to the nearest telephone box to call the police," Francis went on, "would you try and stop me? Shoot me even?"

"Don't be stupid," Liam said and pushed himself into a sitting position. He looked at Francis directly. "You aren't going to do that, any more than I will grass you up. I took you in, didn't I? I was taking a big chance doing that, letting another person share my world."

Francis watched as his friend sipped from the bottle again.

188

"If I thought for one moment that you would, mind you, then who knows?" Liam said pointedly, and Francis wasn't sure if he was being serious or not.

"Great."

"It's all well and good you being all preachy, getting worked up over things that have nothing to do with you. The Liam Brennan back then is different to the Liam Brennan of today. Just like you aren't the same person you were twelve years ago, boy."

"The difference is that you murdered somebody and I didn't."

"So why the hell are you obsessed with that kid's murder? Why are you so fixated on raking it up? You've been cleared, you have nothing to prove to anyone. But you go over that fecking file, looking for answers that aren't there. You say my life is ruined, and you're right, I'm a complete wreck. But mine is ruined because of what I did, whereas yours is self-inflicted torture."

Liam staggered to his feet. He wobbled about and it was fifty-fifty as to whether he'd stay upright, but after a moment he steadied himself.

"You have a chance to move on, to start afresh here with me. That's why I've taken you under my wing, Francis bloody Bailey. Do you think *they*," and he pointed vaguely at the world outside, "do you think *they* will ever let you move on? They'll never offer you the chance that I'm offering you."

Liam waited for him to reply. Francis was temporarily lost for words.

"To do that, there's one thing that you need to do. The first step, boy."

"What?"

Liam held his gaze for several heartbeats and then he shambled past and lumbered over to the table. For half a second, Francis thought he was reaching for the gun and a jolt of terror squeezed his heart, but then he watched as Liam grabbed the case file off the tabletop. Before Francis could say anything, his friend barged by him and disappeared through the door and down the steps. Francis dashed outside after him.

Liam was kind of running and tottering towards the barbeque and looking like he could go over headfirst into the orange embers, and Francis called out a garbled warning to his friend before it struck him what Liam was about to do.

"Shit! No, don't!"

It was too late. Liam was throwing the file onto the embers and immediately flames whooshed up to swallow and engulf the papers and police reports, eagerly devouring them in a lascivious frenzy.

Francis cried out in dismay. He raced over, hoping to snatch the file out of the flames, but he saw that already they were all afire, the pages curling up and turning to grey ash.

"What have you done?" he shouted.

"I've done what you should have done days ago," Liam laughed. His eyes burned red as fire danced in them.

"You fool! You fool!" Before Francis could stop himself, he lashed out with his good hand and caught Liam a glancing blow over his bearded jaw.

Liam struck back reflexively and hit Francis with a sharp backhand, drawing blood from his lip and nose and sending him crashing down onto the grass.

He lay there, stunned and breathless. He was certain he was about to take another beating but this time from a friend, and he cringed away.

"You see?" he heard Liam shouting at him. "It's all going wrong, all because you went looking into things that don't concern you. Now look at what's happened. Everything is going to shit!"

Francis wiped at his mouth, smearing blood over his chin.

"Do you think this is what I wanted?" Liam continued. "All of this effin' and blindin'? Look at the state of you, lying there covered in blood and snot. All I wanted was a mate."

Francis spat a tooth out of his mouth and managed to say, "You moron, you didn't have to burn my stuff. Why would you do that?"

"Because I was sick of hearing you shitting on about that girl. You were giving me a right pain in the bollocks listening to you, you clown."

He glugged away at the last dregs of booze in the bottom of the bottle and then lobbed it into the trees. Uncapping the second bottle, he turned and stomped back up the steps into the caravan.

18

B Y THE MIDDLE OF THE afternoon, Francis was back at Wainhouse Terrace. He found the same spot where he'd spent his first night living on the streets. The half-burned candle was still on its small ledge and a dark circle of cinders marked the spot where he'd built his campfire. Empty food tins lay about.

After their fight, Francis had silently packed his things, shoving everything into the Adidas sports bag. His nose and mouth had stopped bleeding but he could taste iron in the back of his throat. Liam was back on the couch, looking out the window. No words were exchanged between them. Francis left the caravan with no fuss and as he'd walked away across the field, he heard the TV come on with the volume turned up loud. He didn't look back.

After a long walk, he reached the crumbling Victorian promenade. He was just in time, for five minutes after arriving, the fickle English weather sulkily took a turn for the worse. The heavens opened and rain poured down.

Others were sharing the shelter with him. A handful of people like himself; impoverished, living a nomadic lifestyle and poor as a church mouse, all of them dossing down for the day. He watched out of the corner of his eye as one of them, a skinny and gaunt woman with lined features and haunted-looking eyes, injected herself. She was soon fast asleep, curled up and trembling in her sleeping bag. With her were two male friends;

one was drinking a bottle of meths, the other a bottle of Brut aftershave.

They were some distance away, so Francis ignored them.

He decided to remove the sling from his arm. It was restricting his movements and, if he took a few painkillers, the dull ache hardly bothered him. What's more, it left him feeling vulnerable, somehow, which was something he found an unnecessary risk under his current circumstances.

He watched the rain. It came down in sheets. It was like being behind a waterfall and soon, the littered ground outside was ankle-deep. Inside the lower arcade, water leaked through the decaying brickwork in the arched roof and was soon dripping down so that large puddles spread across the dirty concrete floor. Francis was forced to move further back, away from the entrance and the deluge.

He had no idea what to do now. The fallout with Liam and losing the file, with all its important details of the case, had completely blindsided him.

He could go home. He should go home, if only to alleviate Mum's worrying, for which he now felt ashamed. Yet if he did that, he would be back to square one and would have achieved nothing.

Another option was to just take off and start over again somewhere new. He still had his bus and train ticket so getting around shouldn't be a problem. Maybe he could head for the coast? He'd always liked the idea of living by the sea. Morecambe was nice. Blackpool might be better. Surely he could get a job there working on the pier or in an amusement arcade? Then he could afford to rent a flat or a bedsit. He could even change his name.

All kinds of fantasies and pipe dreams filtered their way through his daydreaming mind. Maybe losing the file wasn't a bad thing. Liam might have done him a favour, although he was still furious with him for chucking it into the flames. Perhaps it marked a turning point, the moment when he finally put the whole saga of the murder of Susan Ross to bed.

He fervently wished that to be so.

Francis wasn't aware of having drifted off to sleep. The next thing he knew, his eyes flickered open as he came awake, roused by whispering voices.

It was dark outside but he could just make out two figures crouching over his Adidas bag, unzipping pockets and hurriedly going through his belongings.

Francis became fully alert as he realized they were stealing his things and he shouted out, "Hey, leave that alone!" as he jumped up.

One of the figures, a scrawny and spotty youth of no more than sixteen or seventeen, spun around and light flashed on a blade, making it scintillate like a minnow in a pond. The kid thrust the knife towards Francis.

"Fucking keep back," he hissed. "Come any closer and I'll use this, I swear."

Francis froze, his mind hurriedly weighing up the benefits between trying to stop them or meekly surrendering his things.

"But you can't do that, please."

"This is our spot. You can't just fucking come here, man. It's our place, not yours. Fucking twat!"

The other person, an older man with a lank ponytail, continued to go through the bag, pulling out clothes and chucking them onto the wet floor.

"We're going to take what we like and there's nothing you can do to stop us," bragged the teenager. "It serves you right for coming here. This is our spot," he said again.

"I got food, some tins and packets of biscuits, Manny," the other was saying excitedly. "There's some good scoff in here. There's a wallet too, bloody Nora..." and he gave a low whistle. "Holy mackerel, there's a shitload of money. We struck gold, kiddo."

He held up a handful of notes and pumped the air, giggling like a child on Christmas morning.

The teenager's eyes nearly popped out of his head. There was only thirty quid or so in the wallet, but it was more money than they'd seen in some time, apparently. Then he remembered Francis, who was standing and watching helplessly as they robbed him.

He turned the blade in his hand in a slow corkscrewing gesture. He had a cold, flat-eyed look in his eyes.

"Now eff off. This stuff belongs to us now. Eff off and find somewhere else to stay, you ugly slob."

Francis stumbled out into the pouring rain, the downpour washing away his tears as he shuffled through the night. He was soaked to the skin before he'd even climbed the stairs to the top level of the promenade.

He'd lost everything. His money and bus pass, all the contents of the Adidas bag, including the metal strongbox with the knife and the air pistol, as well as the embroidered handkerchief in the front zip pocket. They'd even taken the keyring from his belt loop and stolen the watch off his wrist whilst he'd slept.

He owned no worldly possessions except the clothes that he had on his back.

The rain dashed against his face so hard that it stung his cheeks and his hair became bedraggled so that it was plastered to his forehead. It bounced off the roofs of parked cars, creating misty halos around their bodywork, and it ran in rivulets down the gutters.

Francis hunched his body in a vain attempt to ward off the torrent. His eyes were cast down. Both shoes were leaking and soon his socks were waterlogged so that each step he took made loud squelching noises.

He had no idea where he was going and after an age, he glanced up to see he was passing a row of shops. He saw one deep-set doorway outside Radio Rentals and Francis went across and lowered himself down in the entrance, his back against the door.

He stayed there for a long time, shivering, dozing one moment and awake the next.

The rain relented briefly.

A few pedestrians ventured out. One man was giving his dog a late-night walk and he stopped near the shop doorway to allow the pet to cock its leg and pee. Then he noticed Francis in the shadows, hunched up in his coat, and he hurried away.

A group of men walking home from the pub saw him and one of them spat at Francis before they carried on, laughing loudly.

The rain returned and washed the spittle from Francis' face.

In the distance, police sirens troubled the night.

•   •   •

His mind started to drift. Maybe he was coming down with a fever and was delirious. Or maybe he was just cracking up.

Voices from the past came to him. It was like cold fingers were probing through his thoughts, caressing, seeking out his worst nightmares.

"*Hold him down, keep the little sod still.*"

"*I'm trying, Boss.*"

"*Well try harder. Now use this. Don't hit him with it there, you fool, it will leave bruises! Take his shoes and socks off and hit him on the bottom of his feet.*"

"*Gotcha.*"

In his semi-conscious state, Francis imagined he could feel the agony of the blows, for they were ingrained in his memory.

"*Effin' bastard. It isn't having any effect on him. What shall we do?*"

"*Take some of those paper towels, Pickford. Screw them up into balls.*"

"*Right, Boss.*"

"*Open the bastard's mouth. We'll break him, don't you worry.*"

Francis gagged at the recollection of DS Wolfe shoving the scrunched-up paper towels down his throat. In his fevered mind, his airways clogged up once more, and he convulsed as he went into spasms.

"*Just sign the damn confession! Sign it and all of this will stop!*" Wolfe had shouted.

Francis shook his head. He was no longer squatting in the shop doorway but was back in that police interrogation cell.

"*If you don't, I'll send Pickford around to your house. Then we'll see how long your old man holds out, eh? And your dear mother, bless the old bag.*"

"*Or I might just burn your gaff down with them still inside,*" Constable Pickford threatened.

"*Write your name on the blasted paper, will you?*"

•   •   •

"Howsagoin?"

Francis came back to the present and looked up. A man in a heavy coat was leaning into the shop doorway. His hood was up against the rain, but he peeled it back to reveal a familiar face.

"You?" Francis croaked.

"I've been looking for you all night. Was beginning to think that I wouldn't find you, boy."

Francis just shrugged and glared back.

"You need to come back to the caravan."

"Why? What's the point?" Francis asked.

"Because something has happened. Something you need to hear about," Liam informed him.

PART 4

<u>THE MISSING</u>

19

O N THE EDGE OF TOWN and overlooking Crag Lane with its fine views over the open countryside was the area's most notorious and run-down council estate. Centered on Furness Drive and The Grove, it was a scar on the local landscape, like a festering open wound. Neglected for decades by successive town councils, the area was a claustrophobic slum of high-rise housing and tenement blocks filled with families on low incomes. Blighted with high levels of unemployment, petty crime and anti-social behaviour, it soon attracted a reputation as a no-go zone, a little fiefdom of drug dealers and hard cases where even the police rarely ventured. Kids here didn't bother going to school, preferring instead to spend their days riding around the playing fields on stolen motorbikes or setting cars alight and their evenings hanging around the shadowy back ginnels sniffing bags of glue.

Unless you called the place home, anyone with an ounce of common sense didn't venture here.

Most of the time.

The man in the pale blue Bedford Van drove slowly along the Furness, his soft eyes looking for a turning. It was just after nine in the morning and most of the estate's residents had not risen yet, which meant the area was mostly deserted. The only person he saw was a youth with shorn hair watching his Pitbull having a crap on the concrete playground.

He spotted the road and swung the campervan's steering wheel over. Slowing down, he pulled up to the curb and stared out of the windscreen at the building up ahead.

Of all the housing blocks, York House was by far the worst. A crumbling and damp and miserable hellhole, half of its twenty-odd flats were empty shells, their windows smashed and the rooms gutted and sprayed with graffiti, home to rats and pigeons. The few people who still lived here had, over the years, become absorbed into the morass of despair, so that they felt devoured by it, living an impoverished life from which there was no escape.

The driver was hyperalert and watchful as he continued to observe the tenement block and his surroundings. He plucked up the piece of paper resting on the passenger seat, again checking that he had the correct name and number. FLAT 16, on the second level.

Popping the van door, he quietly climbed out, his brown leather jacket creaking when he stirred.

As he passed through a gap in the wall and crossed over the concrete walkway to an outside communal staircase, he spent a moment again trying to justify what he was about to do.

Whenever the impulse came over him, he always went through the same internal struggle. It was all a charade, of course. A pretence, a feeble attempt to talk himself out of it. By the time it reached this stage, the decision was already made. The die was cast. Everything was in place and there was no fighting off the feeling.

After all, he wasn't doing this for his benefit. If he had a choice, he would not be here but would be back home with his family. But he didn't have a choice anymore. In truth, he never really had.

He reached the staircase and climbed to the top level, stepping around the litter on the steps.

Walking along the landing, the driver counted off the door numbers and drew to a halt outside the last flat. Straightening his tie, he knocked lightly on the door and waited.

After a moment, he heard an internal door open. Then a blurred shadow appeared beyond the frosted glass. The door opened.

A woman with pinched and pale features peered at him through the narrow gap.

"Yes?" she croaked. She'd probably only just woke up, the driver guessed.

Reaching into his suit pocket, the driver showed his ID badge.

"Good morning, Mrs Underhill. My name's Donald, from Vale Respite Care. I believe you've been expecting me?" He flashed her his best smile.

"What? Oh, yes. Sorry, I thought that you wouldn't be here until dinnertime."

"We prefer to pick the children up bright and early. Our charity policy is to give parents in your circumstances as much time to themselves. As well as to allow the children a break from all of the stress, of course."

The driver made a show of looking at his watch.

"I can come back later if you like?"

"No, no," the woman said hastily and opened the door wider.

She did not look good, the driver observed. Skinny to the point of being anorexic, dark shadows underneath her watery eyes, a bandana over her head. All flesh and bones and already smelling of death from the cancer riddling her body. She should be in a hospice, he figured. People could be strangely stubborn;

they would rather put their family through the torture of watching them slowly die at home before their eyes. In this case, the woman was a single mother with one daughter, who at the age of just ten was already caring for her parent during her final months of life.

Cruel bitch, he thought as he stood waiting, the smile still on his face, his blue eyes sparkling. He wondered what the mother would look like in her coffin.

He looked at the paper form and read the name written there.

"Is Mary ready? The foster family is looking forward to meeting her and having her stay with them for a short time."

"Just give us a moment, will you?" The mother turned and disappeared inside the flat.

The second she was gone, the pleasant smile disappeared from the driver's face, replaced with a sneer of contempt.

After five minutes, she reappeared, this time with a girl in tow. Quite tall for her age, she was wearing a purple and blue windbreaker jacket and black jeans. Long brown hair parted in the middle framed a freckled face with small features. She was holding an overnight bag.

"Hello, Mary. It's nice to see you. We have a bit of a drive, so perhaps you'd like to hug your mum goodbye and we will be on our way. How's that sound?"

Mary gave him a nervous smile and then turned to embrace her mother. It seemed like a one-way hug to the driver. The mother didn't seem to care too much about her daughter going away.

She gave the girl a perfunctory kiss on the top of her head and stepped back into the hallway.

"We'll have Mary back in a few days, all rested up," the driver informed the woman, but she merely nodded and was already closing the door.

Mary looked down at her feet and chewed on her bottom lip, the sadness in her young eyes evoking a brief feeling of pity inside the driver. He wrapped an arm around her narrow shoulders and steered her along the landing. "Come along."

They reached the bottom of the stairs and crossed over the walkway. The girl noticed the campervan for the first time and her face brightened up.

"A Scooby-Doo van. Are we going camping?"

"Oh, didn't your mother tell you? Mr and Mrs Yates, the kind couple who you will be staying with, well they own a smallholding, that's a little farm. They have horses and piglets and geese and all sorts of things there. They also have two teenage girls of their own who I'm sure you'll get along with just fine. They are such a loving family. They're hoping to take you and their girls away tomorrow, perhaps to a campsite in the Lake District, so I said that I would drop the campervan off for them. Won't that be fun?"

They reached the campervan and the driver unlocked the rear door. He slid it open and, taking Mary's bag, placed it in the back.

"How will you get back home, after you've dropped off the van?" Mary asked curiously.

"Not to worry, it's all taken care of," he replied and, after having a quick look around, reached back into the van and removed something from a cardboard box resting on the upholstered seats.

It was a small grey metal canister about nine inches long and with a rubber hose sticking out of one end.

"What's that?"

"Just a little surprise," he whispered, and then suddenly he grabbed the girl by the back of the head with one hand and pressed a circular mouthpiece over her nose and mouth with the other. She gave half a scream and tried to squirm away, but he pushed it firmly against her lips, holding her hair in his strong grip. The driver pulled a small trigger at the top of the canister and there was a loud hiss and then the sweet smell of Halothane gas filled the air.

The girl pulled back as she suddenly started to panic, but her struggles lasted for only seconds before the anaesthetic took effect. Her body sagged and her legs gave way.

The driver caught her in his arm and, keeping the mask over her face, he dragged the girl through the van's doorway, ducking low to keep from banging his head on the roof. There, he gently laid her down on the long seat. He reached back and quickly slid the sliding door shut, then turned to the girl again. Finding the mouthpiece's elasticated headband, he looped it over the back of her head and pulled both ends to cinch it tight, so the mask fitted snuggly against her face.

The girl drew in long and deep breaths, filling her lungs with the incapacitating gas from the canister.

Once the driver was satisfied that she was fully asleep, he climbed through to the front of the van and slowly pulled away from the curb.

20

THE EASTERN HORIZON WAS JUST starting to lighten by the time Liam and Francis returned to the caravan. It was still drizzling and the two goats had sought shelter beneath the makeshift awning. They were curled up beside the smouldering barbeque, seeking its warmth.

Inside, Liam spread out yesterday evening's edition of the Brighouse Echo on the table. In huge bold type, the front page headline simply said:

Missing.

There was a concise summary of the story, describing how a local girl named Mary Underhill had been missing for several days, and that the police were increasingly concerned for her welfare. They were appealing for any help from the public who may know her current whereabouts. She was described as vulnerable and highly emotional due to her mother's poor health and although they had not ruled out the possibility that the child may have run away or harmed herself, they were at present treating it as a case of abduction. Police were currently searching for a suspect.

Beside the story was a grainy, black and white picture of the missing child.

The story continued in more detail on page five and Francis skimmed his eyes over it. At the bottom was a press photograph of Mary's mother, who looked like she was wasting away before the cameraman's lens as she stood in the doorway of their council flat with a blanket draped about her bony frame.

Below was a quote – *"Please bring my baby home."*

"How long has she been missing?" Francis asked as he sat down at the table and re-read the feature again more slowly.

"Since the day before yesterday," Liam answered before he realized a new day had just dawned. "Actually, make that for three days, now."

"Why on earth did her mum wait so long before calling the police?" Francis shook his head in disbelief. "The girl is only ten years old."

"Apparently there was some confusion. Mary had gone away for a few nights to stay with a temporary foster family – all pre-arranged with her mum's consent, due to the woman not having long to live, it seems. It was been done through some kind of charity foundation that helps children with terminally ill parents."

Liam tapped the newspaper where it described what he'd just summarized.

"Anyway, when Mary didn't come back on the day she was due home, her mother telephoned the foster family to find out where her daughter was. The foster family was taken aback. Mary, they told the mum, had never even arrived on the arranged date. They assumed Mrs Underhill had postponed the visit. A second phone call to the charity foundation revealed that indeed, they had received a message explaining that the visit was cancelled, left by a gentleman named Donald. The man gave no surname, but he had the correct credentials. The police now think they were fake. It was then that the mother raised the alarm."

"And this *Donald* is the suspect mentioned in the paper?"

"Yes. An eyewitness on the council estate has told the police he saw a blue campervan drive by him while he was exercising his dog and then drove past again ten minutes later. Amazing that anyone from that place volunteered any information to the police," Liam added with a low whistle.

Francis rubbed the bridge of his nose. He had pain behind his eyes and his brain was in a spin.

"I came to find you before the police picked you up off the street."

"Me?"

"Yes. The girl went missing soon after you walked out on your mum and your sister, so they are bound to put two and two together—"

"And come up with five," Francis finished for him. "Thanks, Liam."

"As far as the police are concerned, you are still their number one suspect, their only suspect in their minds. Even though," and Liam flicked the paper to page six, "they are linking Mary Underhill's disappearance not only to the murder of Susan Ross in 1972 – again, they are convinced you killed her – but also to a series of unexplained deaths and disappearances of more girls going back over the years."

Francis leaned over the newspaper and read the report with renewed concentration.

There was scant detail about the girls Liam was referring to, just a list of names and a few particulars.

IMOGEN HUGHES – AGED 8. MISSING SINCE 1971. CURRENT WHEREABOUTS ARE UNKNOWN. DAWN PRESTON – AGED 12. ABDUCTED AND MURDERED IN 1978. REMAINS DISCOVERED ON LOCAL PLAYING FIELDS.

REBECCA HOBAN – AGED 9. ABDUCTED AND MURDERED IN 1981. REMAINS RECOVERED FROM CANAL.
DEBBIE LEE – AGED 13. MISSING SINCE 1982. CURRENT WHEREABOUTS ARE UNKNOWN.

"If they are all connected, then three of these cases happened whilst I was in prison, for crying out loud!" Francis said.

"That won't stop the police coming for you and framing you for taking this Imogen Hughes, who's been missing since '71, and the new one, Mary Underhill, who was abducted just the other day. They tried it with the murder of Susan Ross and ultimately failed, now they'll try for a second time. It plays into their hands perfectly."

"Shit."

"Precisely," Liam agreed.

"The paper doesn't say why the police are connecting them all. They must be holding that info back. Susan was taken at some point on her way home from school, but Mary Underhill seems to have been taken willingly from her home right before her mother's eyes. Do you think that whoever is responsible for all these missing and murdered children was known to them?"

"Probably. It would explain how they just disappeared without causing a big scene. Snatching a child off the street is bound to draw attention. Easier for the abductor if he were able to entice the children away by first establishing some kind of trust with them. They'd be less wary if he is a friendly, even familiar, face."

Francis scrutinized the newspaper, flicking back and forth between the pages.

"I can't see anywhere where it describes this man, this *Donald* person. The mother got a good look at him when he called around to pick Mary up."

"I'm sure she is working with the police. They might issue a photo-fit in a day or two. Let's hope that you don't fit his description," Liam answered with a gentle pat on his back.

Francis sighed loudly and closed the newspaper, folding it in half before sliding it away.

"We need to find out more about these other girls. Who they were, where they lived, how they were snatched? What links them? Why did the abductor choose them in particular? Three of them were later found dead if you add Susan Ross' murder to the list. Susan was manually strangled but only after she'd been held somewhere for several days. There was no sign of a sexual thing going on, according to the autopsy report. Were Dawn and Rebecca killed in the same manner? I'd also like to learn more about the locations where their bodies were dumped. As for the two girls who are still missing and have never been found—"

"Make that three," Liam interjected. "Imogen Hughes, Debbie Lee and now Mary Underhill, remember?"

"Of course. Unless the abductor took them for other reasons, I think it's safe to assume that they are dead too. Their bodies just haven't been found yet. But if we can establish some kind of pattern, then it might lead us to the psycho who took them."

"We could, you know, just leave this alone. We have that option, Francis."

Francis looked at his friend and they exchanged brief smiles.

"You know me better than that," Francis responded.

"I guess finding the bastard responsible will finally put to bed all the innuendo and rumours still swirling about your innocence, boy. Not that that's your only motive, I'm sure."

"Get stuffed, you maggot," Francis said in his best Irish accent, and they both laughed. "But I'm glad you changed your mind about helping me get to the bottom of this."

Liam waved the comment away, then said sheepishly, "This latest development sort of changes things, doesn't it? So it seemed the right thing to do. I'm sorry for burning the file, as well."

Liam came to his feet.

Francis followed suit, asking, "So where do we start? How are we going to proceed?"

"We go back to the beginning, don't we? Back to the abduction of the first girl, Imogen Hughes in 1971. Then we work through them all one at a time. The killings and kidnappings of all six girls in a thirteen-year period up to the latest a few days ago."

"Sounds easy."

Liam hesitated a moment, as though undecided on whether to say something more, and Francis noticed. He waited.

Liam made up his mind.

"There is one more thing that I think you should know, Francis. It's about the police investigation. To be more accurate, about the main detective running the show now. Appointed by the Assistant Chief Constable of West Yorkshire Police himself to lead the inquiry into the abduction of Mary Underhill."

Francis had a horrible feeling he wasn't going to like what he was about to hear.

•   •   •

Sitting in the cramped police panda car, Detective Inspector Glen Pickford was reminded of a bitterly cold morning three years ago. He remembered it clearly. Monday in early January, when a light dusting of frozen snow covered the path and the steep driveway leading to the house on the hill. A house that would forever be remembered as the home of Britain's most notorious serial killer, a lunatic more feared than his Whitechapel namesake.

The coppers at Millgarth HQ and Dewsbury nick, where the murderer was still undergoing interrogation, had called him J.R. The name had nothing to do with the guy in the big cowboy hat on the telly, wheeling and dealing and screwing his rival's missus. No, the nickname was in reference to the killer who had menaced the streets of London's East End in the autumn of 1888. Jack the Ripper.

Sutcliffe. Peter Sutcliffe. The Yorkshire Ripper, who far from being the blood-soaked maniacal madman the people of this county were expecting, turned out to be a short and skinny bloke with a bad beard and a squeaky voice.

Sutcliffe and his equally bonkers wife lived in a nice, detached house on Garden Lane, Bradford. The skinny bloke had just coughed up to the crimes that had been haunting the north of England for five long years – "We've got him!" went the message to poor old George Oldfield – and the following day, a team of officers led by Pickford had been dispatched to the Sutcliffe's marital home to begin the search for clues and potential murder weapons, of which they found plenty.

Before entering the home, Pickford had hung back momentarily, sitting in his squad car like now and staring up at the house on the hill, wondering what kind of hellhole awaited them. He'd imagined all sorts of things, from blood-soaked clothing to creepy trophies taken by the killer from the corpses of his victims, possibly a collection of violent snuff movies, or maybe even a torture chamber in the cellar. Instead, and a little to Pickford's disappointment, all they found was a cold and sterile dwelling devoid of all the comforts that made a place a home, freshly decorated in caramel wallpaper. Mrs Sutcliffe, a mousy little thing, had remained in the front room watching a German-language TV show while Pickford and the rest of the team searched through her home.

Later that evening, Pickford had returned to Garden Lane with Sutcliffe himself, where the killer showed the police various items of clothing he'd worn while carrying out some of his attacks. Sutcliffe was handcuffed to Pickford throughout. At one stage, the mousy wife had joined them upstairs. She wanted her husband to have a slice of Christmas cake that she'd just baked. Flabbergasted and bemused at the ludicrousness of it all, Pickford agreed. And so the three of them, Pickford, Sutcliffe and Sutcliffe's oddball wife, found themselves sitting at the kitchen table, the two men still handcuffed together so that each time the killer raised the slice of cake to his mouth, Pickford's arm went up and down in unison, a sight that caused a few stifled giggles from the other coppers. And all the while, forensics were removing exhibits that would help strengthen their case, things that included a sweater speckled in blood spots and a hacksaw from the garage.

Sitting in the car outside a different but not dissimilar house a few years later filled Pickford with a strange sense of déja-vu. It also brought to mind the last time he'd been here with his then-boss, the late DS Wolfe. On that night they'd arrested Francis Bailey and carted him off to Halifax for some rigorous questioning about the murder of Susan Ross. Now, here he was again, dealing with a different missing girl but looking for the same dangerous deviant.

The only problem was that the bastard had vanished off the face of the earth. Unless he was hiding somewhere in the family home, which seemed unlikely. The freak was one sly and sick weirdo, a screwball misfit, but he wasn't stupid. Not by a long shot.

The justice system might have been fooled by his dewy-eyed act and his lawyer's slick words in court, but Pickford hadn't fallen for it. He knew it was nothing but a front, constructed over many years, to hide the real monster lurking beneath.

Pickford reached for the patrol car's CB radio and toggled the switch.

"Are you in position?"

There was a hiss of static and then a tinny-sounding voice came back to him.

"Yes, DI Pickford. We have the back door covered, as well as the rear of the garage."

"Good. I don't think the little twat is in there, but best to be safe than sorry. When you hear the front doorbell ring, make your way inside. I don't want to fuck this up, you understand?"

"Not to worry," came the reply, which sounded somewhat too laid back to Pickford. He'd have to have a word with the brazen young constables later, instil a bit more of a professional ethos into their tiny brains. Then he remembered that, not too many years ago, he himself had been an impertinent and maverick copper and the recollection brought a thin smile to his lips.

He opened the car door and dragged himself out with a groan. His knees creaked more and more, these days. He should remember to take those cod liver oil tablets his wife had bought him. He was in his forties now and no longer the sprightly young constable who liked to have a rumble with the chuffing toerags that he nicked. Although, he reflected, those days weren't completely behind him. He was still fit enough and the extra timber he carried and the tight suits he wore still had a sobering effect on most of the wazzocks he hauled into the cop shop.

Quietly closing the door, he walked up the driveway and past the flower beds to the front entrance and pushed the doorbell with a stubby finger. He heard the chime sound inside, an annoyingly cheerful melody, so he kept the button depressed so that it played over and over, only releasing it when the door opened.

A youngish woman answered. Long hair with blonde highlights, white blouse, fit-looking Pickford decided, before realizing this would be Bailey's sister. One of the two fools who had fought their silly legal campaign to get a murderer cleared. The sister and the mother. There used to be a third member of the Bailey Appreciation Society up to not too long ago, the twat's father. But the doddery old fart had popped his clogs a while back, leaving the women to man the barricades.

This should be a piece of piss.

Pickford pushed her aside and stomped into the entrance hall, looking around and saying loudly, "Where is he, then? Come on, tell me!"

"Who?" the sister squawked. "You have no right to just walk in here. Who the heck are you?"

"Don't give me that. You know damn well who I'm talking about, and you know who I am. You're hardly likely to forget, are you?"

From the kitchen came a series of loud bangs. The others were inside, then.

The quavery and frightened voice of the mother reached them, followed by crockery shattering on the floor. Nice one, lads, Pickford thought in an almost fatherly way. Keep it up.

"Mum?" called the sister anxiously. "Mum?"

"Never mind her, she's as tough as old boots that one."

Pickford stepped up close to her, so near that he could smell the shampoo in her hair. She must have recently showered. A shame they hadn't burst in five minutes sooner, he thought, then he would have had the pleasure of dragging her out of the shower cubicle.

"I'll ask you again, and mark my words this is as friendly as I'm going to be, is that clear? Where is that retard brother of yours?"

Credit to her, she stood her ground and scowled back at him, saying nothing.

"Is he here? Or is he hiding somewhere else? If that's the case, and if you've been helping him, then I have grounds to book you with assisting a wanted murderer to evade arrest."

Again, she refused to answer.

A commotion at the other end of the entrance hall drew their attention and they both looked around in time to see one of Pickford's men manhandling the frail old mother through from the kitchen. The old bat was crying and her silver hair was awry. Her knitted blue cardigan trailed on the carpet.

The woman in front of Pickford screamed and ran down the hall, calling out. The two fools hugged and started to bawl, a sound that was music to Pickford's ears.

Another one of his men joined him.

"There's nobody in the garage or the garden shed, sir. PC Keeble has checked the cellar and the kitchen too."

"Alright, Jacko. Run upstairs and have a poke around. Look everywhere, the cupboards, the divan beds, wherever that twat might be concealed. And check outside the bedroom windows. I doubt the fat slob could shinny up the drainpipes, but you never know. He's a slippery cunt is that one."

The young officer nodded, all breathless and excited as he ran up the stairs.

"And if you don't find him, start tearing the place apart looking for any clues as to where he might be holding that lass," he added loudly.

Turning his attention back to the women, Pickford gave a shake of his head and granted them a sad little smile. Then he went through to the living room, beckoning his man to follow with his two charges.

Inside the front room which overlooked the garden and driveway, he was amazed to see that it was exactly as he remembered. Nothing had changed at all; the same décor, the same chintzy furniture, even the TV was an older model. The only thing he spotted that was different was a video recorder on the carpet below the TV stand and an oak cabinet with lines of VHS tapes behind the smoked glass.

Mrs Bailey and her daughter – Pamela, he recalled – were paraded before him.

"You're not making this any easier, you do know that don't you?" he told them. "For yourselves or him. Actually, you are just making things a hell of a lot worse. So my advice to you is this: if you know where he's gone or what he intends to do next, now is the time to tell me."

Mother and daughter were both crying uncontrollably now, their cheeks damp with tears. Seeing a box of tissues on the coffee table, Pickford snatched out a couple and offered them over. They dabbed their eyes.

"If you help me, if you have any information that you feel is relevant, then you have my word as a police officer that when we find Bailey, we will go easy on him. I will instruct my men to stick rigidly to the rules, that there's to be no funny business from them. No accidental falls down the stairs, no walking into walls, if you get my drift?"

This time, Patricia broke off from her snivelling to glare at him. *What?* she mouthed in stunned disbelief.

He didn't blame her for not trusting a word he said. Which was precisely the reaction he was hoping for. It was all part of the mind games that a veteran copper such as him employed. It might be 1984, he told himself, but sometimes the Old School methods of questioning still had a place in modern policing.

"I see," Pickford murmured, filling the void.

He looked around at his surroundings, weighing up his options.

The police officer reappeared just then, poking his head around the doorframe.

"Nothing, sir. The suspect has well and truly scarpered."

"I thought as much, Jacko. Well, you and the boys better start going over the place. I want every inch of this house searched, top to bottom. Every room, every effin' wardrobe. Pull up the floorboards and the skirting, look for hidden hidey holes, and dig up that shitty vegetable patch in case anyone is buried down there. Search the car. Contact British Telecom and get their boffins to trace any calls that have been made from this number, see what bloody Buzby has to say. The whole works. Get on it, lad."

Jacko disappeared.

"Keeble!" Pickford hollered, making the two women cringe.

A pair of heavy footsteps thundered down the hallway and another officer appeared.

"Get a bin bag and start bagging up these video cassettes, will you? When we get back, I want you to go through them. I don't care what it says on the labels, I want to know what they really contain. If it means that you have to sit through endless hours of The Care Bears or ruddy Conan The Barbarian, then hard luck."

Pickford glanced over at Mrs Bailey and her daughter.

"You could have avoided all of this chaos. All I wanted was to ask you a few questions, but my patience has worn thin, ladies. The clock is ticking, we have a kidnapped young girl to find, the abductor has slipped away and you are refusing to offer the police any assistance. If that's how you want to play this, then I'm happy to play along too."

Pickford turned to PC Keeble.

"Cuff them both."

Then he reached into an inside pocket of his suit and pulled out the Swiss Army knife he liked to carry. Teasing out a small blade, he proceeded to rip apart the furniture upholstery.

21

LEAVING THE CARAVAN WAS RISKY because of the danger that someone might recognize him, but Francis insisted that he wanted to go.

"We'll have to try and disguise you, in that case," the Irishman said.

He went into his bedroom and came back holding a paint-splattered green jacket that looked like it had come from the Soviet Army.

"Try this one. I found it outside an Oxfam shop."

Francis removed his duffel coat and slipped it on

"This, as well," Liam said, passing over a woollen Def Leppard hat.

"I stink," Francis complained once he had changed. The clothes whiffed of piss and mildew.

"Good, it will mean people will give us a wide berth."

It seemed to work. They hotfooted it down the steep banking and through the streets without incident, and twenty minutes later found themselves going by St Martin's Church and marching up to the library door. This time it was open.

Inside the old building, they went straight past the counter to the reading room in the back. A gent was sitting at the huge oak table doing a crossword. He looked at them disapprovingly.

They ignored him, something that Francis found easier to do with each passing day.

In the corner they found a microfilm reader and while Liam went to find the newspaper reels for the dates in question, Francis sat on the stool and familiarized himself with the controls.

He took a moment to consider what Liam had told him a short time ago. Pickford, the eager young constable who had taken to interrogating Francis alongside DS Wolfe with frightening enthusiasm, was now a Detective Inspector and in charge of the investigation into the missing child, Mary Underhill. He may have moved up the chain of command, but Francis was sure he'd have lost little of his sadistic streak. If anything, his new powers would leave him convinced he could get away with even more, shielded as he was by the public support of the Assistant Chief Constable.

Francis didn't know what his appointment meant for the case overall, but should their paths cross once again, as they could well do, then he dreaded to think what might happen.

Liam returned, interrupting his thoughts.

Placing several cardboard boxes on the counter, he lifted one of the lids to reveal a pair of round reels. They were dated and indexed.

"These cover the dates we need. Microfilms of all editions of the local newspaper. They should contain any reports on the murders and disappearances of the girls."

They fished out the reel for early November 1971 and placed it on the spool wheel. Sliding the end of the microfilm into the machine, Francis proceeded to use the round dial to glide over the black and white newspaper pages until he came to the main headline dated November 5th. Bonfire Night. The night Imogen Hughes was abducted.

There was nothing. No mention of the incident. Just some story about vandalism in a local cemetery.

"Idiot," Francis said to himself. "The story won't have been in until the following day's edition."

He scrolled forward a day and sharpened the focus.

Fears for Safety of Missing Girl

An eight-year-old girl is the subject of a large police search.

The child, Imogen Hughes, was last seen when she left her home at Rooley Heights at 4.45pm yesterday.

Imogen was supposed to call at her friend's house five doors down, where her friend and her parents had arranged to attend a local bonfire in nearby Pinfold Lane.

Imogen never arrived at her friend's. Eyewitnesses have come forward to say they saw the missing child walking, alone, down Hudson's Passage, a five-minute walk from her home, shortly after 5pm.

Police now think Imogen may have decided to go elsewhere without her mother's knowledge. She has not been seen since. Police say that they are still hopeful the child will be found

safe and well, but they have not ruled
out the possibility she may be the
victim of foul play.
Anyone with any knowledge of Imogen's
whereabouts should contact the police
immediately.

There was a very small photo of Imogen together with a brief description but very little else.

The following day's edition contained the headline:

Police Widen Search for Missing Imogen
Volunteers help scour local countryside

The search for missing schoolgirl,
Imogen Hughes, has entered its second
day as her family grows increasingly
desperate for any news.
Imogen has not been seen since the
evening of November 5th and police are
now openly stating that this is being
treated as a case of child kidnapping.
They have given no reasons for why
they think Imogen was taken against
her will, but admit that no further
sightings of the young girl have been
reported.

Imogen's father, who no longer lives at the family home, returned today from his job on a North Sea oil rig to offer comfort to his former wife.

For the next few days, the newspapers had contained little new information about the case, other than that the search was continuing. Francis guessed there'd been nothing much to update readers with and, although looking back at events from the present-day gave him and Liam the benefit of hindsight, it was still frustrating to see how quickly the story was relegated to second place behind reports of council corruption on plans for a new hospital and a feature about the local football league's match schedule.

They skipped forward until they found this:

Mystery Deepens on Kidnap Case
Parents' anxious wait for news as police wind down their search

Over a week after a local girl, Imogen Hughes, aged 8, was reported missing by her mother, police admit to having little choice but to wind down the large-scale search.
"There have been no fresh sightings of the child," a Police Inspector is

quoted as saying this morning, "and sadly, very few clues regarding her uncharacteristic disappearance. Therefore, with great reluctance and unless more information is forthcoming, we will have little choice but to reduce both our search and our door-to-door enquiries over the coming days."
Prayers are to be offered for her safe return at this Sunday's church services, but for the time being, Imogen's fate remains a perplexing mystery.
Her parents are being supported by police family liaison officers and social services.

"It's not a lot to go on," Liam said, having read the reports over Francis' shoulder.

"Which girl is next in chronological order?" Francis asked.

"Well, as far as the cases go, Susan Ross comes next. She went missing and her body was found in the woods near your home in the autumn of 1972. As we already know everything there is to know about that case, we might as well jump forward to the next one. The abduction and murder of Dawn Preston six years later."

They removed the microfilm reel and replaced it with the one dated 1978.

After a couple of minutes of searching, they found the correct front-page edition:

Body Found at Brookfoot Playing Fields

Murder investigation opened after discovery of Dawn Preston's remains

Postmortem reveals death by strangulation

The body of a young child has been found by a member of the public whilst out walking his dogs. The grim discovery was made yesterday evening, and the victim has been positively identified to be 12-year-old Dawn Preston who has been missing from her foster home for nearly three months.

A postmortem conducted overnight revealed the cause of death to be strangulation, and as a result, West Yorkshire Police have today formally launched a murder investigation.

The site of the find, in shrubbery on playing fields close to Holmes Road Timber Merchants, has been sealed off and local enquiries are underway.

They read the rest of the feature which mostly comprised an interview with Dawn's foster parents, a middle-aged couple originally from Scotland but who had moved to England some twenty years ago. Unable to have children of their own, they had instead provided safe and happy environments for many children over the years.

Next on their list was Rebecca Hoban, aged nine when she vanished in 1981. It was a similar tale to the others. Snatched off the street while playing hopscotch, there'd been no further signs of Rebecca despite a large police search and a reconstruction screened on the BBC Look North TV programme. Then early one frosty morning in February, there came the shocking news:

Canal Horror
Corpse pulled from frozen water
Poor Rebecca's last resting place

The story summarized the frightful discovery of Rebecca's body in frozen canal waters near the Standard Wire workshop at Sterne Mills. Men arriving for work had spotted what they first thought was a shop window mannequin tossed into the water, but on closer inspection, they realized it was the fully clothed corpse of a young child. They had pulled the body clear of the canal, much to the police's frustration because vital forensic clues became compromised. The cause of death was unclear as there was disagreement on the age of several injuries spotted during the autopsy – a broken arm, for example, had signs of two separate fractures, one old and one more recent. One thing the pathologist was sure of was Rebecca had been murdered sometime in the previous twenty-four hours – but around five days after she first disappeared. Where had she been during the intervening period?

When reporters commented on the similarities not only to the Imogen Hughes and Dawn Preston cases but also to the murder of Susan Ross in 1972, the police had angrily ruled out such a link:

"We are not connecting the killing of Rebecca Hoban to the brutal slaying of Susan Ross. We have the monster responsible for that murder safely behind bars," Detective Inspector Wolfe of West Yorkshire Police stressed.
Francis Bailey, now aged 27, is serving a life sentence at Wakefield Prison for the 1972 killing of Susan Ross

the report concluded.

Until today, Francis had known very little about these other cases of missing and murdered children. Reading the details now it seemed astonishing that they had never previously been linked. Was that a huge oversight or a deliberate ploy by the police? Connecting the cases would inevitably have set off alarm bells regarding his own guilt. Many people, some with lots of influence, were already starting to ask awkward questions concerning his conviction. Unless the police were willing to admit to having framed an innocent man, was it best for the public to believe the abductions and murders were the actions of different offenders?

The disappearance of girl no 5 – Debbie Lee – had received very little coverage in the local press. Just one brief mention:

Runaway Teen Believed to be in Capital
Troubled Debbie Lee fled her unhappy home, police believe.

There followed a cursory report on the missing girl, who was believed to have run away from her home at Holywell Green during the first week of January 1982. Subsequent investigations unearthed a violent home life living with her drunken father and a heavily pregnant mother, as well as medical reports that Debbie self-harmed and had twice left home before. It was hoped that, as in the past, she would return after a few days. On this occasion, sadly, she did not. There followed vague eyewitness reports that she may have been spotted in London, yet these leads went nowhere and the trail ran dry. After a few weeks, the investigation was, as in the Imogen Hughes case, gradually wound down with no conclusions.

Reading the short piece reminded Francis of some aspects of the Susan Ross case, especially regarding the two girls' sad upbringing and rumours of abuse. Thinking about the others, they too contained similar elements. They had all been under the supervision of social services or living with foster families.

Ditto the latest disappearance, that of Mary Underhill three days ago. She had been due to spend several days with a family who took in children temporarily as some kind of respite break for kids with poorly parents.

Francis was just about to remark on these commonalities when Liam drew his attention to a separate but linked story, breaking into his thoughts. He followed Liam's pointing finger. On the screen he read the following, dated the same day as the runaway teen piece:

Ripper Squad Detective's untimely Death

A top West Yorkshire Police Detective has sadly passed away after being taken ill during a New Year's Eve party.

Detective Inspector Wolfe, best known as the copper who helped convict murderer Francis Bailey for the killing of Susan Ross nearly a decade ago when he was a newly-appointed Detective Sergeant, is believed to have suffered a heart attack. In more recent times, he was part of the Ripper Squad led by George Oldfield that captured notorious serial killer Peter Sutcliffe just last year.

Known as a no-nonsense kind of police officer with an extraordinary gift for

solving crime, his energy and dedication resulted in many a dangerous criminal doing time behind bars.
Fellow cop DI Glen Pickford, who worked alongside Wolfe on both cases, paid this short tribute.
"Detective Wolfe was a throwback to the days of proper policing, your traditional Crime Buster; he was hard but fair, and his record speaks for itself. The people of West Yorkshire will surely miss his granite commitment to making their streets a safer place."

"He's the bastard who had you banged up, right?" Liam asked, tapping DI Wolfe's picture.

"Him and Pickford, yeah. My mother told me he'd passed away."

"It must have been satisfying to hear."

"It was," Francis admitted, "but in a bitter-sweet way. His death meant he avoided facing accusations of corruption. As far as the people of West Yorkshire are concerned, he's a hero, an old-fashioned kind of copper who got things done. It makes me sick."

After Francis told Liam of the one thing all the cases had in common, the running theme of neglect and unhappy childhoods blighting the girls' young lives, they sat there for a moment. Both men fell silent as they considered their conclusions.

Liam broke the hush.

"There's something else that we also need to take into account. Out of the six girls who have been taken, three have been found dead and three more are still missing, right?"

Francis nodded.

"The dead children, Susan Ross, Dawn Preston and Rebecca Hoban, were all kept alive for several days after they were abducted before being killed and their bodies dumped. We have to assume Imogen Hughes and Debbie Lee are both dead after all of this time, as well. But there's a chance, only a slim one admittedly, that the girl taken three days ago—"

"Mary Underhill?"

"She might still be alive, might she?"

"Yes, it's been preying on my mind."

They switched off the microfilm reader and packed away the reels.

"You know, when I worked at Susan's school, there were lots of rumours about the poor girl even before she went missing. I thought it was just tittle-tattle spread by the other children and then picked up by staff members, silly gossip really."

"What kind of gossip?"

"About her background, her personal life at home. There was talk of trips to the hospital, sick notes to keep her off PE classes, and injuries spotted by the school nurse. She was very sad, that much I do know. If true, then it all confirms this pattern of ill-treatment."

Francis thought for a moment.

"Her case worker at Social Services often came to the school to talk things over with Susan's class teacher. I saw them a few times, discussing the matter. I never heard what was being said, but her social worker seemed very concerned for her wellbeing. Nothing ever came of it, though."

"Even after her murder?" Liam said with surprise.

"The police decided it was irrelevant. By then, they'd fixed their sights on me."

"What did your lawyer have to say about that?"

"He wasn't happy. He intended calling on the social worker to give evidence, but it turned out the social worker's wife, who was in a wheelchair, was due to have an operation and the whole idea was left to hang."

Liam glanced around. Other than the man doing the crossword, there was nobody else but them in the reading room. "Where are you going with this?" he asked.

Francis shrugged and then said, "It would be interesting to hear what he has to say about Susan Ross' home life. If he's still alive."

"Do you recall his name?"

Francis closed his eyes in concentration and tapped a knuckle against the side of his head. Then he sat up and nodded, fixing Liam with his gaze.

"Roy Kilinkski."

"Unusual surname. There can't be many Kilinski's in the phone book. Wait here."

Liam went over to the front counter. The librarian was chatting on the telephone and had her back to him, so he reached over and plucked a copy of the local phone book off the shelf and then went back to the reading room.

He flicked through the pages and then ran his finger down a list of names. "Kidder... Kiely... Kilburn... here we are, Kilinski R. Current address is," and he turned the book to show Francis.

"Not too far away, then. Should we telephone first and explain things?"

"We could, but if he recognizes your voice it might make him clam up. You're not the most popular person around these parts. Also, if the police are looking for you, what's to stop him from tipping them off before you arrive at his home?"

"Right then, we'll call around for a chat, try and catch him on the hop."

Liam closed the phone book with a loud thud, making the man doing the crossword jump and causing his pen to scrawl over his newspaper. He scowled irritably in their direction.

"When you get there, try and keep it friendly, like you are just curious. Don't get into anything too heavy. And keep your hat on. Remember to stay incognito."

"You're not coming with me?"

"No," Liam said with a small shake of his head. "There's something else I want to check out."

22

DETECTIVE INSPECTOR PICKFORD WATCHED FROM the upstairs landing as his men searched the upper floor. They'd gone over the place like locusts, ransacking the entire house room by room. There was little finesse to their search. The idea of finding and preserving evidence had quickly gone out the window. Not that Pickford was over-fussed. He hadn't been expecting to find anything of worth in the first place and this whole episode was never meant to be that kind of search, anyway.

The lads had done a thorough job of wrecking the place, though. Grant them their due in that respect. They'd pulled out drawers, tipping their contents onto the floor. They'd peeled back all the carpets, lifted the floorboards and torn away the wallpaper from the walls. Clothes and bedding were strewn everywhere, along with broken units and shelving. Pieces of shattered vases crunched underfoot. The staircase banister was splintered where someone had decided, just for the fun of it, to kick at the wooden struts with their heavy shoes. Flat-footed bastards, Pickford thought absently.

They were currently going through the bedrooms. One of the younger constables was riffling through the young woman's underwear drawer. He had a bra on his head and was twirling a pair of frilly knickers around one finger. His mate was sitting on the bed, bouncing up and down as if testing the mattress. The pair laughed loudly.

Pickford let them have their fun and went back down the stairs.

Mrs Bailey and her daughter were in the hallway. They were still handcuffed and their faces were pale and drawn; they looked like all the fight had gone out of them. The old woman was trembling. With a bit of luck, the upset might finish the old bat off, Pickford mused as he stepped through the front door.

Teams of officers were going through the garage while behind the house, Pickford knew more of them were digging up the back garden. A few neighbours had gathered to watch the spectacle. They looked to be enjoying the show.

He went down the garden path, strode over the pavement to his panda car and climbed in, his heavy bulk making the vehicle sink down on one side.

There wasn't much for him to do whilst his men did their thing. He'd made his point to the mother and the sister, and they'd learned a lesson they wouldn't forget in a hurry; that it was foolish to cross paths with him. Now it was all a matter of letting them think about their situation and see whether or not it caused them to reconsider. Previous experience told him that, invariably, suspects or acquaintances of suspects quite often blabbed once they understood beyond any doubt that the game was up. Sometimes the relatives of suspects were harder to crack, especially Mums for some reason, but eventually even they would cave in.

Pickford sat back as he prepared to wait them out, but just then his car radio came to life. He lifted the CB mike and toggled the transmit button.

"What is it, Gloria?" he asked the woman manning the desk over at Halifax nick.

"I have an update for you, sir. It could be important."

"Really? Try me."

There was a little pause – Gloria went in for dramatic pauses – and then she said, "We have a possible sighting of Francis Bailey."

"You've just made my day, Gloria."

23

SCREENED FROM THE ROAD BY a large and overgrown privet hedge, the bungalow was easy to miss. Francis walked right by it before he realized he'd gone too far. He doubled back and after searching for a moment, he found the front gate, which was nearly hidden amidst the foliage. He had to push his way through the prickly branches to get to the handle. With some effort, he shouldered it open and went through.

Roy Kilinski's home was in the leafy suburbs on the outskirts of town, just opposite the entrance to a garden centre. There was a shop and a bus stop around the corner, while a few minutes away was The Peace Gardens with its war memorial and fountains and park benches. It was a nice area to retire to, Francis thought, as well as being ideal for Kilinkski's disabled wife.

The garden, like the hedge, looked a bit worse for wear, though. Francis paused a moment to take in the uncut grass and the dandelions. A path cut through the centre of the lawn, the stone flags starting to disappear beneath encroaching weeds. Over at the corner of the house stood a weeping willow tree with a carpet of unraked leaves around the trunk.

There was a wheelchair ramp sloping up to an entrance porch, and as he walked towards it, he noticed the drawn curtains to the right and the closed kitchen blinds to the left.

Stepping into the wide porch, he adjusted his Def Leppard hat to make sure it fitted snuggly, and then rapped on the door.

While he waited for somebody to answer, he went over his plan again. Francis reminded himself to keep things low-key. He was here to simply make a few enquiries about Susan and her background. Don't mention the court case directly, he told himself, as it might rouse suspicions. Hopefully, the man might not recognize Francis in his disguise. If Kilinksi became curious and wanted to know why he was seeking information, just say he was a friend of Susan's family and they had asked him to pop round the next time he was in the area, just to clear up a few loose ends. Susan's mother wanted some closure to the whole tragedy. Then maybe compliment him on his home (don't mention the untidy garden) and enquire about his wife's health. Most of all, keep smiling.

He knocked on the door again, louder this time, but when nobody came to the door Francis suspected there wasn't anyone home.

Pursing his lips, he decided to try the back in case the homeowners were outside and enjoying the break in the weather. He walked by the curtained window (he could see nothing through the large plate glass) and, ducking beneath the low branches of the willow tree, he went around the corner of the house.

The pathway led down the side of a rockery filled with neglected winter honeysuckle and hardy alpine plants, then there was a large stand of rhubarb which looked like it hadn't been touched in weeks, and rounding the corner, Francis spotted the half dozen bottles of milk and three cartons of eggs on the back doorstep.

Feeling sure that the place had been empty for some time, he nevertheless tapped on the glass panel of the rear door.

There was still no answer and Francis was contemplating what to do next when a bald head popped up over the fence dividing the back garden from the neighbours' property. A pair of large eyes blinked down at him owlishly through thick-rimmed, round spectacles.

"He's not here," the middle-aged man announced, pointing at the Kilinksi's home with a pair of secateurs.

Francis took a few paces closer to the fence and smiled broadly.

"Do you know when Mr Kilinski will be back?" he asked pleasantly.

The man shook his head and then shrugged. "I have no idea and I don't rightly care."

"Sorry?"

"That one," the neighbour told him, nodding at the backdoor as though Roy Kilinski was standing right there, "is a miserable and peevish old blockhead. A horrible little man with no manners. I've lived here for seven years and not once in all that time has he so much as said hello or good day. His wife, well, she was even worse. Always whining and whinging, blaming the world for her woes. It's not my fault she ended up in a wheelchair. I wasn't the fool who crashed into them, was I? I tried my very best to be neighbourly but when they declined to join the Rotary Club of which I'm the chairman, well that's when I decided enough was enough and I've left them to their own devices ever since. Good riddance that they are no longer my problem, although I shouldn't speak ill of the dead."

Francis shook his head. "I'm a little confused. A car accident? Mrs Kilinski has passed away?"

"Yes. Three or four weeks ago. She never recovered from the car accident, either physically or emotionally. Losing their daughter must have been difficult, I concede, and then her becoming wheelchair-bound for the remainder of her life must have been hard for the two of them. Alas, the lady succumbed to her injuries and left this mortal coil, then the husband, the horrible little man, moved out a few days later. He's gone. Hopefully for good."

"Their daughter died in this car crash?"

The neighbour nodded.

"Can you tell me about it?"

"Well, actually I wasn't here at the time, I should clarify. I was living over near Batley Park with my, my erm… my friend, Malcolm. I moved here in the summer of 1977, three days after Virginia Wade won Wimbledon. The Kilinski's were already here, of course, just him and her. She was in her wheelchair thing by that time because the car crash occurred, I later found out from Agnes Whitehead at number fourteen, all the way back in 1970."

The neighbour paused for a moment, like he was reluctant to continue, which Francis knew wasn't the case; he was dying to divulge what gossip he knew about the people next door.

"Please, go on," Francis indulged him, smiling warmly.

"Well, the crash happened one evening. The family, him, her and the daughter, had been out with friends over at The Blue Ball Inn in Norland. Do you know it?"

Francis nodded.

"Me and Malcolm often went there, we used to call it *pop and crisping* because we never partook of alcohol, we preferred to have lemonade and a packet of crisps. The ones where you had a little blue bag of salt that you sprinkled on yourself. The Kilinski's, in contrast, did enjoy a good tipple, according to Agnes anyway. On this night, Mr Kilinski must have had one too many because, on the way back, he swerved their car over to the wrong side of the country road just as another car was coming in the opposite direction and..."

The neighbour snipped at a rose branch with his secateurs.

"...just like that, the daughter was killed instantly and the poor mite's mother was left with a broken spine. Tragic."

"How old was she at the time? The kid, I mean?"

"Nine, maybe ten. A bonnie lass, by all accounts. Before the accident, I mean. The silly sausage wasn't wearing her seat belt, so she went straight through the windscreen. They had to scrape her off the tarmac with coal shovels, they say."

Francis cringed as images crowded his thoughts.

Unperturbed, the man over the fence went on.

"Mrs Kilinski was lucky to survive, if you can call it lucky. She barely made it past the first few days. The wonders of modern medicine ensured that, somehow, she scraped through. Only to be confronted with a future filled with hopelessness and grief. She was paralysed from the neck down. Unfortunately, it never stopped her carping voice. Morning, noon and night she henpecked her poor husband. I could hear her non-stop shrill voice pass right over this very fence and through my conservatory. What a nightmare!"

He waved his arms in the air dramatically like it was all too much for him.

"Sometimes I think she wished she'd died alongside her daughter. It's no kind of life, is it? Having to depend on other people for every little thing, being pushed around like a baby in a pram. I say this with no ill-feeling, my young man, but that woman withered away on the inside just like her shell withered away on the outside."

Francis let him drone on as he took another look at the house and back garden.

When there was a break in the neighbour's commentary, he edged towards the corner of the house.

"Well, thank you for your time," he said politely and turned to go.

"Are you a relative? Of the Kilinskis?"

Francis looked around.

"You look vaguely familiar. They didn't have many callers, unsurprisingly, but perhaps I've seen you visit in the past?"

The bespectacled man looked him up and down as though only just noticing the scruffy and smelly clothes.

"I'm just an old friend, that's all."

"I see. Well, in that case, if you positively must talk to Mr Kilinski, I might happen to know where you can catch him."

Whilst Francis was learning about the tragedy that befell the Kilinksi family all of fourteen years ago, Liam was walking through the wrought-iron gates of Wainhouse Terrace cemetery.

It was years since he'd been here last. On several occasions in the past, he had found himself sleeping in the bottom arcade with the other street people. That was in the early days, shortly after falling on hard times and pitching up in this part of England. Since then, experience told him that to survive, he would need a roof over his head. The junkies and loonies who frequented this spot only lasted for one or two winters, before bronchitis or pneumonia claimed them.

A short time staying at The Salvation Army drop-in centre was followed by spells living in various homeless shelters. But they always ended the same way; with him being told to leave due to the heavy drinking and the fights.

Eventually, two years ago, he'd stumbled over the abandoned caravan in the field and after fixing it up the best he could, it became home. The goats kept him company.

The cemetery had changed little. Other than a few extra headstones (he knew one of the graves contained Francis' dad, but he didn't have time to search) and an extension near the car park, it looked mostly the same.

He spotted a groundsman gathering dead brambles, so he went over, threading his way between the memorials and gravestones.

As he approached, Liam caught the mouth-watering aroma of tomato soup; a thermos flask and a sandwich box were resting on a low wall.

"Hello there, Chief!" he called out.

The worker caught sight of Liam and pulled a set of Walkman headphones away from his ears, saying, "How do?" and nodding brusquely.

Liam held back because he was well aware that his appearance, not to mention the unwashed aroma that hung about his frame like a fetid miasma, often made people nervous. Indeed, the groundsman gave him the once over and Liam knew he came up short in the other's estimation.

Removing his flat cap and scratching his scalp, the man shook his head. "I have no spare change if that's what you are after."

"Oh, no. I wouldn't bother you in that way whilst you are working," Liam stressed, although a couple of quid wouldn't go amiss, he thought to himself. "I was hoping you could help me."

"In what way?"

"Just a piece of information. Have you worked here long, sir?"

"A fair while, aye. Nigh on twenty years. Afore that, my old man was the gardener slash gravedigger slash handyman around here. Now I live in the old Lodge House over yonder by mi'sen, and I keeps the place tidy in between helping with the burials."

He tied the top of a black bin liner that he'd filled with brambles and deposited it next to a row of similar bags.

"Is it a particular grave you are looking for?" he asked Liam.

"In a way, I think."

"You think? That's an odd thing to say."

The groundsman waited for him to go on, so Liam carefully explained the reason for his visit. He asked about the reports of vandalism in the cemetery that he and Francis had chanced upon whilst searching the microfilms of old newspapers in the library. He knew that it was a long shot, that nobody was likely to remember a small incident from many years ago. The tiny story appeared in the paper the day before news of Imogen Hughes' abduction broke, and it briefly described reports of teenagers desecrating the burial ground. Nobody was ever arrested. Repairs were made and it was quickly forgotten. At least, that's what Liam assumed. He wondered why he was even here, why he thought it important.

"This happened in 1971, a day or so before Bonfire Night," he finished.

"I knows when it happened, alright."

Liam looked straight at the groundsman.

"You remember it?"

"Of course I do, you daft 'apeth. I had to tidy the mess up, didn't I?"

The groundsman took a seat on the low wall. Unscrewing the plastic cup off the thermos flask, he half filled it with steaming tomato soup. He slurped at the tasty beverage.

"It was more than just a bit of vandalism, mind you. The paper made out that it was unruly yobs messing about, tipping over a few headstones, but I tell you, pal, it was far worse than that. The council and the police hushed it up. Can't say I blame 'em, like. Who the heck wants to read about that sort of thing happening around here?"

"What sort of thing would that be, Mr...?"

"Cartwright, Harry Cartwright."

"What sort of thing would that be, Mr Cartwright?"

The groundsman chuckled quietly and sucked in his breath between stained teeth.

"Do you smoke?"

Liam reached into his coat pocket and found a crumpled packet of ciggies. He shook one loose and offered it to the groundsman, followed by a lit match.

The man puffed away for several seconds.

"I'll tell you what I know, alright pal? What I saw. Because I remember it well. After that, you can make of it as you wish."

Liam pointed at the wall alongside the groundsman. "Do you mind?"

"Free country, innit? Park your arse down."

When Liam was seated, Mr Cartwright explained further.

"I was late for work that morning. Slept in. Don't know why, 'cause normally I'm an early riser, me. Was probably on account of watching the gogglebox the night before. I liked me cowboy series back then, especially that *Alias Smith and Jones,* and they always repeated 'em on BBC 2 late on, before bedtime, like. Anyhow, whatever the reason, I didn't wake up until after eight, and I was supposed to have started work by then. Luckily, like now, I didn't have far to commute," he said with another chuckle.

"Anyhow, I skipped breakfast because I had lots to do, so's I gets me clobber on, me wellies and me blue overalls, and on the way out I grabbed a few tools from the lean-too."

He drank from the cup some more.

"It was a foggy morning. Always is around Plot Night, because some folks have their bonfires a few nights early, don't they? A foggy November morning in a cemetery high up in the Pennines. Was enough to give you the wobblies. Still, I makes me way along the path when suddenly summat catches me eye. A mound of freshly dug earth, right smack bang in the middle of the cemetery where there shouldn't have been one. So I wander over, thinking some bastard kids have been messing about during Halloween a few nights earlier, but even as I thought that I knew that couldn't be right, because I would have seen it before then. You couldn't miss it."

The groundsman dragged on his cig, the smoke coiling in the air like some lost spirit seeking out its final resting place.

"And sure enough, me worst fears had been realized. There was a great big sodding hole, a long oblong trench right over a grave, and at the bottom was the coffin. What was left of it, anyhow. It was mostly rotten splinters and the lid was flung away and, argh, it's giving me the shivers just thinking about it all these years later. Grave robbers, can you credit it?"

"Was the coffin empty?"

"Of course it was, you prat. They wouldn't be very good grave robbers if they'd left the smelly cadaver behind, would they?"

Liam shrugged, saying, "They might have done it to steal valuables."

"This isn't some tomb from Ancient bloody Egypt! We're not talking Queen Nefertiti, are we? This is Yorkshire. That kind of thing doesn't happen around here. I'm glad I skipped me black pudding that morning, pal, otherwise I'd have been spewing up all over the shop."

"It must have been a frightful sight?" Liam commented.

"And some. Bleeding hell, you're a bright spark, aren't you? So what do I do? I runs, no I sprints, back to the house and dial 999. The police arrived and had a shufty around, took a few photos, and then within a couple of hours I'm been told to fill the hole in and tart the grave up again, make it look all spick and span. Then I was ordered to keep me gob shut. So's I did, 'cause I like me job. Then, later that day, a report appears in the local rag with all this nonsense about teenage vandals causing a bit of harmless mischief in a local cemetery. Like I told you, they hushed it up. Don't ask me why, they just did."

Liam cast his eyes over the monuments and tombstones. On a peaceful day like today, it was difficult to visualize the horrible deed of a corpse being dug up from its burial place.

"Can you remember which grave it was? Who was buried there?"

The groundsman drank the final dregs of tomato soup and shook the droplets from his cup before screwing it back on.

"Follow me."

He led Liam to a segment of graves near the south-facing slope that overlooked the town. Off in the distance, trucks and cars trundled along the motorway that cut across High Moor. A stiff wind buffeted the exposed spot.

The groundsman pointed a finger.

"That's the one," he said, indicating an upright slate grave marker. "I did my best to make it look presentable, but nobody's been to pay their respects for years, now. It's left to me to maintain all of the graves."

The inscription was faded and filled with lichen, so Liam crouched down and scrubbed at it with his hand.

"Not that there's anyone down there any longer," the groundsman added. "They never did recover the body. Ghouls!"

He gave a theatrical shiver.

Liam read the name and date on the headstone and so taken aback was he that he rocked back on his heels. It felt like a stone had dropped into the pit of his stomach.

24

CONSCIOUSNESS RETURNED TO MARY UNDERHILL in various shades of grey and black.

In her dreamy state, her mind struggled to comprehend what was happening. It felt like she was deep underwater. As though she'd been diving below the sea and was now struggling to get back to the surface before she ran out of air.

As she rose, the watery depths changed from impenetrable black to a murky grey and finally a shimmering pale opaqueness that beckoned her on. The ceiling of daylight above was dazzling.

Mary opened her eyes and the world about her wobbled and tilted. Her head felt too big and heavy, and a deep-rooted headache pulsed painfully behind her eyes. She thought she might be sick.

After a moment, the world righted itself and the sensation passed.

Her senses were still dulled. Just constructing basic thoughts was a strain, an effort of willpower. In stages, her memory returned.

Images and recollections flashed through her mind.

A man's kindly face, with an arm around her shoulders.

His soft voice saying reassuring words.

The crinkle of a leather jacket.

A blue campervan parked by the curbside.

Then, the recollection of something being placed over her mouth followed by a sweet smell, before her world had spiralled away to nothingness.

Mary didn't know how long she'd been asleep. Her mouth was dry and she thought she might have peed, so she guessed it must have been for some time. Was she lying on a bed somewhere? Certainly, soft sheets were covering her still-clothed body. She thought she heard traffic, moving fast in the near distance.

Gradually, she became aware that there was somebody else in the room with her. A shifting of the air and a creaking of floorboards made Mary's heart flutter, before a shadow appeared, seeming to suck away the light like a black hole.

Then a familiar voice.

"There, there. There's nothing to be afraid of."

Mary shifted her gaze, seeking out the man who was called Donald. But instead, another face appeared above her, and the sight of it nearly stopped her heart.

It was an old and wrinkled face, of leathery skin turned yellow and brown, the emaciated flesh stretched tightly across cheekbones and forehead. A jaw that hung loose, revealing black and rotting teeth, and sunken, shrivelled eye sockets that seemed like tiny holes. Yet, in contrast, behind them were eyes of such dazzling blue they seemed to shine with luminescence; they flitted back and forth as they studied her.

The cadaverous head was crowned with long, black hair that framed the terrifying face and cascaded down over narrow shoulders. A voluminous blue sleeveless dress with a frilly lace collar mercifully hid the woman's body. There was a smell of damp earth in the air.

She leaned over Mary, blocking most of the feeble light that pushed through a small and dusty window, and spoke again.

Strangely, the mouth didn't move, and the voice seemed distant and muffled.

"Your mother is here, my sweet girl."

Mary quickly looked around, the words briefly filling her with hope. Yet, there was nobody else in the room, just her and the old woman.

"She's missed you. Oh, how much your mother has missed you."

And the bare arms opened out to take Mary in their embrace. A cold embrace, with limbs so skinny they might have been made of bones.

Mary slipped back into the stygian darkness.

When she awoke for a second time, Mary came immediately alert. Her mind was no longer clouded by the lingering effects of the anaesthetic or the sleeping pills or whatever the man called Donald had earlier used to knock her out. Now she was lucid.

She was blindfolded and tied to a chair. Although she could not be sure, she felt she was in the same building as before, just a different room. She could still hear the distant thrum of traffic passing by.

With her clarity of thought, Mary now fully appreciated the danger she was in, and had she not already been seated, she might have collapsed to the floor. Still, a deep dread spread through her like cold black oil, and Mary found herself struggling to get her breath.

She strained her ears, trying to pick up any sounds.

As well as the traffic, she thought she could hear birdsong. And what was that other sound? A rapid tapping. Mary thought at first that it was somebody using a hammer, but it was too fast, the taps sounding more like a drill. Then she recognized it to be a woodpecker.

So, the building or house where she'd been taken was somewhere near or in woodland, with a busy road not too far off.

Not that this knowledge helped her. Tied to the chair as she was, there was no way she could leave. In fact, her binds were wound about her chest so tightly that they made breathing difficult. And her arms were tied to the armrests and her ankles to the chair legs.

All she could do was wait and hope that somebody would come to her aid.

Before the kindly man did something fearfully bad to her.

Sometime later, (minutes or hours, she did not know) Mary heard a door open and footsteps scraping over the floor. There was a pause like someone was standing in the doorway and watching her, before the door was closed again.

"Hello, Mary."

The voice made her jump.

"I'm not going to hurt you. I promise not to harm a hair on your head."

It was the man, the one who had taken her in his blue campervan. Donald. Or was it the old woman, the haggard and ancient crone with the waxy, bloodless face? Mary was confused because the two of them were mixed up in her head, which didn't make sense.

"Would you like me to remove your blindfold? Would you like that?"

Mary's head spun. Not being able to see was frightening, but the thought of looking at the old woman again was even more terrifying. Tears streamed from her eyes, damping the cloth covering her eyes.

Shuffling footsteps drew close and Mary instinctively pulled her head back.

"Please... please..." Her voice trembled with emotion.

Hands on her face made her flinch and recoil.

"Be still, dear, while I untie this."

The knot at the back of her head was loosened and the blindfold fell away into her lap, and when Mary blinked away the brightness, she was relieved to see Donald looking into her face, his features creased with concern. There was no sign of the old crone.

"You've been asleep for such a long time. I think I may have used too much gas on this occasion. Please, accept my sincere apologies. Do you forgive me?"

Mary could not find the words to reply, so she just nodded her head. She could not stop trembling.

She stole a quick look at her surroundings. They were in a dining room, with a table set out with placemats and cutlery. Four chairs were evenly spaced around it. At the end of the table to Mary's right, a young girl sat watching her, a smile on her face.

"You must be hungry. I'm making some lunch, it will be ready soon. I'm just waiting for Mother to join us," Donald explained in a calm voice.

He indicated the girl sitting in the other chair.

"Your sister is here already, see? How wonderful."

Mary wanted to tell him that she didn't have a sister. "Where... where are we?" she asked instead, her voice all thin and raspy.

Donald turned back to her and patted her gently on the hand, saying, "Now don't you worry about that, dear."

Mary looked once more at the other girl. She had blonde hair tied with ribbons and was wearing a floral top fastened up to the neck. Her hands were clasped together and rested demurely on the dining table and she continued to look towards Mary, her gaze one of wonderment.

A buzzing noise distracted Mary then, and her attention shifted to the dining room window. She cringed in revulsion when she spotted a mass of bluebottle flies crawling over the glass, covering nearly the entire pane. More flies hovered and swarmed around the room's lightbulb.

Then she saw something scuttling across the wooden tabletop and her eyes widened in fright. A cockroach! Urgh!

Donald slammed his hand down, flattening the tiny creature under his palm. He turned his hand over to examine the yellow gooey mess for a second, before rubbing the sticky substance on his trousers.

"Melanie," he said harshly, addressing the other girl. "I told you to tidy the house before our guest arrived. Pray do tell me, just what have you been doing all of this time?"

The girl (his daughter, Mary presumed) said nothing back. Until now, her attention had remained fixed on Mary. She seemed overjoyed to have an unexpected friend for lunch.

The whole scene of happy domestic bliss was at odds with Mary's predicament. Everything was somehow out of kilter, and there was a bizarre and fragile nature to the room's atmosphere. Almost as though they were all play-acting in some silly game, some family jape for which Mary was the guest of honour. She was aware that she had been kidnapped and was in mortal danger, so why all of this ridiculous masquerade?

Somehow, it was more frightening than if Donald was shouting and screaming and threatening her with a knife or a gun.

She could smell his sweat, too, like he hadn't bathed in weeks. And there was another underlying odour, one she couldn't quite place. Something sickly-sweet, like the bad aromas at home when Mum returned from her hospital appointments and she was shrouded with the lingering malodor of chemotherapy fluids. It was the rank, gammy stink of something fetid.

"And it's rude to stare," Donald was saying to the girl called Melanie. "Will you stop gawping?"

Mary watched as the man who called himself Donald took up the parental posture most adults adopted when admonishing their children; hands on hips, head tilted sideways, eyebrows raised in exaggerated indignation. He even wagged his finger and started to scold Melanie, but his words flitted in and then back out of Mary's head because of what happened next. Something so unexpected and surreal and hair-raisingly dreadful that she blinked in surprise and her mouth sagged open.

Donald stomped around the table and grabbed a hold of his daughter's face with both hands and peeled the skin away. It came free with a sticky squelching noise, looking like a thin piece of leather in his hands. As though Melanie's face wasn't a face at all, but a mask of flesh.

The girl did not move, did not cry out. She was as still as a mannequin.

Mary sat as if transfixed, mesmerized by the strange tableaux before her, and when the realization of what she was seeing finally hit, a sensation passed through her body akin to an insect crawling up her spine, making her shoulder blades contract.

Beneath the mask was the white skull of a corpse, whose black and empty eye sockets bored into Mary like twin pieces of coal. The jaw, now released with the removal of the face, dropped down with a quiet click so that the smile became a rictus grin.

Donald glided around the table towards Mary, holding his dead daughter's face in one hand.

When he pressed the piece of gossamer-thin skin to Mary's own face, as if to suppress her identity behind this grotesque veil, transforming her into someone new, her young mind snapped.

Mary screamed and screamed.

25

WHEN FRANCIS REACHED THE LAST house on River Street, he allowed himself a moment to go over the directions the nosey neighbour had given him.

This side of town, close to the River Calder and the parallel canal, was crammed with poor-standard housing. Cheap digs owned by shifty-looking landlords offering dingy dwellings to the most unfortunate in society. Row after row of poky terraced houses whose cellars were infested with rats and mouldy with rising damp.

Behind River Street was a clump of soot-stained factories and warehouses. On the front side, across the polluted river, was a huge and sprawling car auction site containing thousands of second-hand automobiles, motorbikes and beat-up vans. Adjoining the large site was a beaters yard where men in overalls custom-built stock cars. It also served as a discreet chop shop where cash changed hands on the sly and mouths were zipped shut.

The area stank of spilled chemicals and burning plastic, and drifting over the water was the continuous sound of metal being hammered and pounded. As Francis watched, a large magnetic crane lifted a wrecked car through the air to deposit it inside a car crusher.

After leaving Roy Kilinski's old bungalow, Francis had returned to the caravan hoping to find Liam waiting for him. There was no sign of his friend. Francis didn't know where he'd gone or what precisely he had wanted to check out, so had no idea where to start looking for him. Instead, Francis had scribbled a quick note explaining his next move. Then he'd left the caravan again.

He turned away from the bleak view of the river and its environs to peer down the street. There was an old and disused gas lamp post standing on the corner, the kind that kids still enjoyed climbing and swinging from the cast iron stanchion arms. Here, River Street ran out and became a rough track with a strip of grass down the middle. Running alongside it was a line of telegraph poles that were tilting so far over they looked like they might fall at any moment. Beyond them was a field and a smallholding.

According to the neighbour, Roy Kilinski, the social worker who had been in charge of Susan Ross' welfare and who might have some important background information, owned a second house somewhere around here. If the set of directions were accurate, Francis should be fairly close. He hoped this time, Kilinski was home.

He followed the rough track and, after a few minutes, he passed behind a stand of trees on the riverbank and left the noisy breaker's yard behind. Soon, the only sound was that of gentle birdsong and buzzing insects.

After five more minutes, the rough track narrowed even further as it ran past a rickety wooden fence, becoming a footpath.

A short time later and the river curled away behind an elongated island and the canal pressed up right alongside what was now a towpath. There was a lock with a lock keeper's hut and a lifebuoy mounted on the wall, then the way ahead disappeared through a tunnel of trees, the low-hanging branches seeming to warn him off from venturing any further. Francis dipped his head below the foliage and pressed on.

Another noise soon reached him. A low hum that seemed to swell and diminish. Francis looked around as he tried to pinpoint its source. Whatever it was, it grew steadily louder.

Then, through the dense trees, loomed the towering structure of a huge bridge. It spanned right over the river, canal and woodland. Francis remembered, now. This was the motorway bridge feeding traffic along the M62 as it crossed the shallow valley north and south, and the humming sound was the traffic passing to and fro.

The bridge was so big that as he drew near, it blocked out the light. He entered the gloom beneath, passing through a creepy, twilight world of shadows and swarms of midges and smelly canal water. Looking up at the graffiti-covered pillars that held aloft the road sixty feet above his head made him go dizzy from vertigo.

Francis emerged on the other side.

After another hundred yards or so, the path veered away from the canal and went up a wooded slope. Francis followed it, being careful of the slippery mud and the exposed tree roots.

At the top, he came out from the woodland canopy into dull daylight. Before him, there was a fence made from strings of wire. One of the posts had been pushed aside and so Francis was able to easily pass through. Then he drew to a halt on the edge of a small pasture and stood still as if he were skewered to the earth.

A narrow potholed road led up to a set of crumbling stone gateposts and a weed-covered driveway, and beyond these was the house. If you could still call it a house, Francis reflected.

At one time in the past, the red-bricked structure would have been a glorious example of Georgian architecture and a grand home for a large and fairly wealthy family. Now, it was a dilapidated ruin. The dormer windows above the cornice, which would have once offered fine views over the open countryside, were now broken and empty openings containing the grimy remnants of dusty glass, and the windowsills were smeared with pigeon droppings. The once-ornate stone balustrade running along the roofline was blackened and cracked with age and had entire chunks of masonry missing. One of the building's two tall chimney stacks had crumbled away and lay in a pile of broken bricks in the garden far below, while the other one leaned at a crazy angle; for how long it would continue to defy the laws of gravity was anybody's guess, because it too could fall away at any time. Most of the lower bay windows were hidden behind gnarled and twisted growths of dead ivy, but those that Francis could see were boarded up to stop local youths from throwing bricks through the glass. So too was the central doorway set in the stone porch. In fact, the whole of the front bay entrance feature and triangular pedimental crown was sagging, looking like an old man whose strength was fading. The ground seemed to be absorbing the large structure and Francis imagined in another decade or so, the entire building might sink from sight forever.

On one side of the house, there was a more recent extension built from sandstone. It had huge quoins at the corners to add strength to the brickwork. These hadn't prevented part of the wall from falling away, leaving a gaping hole. From out of the jagged opening, a short tree now grew, its branches grasping at the sky like a huge hand.

Peeling paintwork and decaying masonry now marked the spot where luxury and elegance could once be found, in another era.

The garden was a wild waste ground of overgrown brambles and thorn bushes. Francis saw, nearly hidden amidst the foliage, the rotten frame of an old wooden greenhouse. And wasn't that a sundial poking out of the tall grass? Also, a water feature now green with slime? Suggestive of the fact that, at one time, the house was surrounded by beautiful ornamental grounds?

It was much worse than the bungalow he'd visited a short time ago. This place looked like it had been allowed to run into wild disrepair for a lifetime.

Francis' heart sank. Surely, there would be nobody here. Roy Kilinski was proving annoyingly difficult to track down.

Still, he thought as he moved towards the gateposts, he ought to at least take a look around.

Abutting the house on this side was a tumbledown garage with flimsy wooden walls and a sagging corrugated tin roof. There was no entrance door, enabling Francis to see inside. He spotted a large, moth-eaten dustsheet covering something, perhaps a pickup truck or a van; Francis caught a flash of blue bodywork through a rent in the cloth.

What held his attention even more was the vintage motor parked alongside. Francis walked up the tangled driveway, his frustration at not finding Kilinski temporarily forgotten.

The car was a Ford Zephyr. It was so badly eaten with rust that the roof and bonnet had holes right through the metal. The engine grill at the front had partially sprung loose so the engine itself was visible within, while the chrome bumper was leaning upright against one wall. Both front headlamps were smashed into fragments, the wing mirrors had twisted out of shape and become speckled with black spots where the silver backing had oxidized, and the car's tyres were all flat.

Francis moved closer. Sliding between the car and the garage wall, he leaned over and, cupping his hand to the driver's window, he peered inside.

The car's interior was, as expected, as bad a mess as the bodywork. The upholstered leather seats were all ripped to shreds and the dashboard, with its once uber-modern radio, ensnared with strings of cobwebs.

Sighing to himself, Francis straightened again.

Leaving the garage, he fought his way through tangles of twiggy bushes and stepped across the lawn. Then he climbed the stairs to the boarded-up front doorway.

He didn't need to go inside. The building was probably an empty and gutted shell. Not to mention a very hazardous place to explore.

So why he found himself gripping the edge of the wooden board with both hands and pulling it open, Francis did not know.

26

IAM PEERED AT THE PIECE of paper, reading the note for a second time. His face was a picture of concern.

He'd found it on the caravan's kitchen table, propped up against a bottle of HP sauce. As well as the message, Francis had included a hand-drawn map and a series of directions, showing the approximate location of Kilinski's second home. Having drawn a blank at the bungalow, he intended to check out this other place.

"Shite, are you away with the bleedin' fairies, Francis Bailey?" he mumbled to himself, wondering yet again just what his friend had got them both involved in.

Things had gone too far. Solving the mystery of the missing and murdered girls, to crack the case once and for all, was one thing. Liam could appreciate why Francis wanted to do that. Why he *needed* to do that. After all, Liam himself had been on his own passage of atonement ever since that night in Templepatrick years ago.

The difference was that his journey had become an endless odyssey mostly spent staring into the bottom of an empty bottle. Whereas Francis had an opportunity to finally lay his ghosts to rest.

But not like this. There was a very real danger that events could quickly spiral out of control and take on a very sinister aspect.

The worst part of it was that Francis didn't know the danger he might soon find himself in.

Liam dropped the note onto the table and pondered his options. He only had the one, which basically comprised him shifting his arse at warp-speed in the hope he could catch Francis before he went and did something stupid.

He spun away and hurried through to his bedroom. Racing around the bed, he yanked away the loose wall panel and dragged out the brown duffel bag. Placing it on the bed, he drew apart the drawstrings and scooped out the oily towel containing his gun.

He quickly checked over the Armalite. It seemed okay. Also in the bag were two magazines with 25 rounds apiece. He clipped one onto the gun's stock just in front of the trigger guard and chambered the first round.

Not counting the few times that he'd practised on the firing range that the Provos used, he'd only ever fired the thing for real on just one occasion. That was when he'd been ordered to kill the informer at Ballyclare, and the memory made him hesitate for a moment. His hands shook.

With any luck, Liam reassured himself, he shouldn't need to use the gun today.

Still, what he wouldn't give to be on the wrong side of nine pints right now.

He returned the gun to the bag and threaded an arm through the bag's handles so that it rested against his back. Then he slipped through the curtain to the kitchen area and opened the caravan's door.

He'd stepped down to the ground and was just closing the door behind him when a movement across the field caught his eye.

It was a car.

A police panda car, pulling to a stop on the other side of the barbed wire fence and hedgerow.

•   •   •

Pickford slowly rolled the panda car to the end of the trackway and parked it as close to the wild hedgerow as he could.

From their vantage point, the Detective Inspector and his two colleagues, officers Jackson and Keeble, could see through the twiggy barrier. The caravan, a neglected old rattletrap with shabby curtains over the windows, was fifty yards or so across a field on the side of this godforsaken hill.

Someone had just opened the door and stepped outside, looking in their direction. Pickford hurriedly turned off the car's engine and kicked himself. He'd been hoping the occupants of the caravan wouldn't notice their approach. Not that it mattered, because they had their man cornered. There was nowhere else for him to run.

Pickford squinted his eyes. The person standing by the open doorway didn't look like Bailey. He wasn't fat enough; was too tall and well built. So, that would be the fucking Paddy; whatshisface? The woman who worked part-time in the library, the sister of that lass who Bailey had exposed himself to in The Upper George just last week, had recognized the Irish pisshead with Bailey and, hearing that the police were searching for the suspected child abductor, had tipped them off. Pickford immediately knew which Irish pisshead she was referring to (it was a small town). He also knew where the drunken Paddy lived.

Police work could be deceptively simple at times, thought Pickford. And he, like his old Boss, DS Wolfe, was a fucking legend.

Opening his door, he climbed out.

It was wild up here, blowing a frigging gale compared to the valley bottom.

The wind was prowling in the east, Pickford observed, and then allowed himself a small smile.

Listen to you, waxing all lyrical.

God, he was good.

Today, he reckoned, marked the end of a long road. They had tried to get this bastard for over twelve years. They thought they had him at one time, banged up and with the key thrown away, only for those pompous judges to let the creep out again. And what happened? Within days of Bailey being released, another girl was snatched off the streets.

Well, the toe rag wasn't getting away with it again.

It was time for some real justice.

This one is for you, Boss.

As for that Irish pisshead, whatshisface? Thingamabob Brennan, that was it. Well, if he decided to get in their way, then he could have his head cracked open with their truncheons as well.

They couldn't waste time fannying around. The missing girl might be in that caravan right this minute.

Pickford leaned back in through his open door, addressing the two uniformed constables in the back.

"What are you two sitting on your arses for? Get out here now."

Jackson and Keeble joined him outside. Remembering that the gaffer could be a stickler when it came to appearances, they put their peaked caps on. It was all about public perception, he would often tell them. The great unwashed needed reminding who was in charge.

All three of them crouched down behind the hedgerow. Looking through the branches, they could see the tall man remaining by the door, standing there like he was undecided on what to do.

"Right then, Bailey must be inside," Pickford told them. "Get your ugly mugs over there and detain the two of them."

"Us?" Jackson and Keeble both said in unison.

"Yes, you," Pickford said, shaking his head.

The two officers seemed sort of nervous and not looking particularly enthusiastic, which royally pissed him off.

"Don't get all mardy with me," he growled. "Go on."

"What if they resist, sir?" Jackson said. "That big guy looks like he could handle himself."

"For crying out loud. Hit him in the family jewels if you have to. Just get over that field and nab them both. Now!" he hissed between his teeth.

Jackson and Keeble pushed their way through the hedgerow, leaving Pickford to wonder why they didn't just use the chuffing gate ten feet further along. It's not like the Irishman hadn't spotted them, was it? They'd already lost the element of surprise. Jesus wept, where did they get them from?

Pickford sighed wearily, then watched from his crouched position as the two police officers closed in on their quarry.

"Bloody Rozzers," Liam said to himself when he saw the two coppers pop out of the hedgerow and start to traipse across the field towards him, waving their arms and hollering at him to stay where he was.

Unshouldering the duffel bag, he turned and quickly went up the steps and into the caravan again.

Slamming the door, he leaned back against it.

"Liam, ye big bollocks. You're in a spot of bother now."

What the hell was he going to do, he thought in a panic? If they nicked him (or worse, if these were the same goons who beat up Francis and left him with a busted shoulder, then they might give Liam a pasting as well) then Francis would be on his own and potentially walking into a whole heap of danger.

Everything was coming apart. Probably had been for several days, ever since he'd befriended Francis.

Liam went back to that day when their paths had crossed in the underpass. He asked himself if, in hindsight, he should have just ignored the dumpy, shambling figure that he'd noticed sheltering from the rain, instead of offering him a drink and a place to stay.

But then, there'd been something about the stranger that elicited a strong sense of empathy from Liam. Francis had looked so hopelessly lost and Liam knew exactly how that felt.

He guessed that there came a time in everyone's life when you had to... what? Make a bloody stand? To stop wallowing in self-pity and do something worthwhile? Shite, he couldn't articulate what he meant. Maybe he was growing old before his time, becoming soft.

"Francis, you gobshite. What the feck have you done to me?"

Liam banged the back of his head several times against the door and then unfastened the drawstrings on the duffel bag.

Pickford saw the door suddenly reopen when Jackson and Keeble were ten feet from the caravan. They both froze as the big Irishman reappeared, and Pickford was wondering why they didn't just grab a hold of him and fling him to the ground when he saw the gun in the Paddy's hands.

Pickford's jaw went slack and a jolt of shock passed through him like an electric current.

Just like that, in a nanosecond, the tables had completely turned. He started to shout a warning to his men, which was a pointless exercise because they knew more than him what was going down.

The two of them spun away, fear etched over their white faces, but before they had even completed the movement the first round rang out. A single shot that blew away the top of Officer Keeble's head and sent his cap spinning away like a frisbee. An aerosol red spray erupted into the air and Keeble was jigging about like he was out on the piss and trying to dance the Cabbage Patch. Then, down he went, hitting the ground and positioned perfectly to give Pickford a clear view into the hole in his cranium right down to the brain.

Jackson fled, screaming and babbling, across the field and the two tethered goats went crazy as the gunshot echoed and rolled across the valley.

"Move it, Jacko!" Pickford managed to shout at last, but he was hopelessly unable to offer any help. He just stood watching the terrifying sequence of events play out.

Jackson nearly made it to the barbed wire fence but just when it appeared that he might reach safety, another round shattered the spring afternoon. He was hit square in the back, the force of the bullet's impact delivering such a thumping blow that he staggered on for several more feet directly into the barbed wire.

271

Caught up in the sharp, tearing barrier, Jackson remained upright, still alive but bleeding to death. With DI Pickford unable to break cover to go to his aid.

Liam closed the door, shutting out the grim sight of the two policemen. He put his gun back into the duffel bag. Notwithstanding what he'd just done, he felt surprisingly calm.

He lit a cigarette and inhaled deeply for several minutes. Then, passing through to the seating area of the caravan, he carefully balanced the smouldering cigarette butt on the edge of a cheap plastic ashtray by the window.

Moving with a quiet purpose, he stepped across to the tiny kitchen. He turned on both hobs of the gas cooker, hearing and smelling the butane gas as it steadily filled the caravan.

Quickly, he scooped up the duffel bag and, after one last look back at the caravan, his home for the last two years, he went through the door once more.

The coast was clear. The policeman lying nearest to the caravan was definitely dead whilst the second one, tangled up in the barbed wire fence, was feebly moving his arms and legs. He had a huge hole in his back so Liam figured he too wouldn't have long to live.

A footpath through the copse of trees behind the caravan offered a more direct route down into town rather than the more circuitous trackway at the front. Before he slinked away in that direction, Liam hurriedly untied the goats and shooed them away.

He set off at a steady pace.

Pickford watched as the big Irishman departed.

He knew that he should call this in and get some backup because events had ratcheted up to a whole new level. Send for the firearms unit and leave it to them. There was a cop-killer on the loose.

That's what he should do.

He hurried across to the panda car and reached inside for the CB radio and he was just about to press the transmit button with his thumb when something stayed his hand.

"Fucking wanker," he mumbled to himself. "Get a bloody grip. Think, think!"

Although his head was in a spin, Pickford wasn't so shaken as to not fully understand the implications of what had just happened.

Any Detective Inspector who was foolish enough to allow two of his men to be gunned down, two brave PCs who had simply followed their superior officer's orders, as well, could kiss goodbye to his or her career. At best, they would be quietly put out to grass or sent to some wild and unforgiving hillbilly patch to see out the remainder of their 35 years' service – somewhere shitty like Hebden Bridge, heaven forbid – which would be a fate worse than death. At worst, they could even find themselves tried for serious misconduct and looking at a long prison sentence.

He'd already veered well away from normal protocol by coming up here with Jackson and Keeble, because no matter which way you swung it, Pickford had allowed things to become too personal. He'd gone rogue.

People might even say he'd gone full Tonto.

There was still a chance that he could salvage the situation.

Possibly.

Pickford returned the CB radio to the car's dashboard.

There was no alternative, he decided. He would have to tidy up his fucking mess all by himself.

First thing's first, though.

DI Pickford hunkered down even lower and slid sideways along the back of the hedgerow to where PC Jackson was strung up in the barbed wire.

The poor bastard was still alive, just about. He was bleeding out and his face was all cut up where the sharp wire was coiled around his head, but somehow he was clinging to life.

Pickford caught Jackson's eye and the PC moaned piteously, his eyes big and pleading, so to stop his racket, the Detective Inspector reached through the vicious barbs and placed his hand over the man's nose and mouth and held it there, ignoring the desperate squirms, until he wriggled no more and sagged lifelessly in the barbed wire.

"It be reyt lad," he told him, straightening Jackson's cap. "I'll see you get a medal for this, you daft buggerlugs."

Pickford risked a quick peek over the top of the hedgerow just as whatshisface disappeared into the treeline and he readied himself to jog across to the caravan and deal with Bailey. A sudden *whoosh* of hot air passing over him threw the Detective Inspector to his knees, however.

He looked up to see the caravan windows all burst outwards in unison and orange tongues of flame curl up the outside walls. The curtains flapped up in the hot updraft, the material all afire.

Pickford looked on as the roof of the caravan was embroiled in a searing fireball.

In seconds, it seemed, the whole caravan was one wild conflagration and a tower of oily smoke spiralled into the sky.

So, Bailey couldn't be inside after all. No way would the Paddy leave his chum behind and set his home alight.

Pickford would follow the big Irishman in the hope he would lead him to wherever Bailey was holed up. Then he could kill two birds with one stone.

27

I T WAS WORSE THAN HE imagined.

Francis squeezed his bulky frame through the narrow gap between the wooden board and the rotting doorframe, his protruding belly briefly threatening to thwart him from gaining entry to the ruined house. His nostrils were assaulted with a strong smell of dampness and decay.

Something fluttered wildly just in front of his face. Bats! He cringed away reflexively, arms shielding his face, but then saw feathers floating in the disturbed air caused by the passage of several pigeons flapping their way up to the ceiling.

Francis caught his breath.

On the floor before him was a gaping hole where some of the bare floorboards had caved in. Francis stared into the opening. The shadows down there were nearly impenetrable, but he guessed there would be a basement or maybe an old wine cellar below the ground floor. Had it not been for the birds, startled into flight by his intrusion, he might well have taken a tumble into the black pit.

The boarded-up door and windows blocked out most of the light coming from the front, but the large hole in the side extension, which extended over two floors and through which the tree grew, allowed some light to penetrate.

He saw that he was in a gloomy entrance hallway. The wood floor was covered in chunks of plaster. A dado rail and wood-panelling on the lower half of the hallway walls had come away in sections, so that it leaned outwards, tearing away the skirting boards. Above the rail, the wallpaper that once decorated the upper half of the walls was all peeling and hanging down in thousands of thin strips, looking like the ribcage of some gutted beast.

Most of the doors along the hallway had been removed. Francis counted at least four openings into various rooms. Next to one of them was a radiator, one of the old cast iron ones with leaf swirls moulded on its upright segments, which had somehow fallen or been pulled from its outlet valve. The floor there was awash with dirty, stagnant water.

Towards the far end of the hallway, a chandelier and ceiling rose had crashed down many years ago, leaving a heap of cobweb-covered shattered crystal fragments, brass stems and finials scattered over the floor, while bare wires and the fixture chain dangled down from the ceiling. The chain creaked as it swung in the breeze wafting through the front entrance.

On Francis' left was a ruined and broken staircase. It was so badly damaged that it looked on the verge of collapse; he feared the steps wouldn't take a person's weight. He didn't fancy checking out the upper floors, deciding instead to take a look in some of the downstairs rooms.

Francis carefully edged around the hole in the floor, then stepped through the first doorway.

He looked to be in some kind of sitting room or a reading room. Most of the walls were covered in tall bookcases. Every shelf space was taken up with dusty old tomes; there were large encyclopedia sets, as well as collections with matching bindings and hardcover classics of literature. Above the cases were more shelves, these filled mostly with paperbacks. A ladder fixed to a set of rollers allowed access to the books near the top, as you might find in an old-fashioned university library.

In one corner, and looking incongruous in this atmosphere of old academia, was an EkcoVision television set resting on a walnut cabinet. Before it was a red-cushioned easy chair with wooden armrests, the only seat in the room. On the floor lay a discarded pair of old boots, like the owner had simply vanished while watching TV, leaving his footwear behind.

Another cabinet had a green tin of paint or varnish on the top.

There was a square rug so mouldy with age that mushrooms had sprouted into life.

Millions of broken shards from the glass bookcase doors crunched underfoot.

Francis backed out and moved down the hall to the next room.

This one appeared to be a dining room, but it was a dining room unlike any other that Francis had seen before.

At first, he thought there'd been a fire in here. Then he realized he was wrong. Everything was grimy with so much dirt and grease that the walls and floor were discoloured with enormous black patches. The cooker and sink and fridge had been reduced to rusty heaps of metal, while the dining table and chairs at the centre of the room were so encrusted with dirt they seemed to grow out of the floor like some alien parasitic creature. Food on the abandoned plates had furred over, creating a haven for crawling insects. Swarms of flies hovered everywhere and Francis swatted them away from his face as he gagged at the stench.

Over the table, the ceiling had mostly gone, leaving a latticework of beams. Francis risked a glance up. The room above contained a bed frame that was balanced precariously on the edge of the gaping opening; it could come crashing down into the dining room at any time.

There was a dresser against one wall. Its lacquer surface had bubbled and cracked so that the once-fine piece was a mass of hairline cracks. China cups hanging on hooks were now nests for spiders and mice.

It was the most squalid and decaying place that Francis had ever seen.

Like the room was somehow decomposing. Putrefying.

He noticed, amidst the room's deteriorating contents, a small fireplace nearly hidden by the dining table and, resting on the mantle, a tiny picture frame.

Francis went across, giving the table as wide a berth as he could, a hand over his nose and mouth.

Bending down, he peered at the framed photograph. It was black and white and seemed to show a man and a woman with a child standing between them, but the glass was so sooty that he couldn't make out their features. Was it Roy Kilinski and his family, before the car crash? Possibly, but as Francis did not know what they looked like, it was nothing more than an educated guess.

He left the dining room, asking himself why he was even exploring this place. It was clear Mr Kilinski no longer lived here. Nobody had lived here for a very long time. What was there to gain from looking around any further except sustaining a bad injury to himself?

There was also something disquieting, eerie even, about the derelict building, as though something bad had happened here. Francis' nerves were jangling more and more with each minute that he lingered.

Still, something drew him on to investigate further.

He skipped the next two rooms, barely glancing into them as he walked by: one appeared to be a walk-in storage closet filled with old brooms and wooden crates, the other a utility room or cloakroom with a clothes horse, a mangle and a white tin bath with chipped paint.

Treading lightly, Francis stepped through the large patch of water from the radiator and slipped into the darkness at the end of the hallway.

In a shadowy recess, he saw a solid-looking door. He turned the handle, surprised to find that it opened smoothly and with no loud horror-movie creak from the hinges.

On the other side, he stopped in his tracks.

The transition, from the front part of the old building to the rear areas, couldn't have been more abrupt. Because while the entrance hall and rooms were akin to a bombed-out and condemned mansion, here the house was clean and well-maintained, if still somewhat dated.

He was in a passage. The floor was highly polished and had a red Baroque carpet down the centre, while the walls and high ceiling were painted in cream. Brass wall lights with glass globe shades shined brightly, their light revealing watercolour paintings lined up above a picture rail. There was a window overlooking the overgrown back garden. A second flight of steps leading upwards, this set intact. A French console table with three slender drawers and a carving of a stag on the top.

Francis took a moment to take everything in. He wondered if he might be imagining things, so sudden was the switch from the ruined residence to a clean home. There was even electricity.

And voices, coming from behind a closed door. So there was somebody here, after all.

He squeezed the handle and stepped through.

The voices instantly ceased, leaving Francis looking into the hushed interior. He thought he might go mad at what awaited him there.

•   •   •

An overpowering mephitic smell greeted him, one that was immediately familiar to Francis.

He found himself thinking of the woods behind his home and the time many years ago when he'd stumbled across the mortal remains of Susan Ross. Francis remembered the carrion crows pecking at her corpse, the carpet of seething maggots, and the pungent aroma of dead flesh.

This was the same, but much worse. The corruption clung to the back of his throat like phlegm and he had to fight the urge to vomit.

He was in a parlour, by the looks of it. There were easy chairs and an octagonal side table with inlaid enamel on its surface. In the corner beside the narrow chimney breast was a small upright piano with the lid up and sheet music on the stand. Tucked into a window nook was a wooden window seat. The fireplace was hidden behind a fan-shaped fire guard, while above the mantle was an ornate gilt mirror inside a mother-of-pearl frame. Other decorations included needlework samplers on the walls, a mahogany cabinet with a glass dome clock, red drapes over the windows, an ornate cornice running around the ceiling and chintzy knick-knacks.

It was like he'd stepped back in time to Edwardian England, but inside a Georgian house with a 1950s car parked in the garage and an EkcoVision television in the derelict reading room. Everything was odd, out of kilter, a crazy mesh of differing eras.

All these observations and impressions passed through Francis' mind in mere seconds because his attention quickly

281

passed on from the room's décor to the two people sitting quietly in the easy chairs.

A lady with long dark hair wearing a voluminous blue dress, and a young girl whose blonde plaits were tied up with ribbons.

Both were quite dead; the smell alone attested to their demise. The girl was nothing but a bag of bones held loosely together by a sack of shrivelled skin. It was like she'd been scooped up in a higgledy-piggledy pile and had her skeleton rearranged into a mock replica of the human form. Something had gone badly wrong with the reconstruction, though, because many of the parts were missing. Even though the corpse was dressed in a floral top and skirt, Francis could see spaces where arm bones and ankle bones and vertebrae should be. They had been replaced with wire joints bridging the gaps, creating a frame that barely held the various parts together, and all encased in a shroud of decayed flesh and flower-patterned clothing. Whoever she had once been, the dead girl was now a dried-up, cadaverous husk.

Worst of all, her face was missing. It had been sliced or peeled away.

In its place was a face of bone with radiant blonde hair.

The dark-haired woman was 'fresher' as her flesh, although it had a stretched appearance like it had shrunk and become taut over her cheekbones and forehead, was relatively whole. A rancid odour hung over her body, similar to when meat was left for too long in the back of the fridge and became fermented. Her sagging breasts must have started to weep and ooze as she decomposed because twin brown stains had soaked through the blue dress. The jaw gaped open lasciviously.

Below the hem of the dress, a pair of shrivelled legs hung limply above the floor, like the muscles had degenerated many years ago, long, long before her death. The sight of them flicked a switch in Francis' head, a recollection of something the nosey neighbour had mentioned earlier when he'd visited the bungalow. About a car crash and Roy Kilinski's wife being left paralysed.

Francis felt the blood drain from his face as everything fell into place, one piece at a time. Finally, he made sense of the mystery that had haunted him since he was eighteen years old. A chain of events beginning way back in the past, further back than the murder of Susan Ross, before the disappearance of Imogen Hughes even, commencing with a horrendous traffic accident and winding their way through the proceeding years to the present; the missing and murdered girls, the inept police investigation, Francis' time in prison, his release and subsequent harassment. Francis needing to confront his past to unearth the truth, following clue after clue until they led him here, to this old, derelict building and the answers he'd been seeking.

Oh God, Francis thought, even as the dead woman in the blue dress began to move, her head turning in his direction, her blue eyes flicking open and seeking him out, and then impossibly pushing herself to her feet, her broken spine crackling and snapping like dried kindling.

A man's voice screeched in fury, spitting and snarling his hatred. Francis watched in dumbstruck horror as the corpse of Mrs Kilinski sprang forward, leaping through the air towards him, the dead woman reanimated and come back to life as a costume of putrefying flesh and rattling bones.

•   •   •

Huge, strong hands around his throat, squeezing his windpipe and threatening to crush the neck bones. A voice shouting over and over, "She's mine! She's mine! You won't take her away from me! My little girl! She's mine..." and the voice fading along with Francis' vision, everything seeping away to a grey blankness.

Suddenly, the pressure around his throat was released and the weight that had been crushing down on his chest was gone.

Francis felt his senses return just in time to hear footsteps pounding up the stairs and crossing the floor overhead. Then there came a shrill, high-pitched scream.

28

FRANCIS ROLLED OVER AND PUSHED himself to his hands and knees. His neck hurt where the man (he was sure it was Roy Kilinski, Susan Ross' social worker, disguised as he was in the ghoulish apparel) had tried to throttle him. He spat onto the floor to try and clear his throat and rubbed at the tender skin beneath his double chin.

Keeping his eyes on the body of the girl, fearing that she too might come 'alive', he crawled across the floor and used the piano to drag himself to his feet. His fingers caught some of the keys, the light musical notes seeming like a bizarre disparity to the chamber of horrors he had inadvertently stumbled upon.

Whilst he tried to regain his breath, Francis listened hard for any further sounds. The house had fallen silent again. No further heavy footsteps thudded overhead.

Francis was certain that Mary Underhill, missing for several days, was somewhere up there. There was no other explanation. Everything fitted.

He ought to get out of here. Make a double-quick exit back the way he had come. Then find the nearest phone box and dial 999.

That would be the sensible thing. Yet the terror he had detected in that brief shriek put the kibosh on that idea, scuttling his natural impulse to flee for his life.

Mary Underhill might well be fighting for her last breath and Francis couldn't leave her to her fate. Not after coming this far.

Taking another look at the dead girl, whom he was sure must be Kilinski's daughter, he tottered over to the parlour door. In the passage once more, Francis spent a moment to get his bearings. The door through which he'd passed from the derelict part of the house to the habitable part was just to his left. There, lay the path to freedom and safety. To his right was the second flight of steps.

Francis again hesitated. The temptation to go left was nearly overpowering and it took a herculean effort not to succumb to the silky voice of reason urging him to save himself. Instead, he went right and tip-toed up the staircase.

Partway up, the steps took a half turn and then continued their ascent. A stair runner cushioned his footsteps but once or twice the wooden risers groaned beneath his excessive weight, making Francis freeze and hold his breath. Each time, nothing happened. The house was deathly quiet. Too quiet.

He passed a stone plinth holding a vase inside a wall alcove and then he reached the second-floor landing.

Opposite him were a small window and an antique blanket box. Francis started down the landing. Just past a Grandfather clock, he came to an open doorway and, ever so cautiously, he peered around the frame.

A bathroom. The floor was covered with a plastic sheet. There was a hacksaw and red stains everywhere and... Oh God... the bath was filled with, with...

Francis turned away, his face blanched of all colour, unable to rid his mind of the horrible things in the bathtub.

A noise further along the landing drew his attention, a sliding or shuffling sound followed by a dull bump.

Francis moved away from the bathroom, his heart beating fast, pounding against his chest. Blood pumped in his ears. His lips were going numb. Each footstep he took drained his resolve. He told himself that, if Mary wasn't in the next room, he would bolt from this hellhole.

He neared a second doorway further along the landing.

The room came into view inch by inch, slowly revealing itself to him.

He saw a chair.

He saw Mary Underhill, seated and bound, with what looked like a rubber oxygen mask over her face and a small gas canister beneath her chin.

He saw Roy Kilinski, wearing his dead wife's skin, standing behind Mary with a knife to her throat.

Mercifully, she was still alive; her chest rose and fell rhythmically as she breathed in what must be some kind of knock-out gas.

The two men watched one another across the room and for many seconds, the only sounds Francis could hear were the quiet hiss from the canister and Kilinski's stentorian wheezing.

Francis noticed something in Kilinski's other hand, something whitish. He thought that it must be some kind of gag.

Just then, the man across from him tilted his head sideways like he was looking askance at Francis in puzzlement, but hidden behind his wife's death mask and with just his blue eyes showing through the twin eyeholes, Francis wasn't certain what expression the madman's face held.

"I know you," came a soft voice.

Francis edged into the room. In his peripheral vision, he saw a small bed frame and rotting floorboards. They must be at the front of the house, in the ruined section.

"You're the man they put away."

Kilinski sighed loudly and his shoulders sagged and for one crazy moment, Francis thought that he actually meant to apologize. His next words ruled that out.

"I saw in the paper that you'd been cleared and released. That was an unwanted turn of events, unfortunately. The last thing I needed was all of these busybodies looking into the case again, raking over the past. It meant that I had to be extra cautious this time."

He nodded at Mary, who was unconscious in the chair before him.

"Do you know, I've saved her in a way? By removing her from a depressing environment."

Francis looked at him in disbelief.

"It's true, although I wouldn't expect you to understand. Nobody understands. Mary wasn't loved by her mother. None of them were, in all truthfulness."

Francis watched as Roy Kilinski seemed to go through a sudden metamorphosis. His voice changed and his body language seemed subtly different, more effeminate, almost like he was no longer Roy Kilinski. Before Francis' eyes, he had transformed into somebody else.

"Go to your room!" he ranted, his speech high-pitched and querulous like a mother scolding an errant child. *"I'm tired hearing your bawling, it's giving me a headache. You're an ungrateful little madam. I work every God's hour to feed you and clothe you and put a roof over your head, and this is all the thanks I get! Charming!"*

Francis was captivated by the spectacle. Despite the terrible danger he and Mary were in, the switch from one personality to another was chilling to behold. It was hypnotic.

"It's not my fault that your father left us. He always did have a roving eye, that one. He is a pathetic excuse for a man. Well,

good riddance, I hope he enjoys himself with his young fancy piece

Head thrust forward, hands on his hips, the bones of his dead wife clinking and jangling together as he angrily remonstrated.

"Now here I am, stuck with you all by myself."

Roy Kilinski slipped metaphorically back into his own skin, his own self. Now he was a calm and calculated child killer again.

"She has cancer, you know," he told Francis. "This little mite's mother. Terminal. She only has a few weeks left. Mary will be better off living here, I think. That's why I chose her, why I chose all of them. Why live with unloving parents when they can be a part of a loving family, in our beautiful home?"

The hand holding the knife stroked Mary's hair, causing the child to stir for a moment. Francis thought that she might awaken, but after a few seconds she grew still and slept on.

"I just want my little girl back, my Melanie," Roy Kilinski continued. "She died because of me, so I'm trying to put things right. I didn't mean to hurt those other girls, but I'm a monster, aren't I? I have to beat down the darkness in my head."

The blue eyes slipped down to the girl before him.

"Soon, she'll be Mary no more."

He held up the thing he'd been holding in his other hand, the white rag-like thing, and Francis saw the slit mouth and blackened lips, the puckered thing that was once a nose, the sinewy strands of flesh at the edges, and he remembered the faceless body in the parlour downstairs of the girl with blonde plaits, and his stomach rebelled and he gagged and retched and he wanted to crumple to the floor and roll up in a ball and plead for the whole thing to be over.

He watched as the madman removed the oxygen mask from Mary's face and brought the edge of the blade to the soft skin of the child's cheek and started to carve...

Francis bellowed in rage and charged forward.

Then they were falling as the weakened floorboards gave way and all three of them plunged into the room below.

29

WHERE THE HELL WAS THE big Irishman, whatshisface, leading him?

Pickford wondered for about the fifth time if thingamabob Brennan had twigged on to the fact he was been tailed and was purposely leading him on a merry dance all around the houses. Either that or the bog-eyed halfwit was lost and not fully compos mentis because they'd been walking for twenty minutes now and Pickford was fair jiggered.

Following his quarry, the Detective Inspector had tried hanging back as much as possible, letting Brennan keep ahead of him by about a hundred yards or so. This was easy enough to do in the woods because the trees allowed for plenty of cover; once or twice, the Irishman had slowed to a halt and taken a look around at his surroundings, making Pickford quickly jump out of sight behind a tree trunk. When they had emerged from the woodland and traversed over open fields and climbed over stiles, it proved harder to avoid detection. Pickford felt like he stood out like a sore thumb and was grateful he was in his civvies even if it was a suit. It wasn't easy shadowing somebody when dressed in a Bobbie's uniform. Then, when they had arrived at the first streets and houses on the edges of town, the opposite occurred. The problem then was to keep Brennan in sight, because he'd suddenly picked up the pace, darting around corners, slipping down covered ginnels and moving more stealthily. Once or twice, Pickford thought he'd lost his quarry amongst the narrow lanes, only to catch a flash of his coat up ahead or the sound of his footsteps echoing up and down the cobbled backstreets.

At least the long foot pursuit allowed Pickford time to think.

Cleaning up this mess wasn't going to be straightforward. Ridding himself of Bailey and Brennan should hopefully be the easy part but after that, there were so many loose ends that needed addressing in order to prevent everything from falling apart. Things like, how to explain two dead coppers and the fire at the caravan?

But then, if Bailey and Brennan were to both come to a sticky end that would take the heat off himself. It would be relatively simple to explain how the Irishman had opened fire during a routine police check, which was kinda true anyway. Then, the two suspects sadly died whilst resisting arrest. Nobody would question that. The big Irishman had just killed two unarmed coppers in cold blood and wasn't about to hand himself over without a fight. Even better, he still had the murder weapon with him.

Then there was the problem of Bailey's silly old mother and his mouthy sister and the state their home had been left in during the police raid. Did Pickford have grounds for barging in and tearing the place apart like that? Without a warrant, moreover?

If they had found evidence during the search linking Bailey to the murders, Pickford might just about get away with it. But they hadn't.

At least, not yet.

Because DI Pickford, clever bastard that he was, maybe had something up his sleeve.

The abduction of Mary Underhill could be his way clear of the clusterfuck of a mess that he, himself, had created.

He was thinking about the blue campervan that was spotted in the vicinity of Mary's home about the time she'd gone missing.

If Pickford could just pin the sighting of that vehicle on Bailey. All he needed was to find it – and it didn't have to be *the* blue campervan, *any* blue campervan would do, then he would simply plant the ignition keys somewhere in Bailey's bedroom and voila! He had grounds for searching his home and in the process of doing so, had recovered indisputable evidence that he was Mary Underhill's abductor.

If he played his cards right over the next few hours then he could pull this off. With a commendation from the top brass to boot. He might even make Chief Inspector by this time next year.

Up ahead, Brennan was moving through the industrial estate that backed up to River Street and the canal. Pickford, who could feel a stitch coming on, knew that after the last row of houses there was just the towpath and then, a half-mile further, nothing but fields.

Where the hell was Brennan leading him, he wondered again?

30

FRANCIS HIT THE DINING TABLE with such force that the air was expelled from his lungs. A sharp pain in his side made him wince and wonder if he had cracked a rib in the fall through the floorboards. Something in his weak shoulder tore.

His bulk – or rather, his flab, he conceded – protected him from the worst of the impact, that and the thick army jacket he was wearing. Still, he, Mary and Kilinski landed directly onto the table in a tangle of arms, legs and pieces of timber, sending the plates of mouldy food and cutlery flying in all directions. Swarms of flies buzzed around their heads.

The table tipped over under their combined weight, sending them all to the grimy, rubble-strewn floor.

Somebody was lying on top of him, trapping Francis. The smell of rancid meat told him it was Kilinski, still clad in that grotesque human skin.

In a panic, he pushed and shoved until the psycho rolled clear. Francis squirmed hurriedly away on his back, the heels of his shoes digging into the floor. When he looked again, he saw Kilinski's prostrate and still form lying unmoving amidst the overturned table and chairs. He must be unconscious, or dead.

Francis craned his neck, searching for Mary Underhill. He found her a few feet away. She was blessedly still asleep and under the influence of the knock-out gas. Her face, he saw with relief, was unmarked. He wiped dust and sweat from his eyes and took a moment to catch his breath, and then he reached across, intending to drag her over. Another sharp pain from his abdomen made him pull up with a gasp instead. He cast his eyes down past his large belly.

The hilt of a knife was protruding from his ribcage. There was a large patch of red soaking through his clothing. As he watched, the bloodstain expanded further.

Panic threatened to overwhelm him and it took a lot of willpower not to surrender to it.

Somehow, during their fall through the floorboards and their heavy landing onto the dining room table, the knife with which Kilinski had been about to carve away Mary's face had become lodged in Francis' body.

His first instinct was to pull the weapon clear and try and staunch the flow of blood. Something told him this could make things worse. Best to leave it in place as it was acting like a plug because, although he was losing blood, it wasn't pouring out. Neither did he think a lung had been punctured as his breathing, although fitful from fright, wasn't laboured.

His internal organs might be damaged but there was little he could do about that other than escape with Mary and get some help, he reasoned.

Francis thought he caught a low moan coming from Kilinski, shattering his hopes that the killer had died in the fall. Another louder, agonized wheeze confirmed this, and it was followed by a sob that shook the semi-conscious man's body.

He and Mary needed to depart from this slaughterhouse before he fully came around. Wounded as he was with a knife sticking in him, Francis, who had never been much of a fighter, didn't wish to be dragged into a brawl with a nutter who wouldn't hesitate to finish both him and Mary off.

It was their one chance to clear out.

Moving slowly and biting down on his pain, Francis clambered to his feet. A wave of dizziness washed over him, but it quickly passed.

Kicking pieces of broken floorboards aside, he reached down for Mary's sleeping form and lifted her slight frame into his arms. More bolts of agony swept through Francis, nearly bowling him over. He grimaced.

Shifting her body so that she was slung over his shoulder in a fireman's lift, Francis made towards the dining room door. Before passing through, he looked back over his other shoulder.

He was rewarded with the diabolical sight of Roy Kilinski pulling himself over the floor after them, slithering free of his dead wife's cloak of corrupted flesh and blackened bones like a snake shedding its skin. In his hand, the killer still grasped the carved-off face of his daughter, Melanie.

The blue eyes were no longer soft and tender-hearted like when he enticed his victims away to their deaths but had an intense and withering glare to them.

Francis could smell the insanity steaming off him in waves.

And the laugh, all brittle and wintry, like the murderer was possessed by a demoniacal wish to destroy life.

Francis fled.

He moved surprisingly fast for a large man with a total lack of fitness and burdened with the girl's weight into the bargain.

He didn't dwell too much on the origins of his sudden stamina. Adrenaline, coupled with the heart-stopping fear of violent death, could boost a person's energy, he figured.

He ran in a breathless, shambling gait, right out the dining room door and down the wrecked entrance hallway, his uncoordinated legs somehow managing to propel him and Mary towards the shaft of daylight pushing through the gap by the boarded-up front doorway.

In their wake was the lunatic, Roy Kilinski.

Francis remembered the hole in the floor. Barely breaking his stride, he jinked sideways and slid around the black pit. He dashed up to the large piece of wood blocking their escape route and, balancing Mary on his shoulder with one hand against her back to keep her from slipping free, he gripped the edge of the wood with the other and pulled.

The tall rectangular piece of timber flexed inwards several inches, widening the gap some more, but then it stopped. Francis pulled again, ignoring the agony in his shoulder. The board wouldn't budge any further. No way was the opening large enough to get himself and Mary through.

Come on, why wouldn't it come free? He pulled and twisted to no avail.

Footsteps approaching just behind warned Francis that their pursuer was almost on them so he wasted no more time with the boarded-up doorway. He scurried across the hallway, past the foot of the wrecked staircase, making for the rent in the mansion's side extension.

This side of the hall was strewn with lumps of masonry and large sandstone bricks where the outer wall had either caved in or, more likely, crumbled away with age over many years, allowing the small tree to take root and further dislodge the extension. Thankfully, the more extensive damage was on the second floor; there the ceiling joists had rotted and later snapped, tearing the stairs in half and ripping away the banister. Down on this level, the remnants of the staircase had shielded the ground floor. There was a slope of crushed, powdered concrete leading up to a narrow rent in the outer wall, and just on the other side, Francis could see the garden.

He climbed the slope and went through the opening, cringing as yet another spasm of pain jabbed through his abdomen. He was hit by a fit of coughing and spluttering and when he wiped his chin his hand came away smeared with red spittle.

Hardly pausing in his flight, Francis clambered down from the opening and picked his way around the concrete slabs scattered over the unkempt flower beds at the side of the big house.

To their rear, he heard Kilinski let out a sudden curse. Risking another quick look, Francis saw that the killer had slipped and gone down on one knee. When he regained his feet, Francis was satisfied to note the tear in the man's jeans and a gash on his leg.

It was possibly the lucky break Francis and Mary needed because he could feel himself growing steadily weaker with each second, his legs trembling more and more, a result no doubt of the stab wound. He tried not to think of the damage he had suffered.

Kilinski was limping badly and this gave Francis renewed hope. He charged around the corner of the house and across the overgrown front lawn, his mouth open wide as he sucked in great lungfuls of air.

If they could just make it to the woods lining the canal towpath, they might have a chance of losing their pursuer.

He passed the tumbledown garage with the rusty Ford Zephyr.

Along the weed-covered driveway and through the crumbling gateposts.

Down the potholed road, the Def Leppard hat blowing off his head.

He galumphed over the small pasture, starting to flounder badly now, his strength slipping away.

At the wire fence, Francis staggered to a halt. His trousers were soddened with blood, the pumping of his heart making the wound bleed freely now.

Just a little further.

But Kilinski was gaining on them again, screaming and hollering and completely at the mercy of his insanity.

Oh God, Francis didn't think they were going to make it.

Over his shoulder, Mary was moving and wriggling as she started to wake up.

Finding reserves of energy that he didn't think he had, Francis went through the gap in the fence and skidded down the muddy path, crashing through the undergrowth and nearly tripping over the tree roots. At the bottom, he followed the canal towpath, but now he was swaying from side to side, his course all snaky as his vision started to dim and shadows edged into his peripheral vision.

He could hear Kilinski laughing, the killer so close Francis imagined he could feel his hot breath on the back of his neck.

The motorway bridge loomed up and then, just before his eyesight blanched away to oblivion, he caught sight of the figure of a man just ahead, someone familiar and pointing a rifle at him and screaming at him to get down, to hit the deck.

Francis fell face-first onto the towpath, taking Mary with him.

There came the boom of a gunshot.

Light bloomed in Francis' eyes, so bright and shimmering that it hurt his head. He saw tree branches and green leaves backed by a blue sky. Then a face hovered into view, that of a scruffy-looking man with a beard and red-rimmed eyes.

Cheeks damp with tears.

Francis peered up at his friend, wondering why Liam was crying and shaking his head from side to side.

He stole a look around.

They were beneath the motorway bridge, the road above humming with passing traffic. Francis was sitting with his back against one of the graffiti-covered pillars.

He looked back at Liam, asking in a croaky voice, "Kilinski?"

"He's dead. Don't you worry about him, you clown. He won't be hurting anyone else ever again."

"And Mary?"

"Not a scratch on her. You saved her. Heaven knows how you did it, but you got her out of that psycho's grip. She's right here."

Francis looked to his right and saw that Mary was indeed with them too. She was awake and looking at him with big eyes. She nibbled at her bottom lip and was trembling from either fear or emotion, Francis couldn't tell which.

"We need to get her home, to her mother."

"In a bit, boy," Liam replied.

Francis frowned. His friend's voice sounded different, somehow. Faint, like he was talking to Francis from afar. The birds in the trees too sounded to be a million miles away. And was that a woodpecker? Way off in another place, another time?

He felt cold.

But calm.

"Look at the state of you," Liam said, pointing down at Francis's abdomen.

Francis followed the finger and saw the handle of a knife sticking out of his body. How had that happened? Francis wondered.

"Did I ever get around to telling you you're an eejit?" Liam spoke quietly, crying openly now. "Ye big bollocks."

They both laughed.

"What am I going to tell your mum, eh? And your sister?"

Francis drew in a shallow breath. "I'm sure you'll think of something," he murmured, suddenly feeling so tired and weak.

They were quiet for a few moments, just content to look at each another. Mary moved closer, her pale face losing its context as her features wavered in and out of focus.

"Do you know what? I think after all of this excitement," Liam was saying, "it's time for me to move on. To start again somewhere new."

Francis watched his friend glance off to the side. He thought he saw his chin trembling.

"You understand, don't you, boy?"

Francis parted his lips to say something back but his thoughts flittered away on the breeze.

He too moved on.

31

A RUSTLING SOUND NEARBY DREW LIAM'S attention away from his friend's body. Blinking away his tears, he turned to see a set of bushes parting and a man step out from hiding.

He looked incongruous in his tight-fitting suit and brown brogues out here by the stagnant canal and, although Liam had never met the man before, he still recognized him from the newspapers.

Liam watched as DI Pickford pulled up sharply, surveying the scene. His eyes widened in shock on seeing Francis sitting on the ground with a knife in his ribs and Roy Kilinski sprawled on the towpath, his features blown away. Both plainly dead.

"Fuck me," he exclaimed in hushed tones.

Then his gaze fell on Mary Underhill, alive and well.

"Fuck me!" he repeated, louder this time.

Liam watched as those eyes turned all flinty, flicking around the scene. Pickford didn't seem to be put off by the gun that Liam was holding loosely at his side; he was too busy trying to piece together what had happened.

"I wasn't expecting this," he admitted, looking back at Liam. "You? It was you all along, not that chuffing gormless sod? You took those girls and killed them? A child murderer *and* a cop killer."

He shook his head in wonder, his nasty features breaking into a grin.

"Jeez, he was innocent all along. Well, I never." He seemed to be almost laughing at the absurdity of it all. "And now you've gone and killed Bailey, too."

Liam didn't have the energy to put him fully in the picture. Let him think what he wanted, he told himself

"And who in God's name is that?" Pickford asked, pointing at the real child murderer lying slain on the towpath.

The copper seemed to shake off his astonishment and Liam watched as he reached into his suit pocket and flashed his police warrant card.

"You're under arrest, you sick bastard—"

He never finished the rest of his sentence. Liam had already raised the barrel of the Armalite and now he squeezed the trigger. The report of the gunshot shattered the air. The round struck Pickford's warrant card, sending it flying away in a hundred pieces and taking the tips of two of the policeman's fingers with it.

Pickford yelped, more in surprise than pain, and he stared at the stubs of his fingers, at the pieces of flesh and fragments of bone.

A half-second later, it must have struck Pickford that standing there like a target on the firing range wasn't the most sensible thing to do, because Liam watched the big copper turn and race back between the bushes and vanish.

He could sure move fast, Liam conceded. Even carrying some extra timber and wearing a tight suit.

"Wait here," he said to Mary Underhill. "I'll come back for you, I promise."

Then he gave chase, following the sound that Pickford made as he crashed through the undergrowth.

He caught glimpses of the large man between tree branches as he pursued him up a steep slope running alongside

303

the motorway bridge. Liam was unaware that their roles had suddenly reversed. Instead of being the hunted, Liam was now the hunter.

The graffiti-covered reinforced concrete pillars grew shorter as they ascended the incline, and where the ground started to level out at the top they were replaced by a low concrete retaining wall. On the other side, zooming by at breakneck speed, Liam saw cars and haulage trucks flash past on the northbound lanes. The noise of their engines was deafening; the roar beat at his ears. The vehicles' passage ruffled Liam's hair.

He'd temporarily lost sight of Pickford. The trees and undergrowth had petered out, replaced with coarse grass that was strewn with discarded rubbish thrown out of car windows. There was nowhere for the copper to be hiding, so where the heck...?

Liam drew to a halt. The ground disappeared in a fold in the earth. Before him there was a gully running across his path and at the bottom was the main British Rail train line between Leeds and Manchester. It ran east to west and this part went underneath the motorway.

Pickford was at the bottom, navigating his way over the sleepers and beginning to ascend the far banking. The copper turned to see how near his pursuer was and Liam was satisfied to see that the man's face was white with fright as their eyes locked.

He raised the rifle and squeezed the trigger, the recoil thumping his shoulder. Heat exhaust from the barrel obscured his vision for half a second, then he saw a small spout of soil kick up just a few inches from Pickford's leg.

"Shit," Liam mumbled, annoyed that he'd missed his target. Still, Pickford panicked and took a tumble. Liam watched as he started to slide back down the embankment towards the railway line, his hands tugging at tufts of grass to halt his descent.

Pickford started up again, so Liam raced down his side, checked the railway line was clear and leaped over, before climbing the opposite bank. He stole a look up to the ridgeline just in time to see Pickford's ample backside disappearing over the top.

Liam crested the embankment. He quickly took in his surroundings. To his right was a narrow access road leading to a large cattle shed with a green roof. Pickford might have gone in that direction but Liam spotted a pair of guard dogs chained up outside their kennels, the bull mastiffs watching him and poised for action. They wouldn't let the copper go past without kicking up a racket, Liam figured.

He switched his attention back to the motorway. The concrete retaining wall had been replaced with an Armco crash barrier and there was Pickford, crouching down on the hard shoulder and trying to stay out of sight. Which was impossible for a man of his size.

Liam calmly covered the twenty yards separating the two of them, holding the gun one-handed by his hip and pointing in Pickford's direction.

Pickford saw him approach. With the lethal flow of traffic zooming past at his back and nowhere left to run, he knew the game was up. He straightened and held out a placating hand, minus two fingertips. His suit was stained with dirt and one lapel was half torn away.

A smirk appeared on his features. Liam wanted to blow it away.

"Listen, Paddy. Sorry, I mean Brennan," Pickford said, having to raise his voice over the sound of the traffic. "It is

Brennan, isn't it? Things have got out of hand here, for both of us, wouldn't you say?"

Liam drew to a halt on his side of the crash barrier.

Pickford ploughed on.

"I don't know exactly what's gone on back there, between you and Bailey. Maybe you were partners in crime with a shared liking for young girls. Frankly, your predilection doesn't concern me. We all need a hobby as they say."

He laughed nervously and plugged away, his words and manner growing more skittish by the second. His eyes kept switching between Liam's face and the gun.

"But there are two dead police officers to throw into the mix, not to mention the fire at your place. That complicates things somewhat, doesn't it? I mean, fuck me, mate. Why the heck did you have to go and kill my men? So, anyway, what I'm thinking is that we come to some sort of arrangement, an accommodation that will be mutually beneficial to both me and you."

Liam slipped his finger over the gun's trigger, a tiny movement that nonetheless Pickford noticed and which made his words speed up so that he was babbling and sweating and trying to catch his breath.

"An understanding, yes? I let you off the hook and you let me off the hook. I will publicly admit that I've made a mistake about your friend, Mr Bailey. Turns out that he was telling the truth, I'll be happy to go on the record as saying. I will also announce that we will fast-track suitable compensation for his family. I have direct access to the Assistant Chief Constable, so I guarantee that it won't be a problem. Then, all of this will be sorted in a jiffy. What do you say, Brennan?"

"Turn around and start walking," Liam said loudly.

"What?" Pickford asked in confusion, his eyebrows pinched together.

"I said, turn around and start walking."

"You're letting me go?"

"Start walking across the motorway."

Pickford looked back over his shoulder at the stream of traffic flashing past him, then said, "I don't understand."

"Walk across all six lanes. Don't run. Walk. If you make it to the other side, I'll let you go."

"You've gotta be kidding me? I'll never get across."

"That's the deal," Liam informed the policeman. He then raised the gun to his shoulder and sighted along the barrel. "Or I can just end it here."

"Okay, okay! Oh shit-fuck, shit-fuck!" Pickford gabbled incoherently as he turned and looked through the stream of cars and trucks towards the central meridian and the far side of the motorway. He placed both his hands against the crash barrier behind him as he braced himself.

Liam waited patiently. He had plenty of time.

"Alrighty, here goes. Do I have to walk, can't I at least dodge about, like in a game of British Bulldog?" Pickford asked loudly.

"You walk. If you break into a run, I'll pull the trigger. I'm giving you a chance here. Now move!"

Pickford nodded his understanding. Liam saw him glance to the right, looking at the oncoming traffic, no doubt waiting for a break in the flow of high-speed vehicles.

Then, with a deep breath, he stepped out.

He made it across the slow lane and then somehow reached the midpoint of the second lane. Two cars honked their horns and glided smoothly around him, their drivers flicking him the finger. But then a huge haulage truck came thundering along, belching smoke from its exhaust, the driver's head bobbing along to some music, and Pickford froze to the spot and watched oncoming death bearing down on him.

Liam turned away from the sight but he heard the impact between soft flesh and hard metal and saw something flying through the air to land with a rustle in some bushes one hundred yards further down the hard shoulder.

Quietly, he retraced his route to the canal, where Mary Underhill was waiting for him.

PART 5

SANCTUARIUM

32

THE FERRY FROM CAIRNRYAN DEPARTED on time.

During the two-hour crossing from Scotland, Liam braved the wind and the driving rain to venture out onto the slippery passenger deck. He shivered at the cold. Even muffled up in a heavy coat and woolly hat, the nasty weather had a frightening bite to it. He reminded himself that it was late October; winter was just around the corner. At least it meant most sensible passengers stayed indoors.

Finding a quiet corner on the starboard breezeway, he waited until he was sure the coast was clear and then tossed the duffel bag containing the gun over the side. He watched as it bobbed and spun about on the surface for a moment before the ship's wash sucked it beneath the waves.

Then he reached into a coat pocket and slipped out a slim bottle of Napoleon Brandy. Unscrewing the top, he took a swig, his first of the day (it was after eleven in the morning, after all). He stayed there for the remainder of the journey, leaning on the rail and watching the gulls hover over the vessel.

Because of a strong headwind and heavy seas, the ferry arrived in Larne thirty minutes late, so by the time it docked at the quayside and it was time to disembark, Liam had drunk all the brandy.

Thus fortified against the elements, Liam made for the bus stop, his chin tucked into his chest to ward off the foul weather.

He waited for almost one hour in the draughty bus shelter. Eventually, the No 154 bus arrived and Liam took a window seat as they turned out of the ferry terminal onto the coast road. He wiped at the condensation on the glass with his coat sleeve so that he could see outside, noticing the Chaine Memorial Tower at the end of its short promontory. It looked exactly as he remembered it from ten years ago. Then, he had been escaping to the British Mainland. Now, here he was going in the opposite direction. Starlings swooped around the tall obelisk, just as they had that day.

The bus headed south away from the town, following the winding country lanes.

There were only a few other people on board and as they stopped off at each village en route their numbers dwindled further as passengers alighted at their stops. Soon, there was only Liam and a pair of teenagers sitting at the back.

He took out a second bottle of brandy and had a few surreptitious sips. This was to steady his nerves, he told himself, because he was growing more jittery the nearer he came to his destination.

A short time after the bus swung into Liam's stop. He walked to the front and jumped down into the roadway, swaying slightly. He waited until the bus pulled away, its gears grinding as it snaked around the narrow lanes.

When the sound of its engine died away, birdsong gradually filled the void.

Liam looked about him.

The village of Templepatrick was tranquil, the main street with its few shops almost deserted. There was a woman laden with shopping bags just exiting a grocery store and a man walking his dog on the opposite pavement. He gave Liam a friendly wave and Liam nodded back, keeping his face hidden within his coat's hood.

He set off.

Head down, he walked at a steady pace for ten minutes and passed no one along the way.

Presently, he came to a large gate. Pushing it open, he went through. On the other side was a straight, stone-flagged path leading through an avenue of trees. Further back from the trees he saw headstones, and at the end of the path, a familiar-looking church built of white stone.

Liam headed down the path and went around the bell tower to the entrance door.

Inside was the porch where he had spent the night after the ambush on the van full of builders, who had actually turned out to be British soldiers. There was the bench where he had rested. Dead ahead, the set of wooden doors leading into the church proper.

Liam turned the black handle, hoping this time they would be unlocked. His luck was in.

The inside of the church was beautifully maintained. The pews were all polished to a sheen that reflected the light from dozens of slender candles in a votive stand by the narthex. There was a strong smell of incense.

A man was standing before the altar. He was slight in stature and his back was all crooked and bent. The wind blowing through from the porch rustled the pages of the prayer books, catching his attention and making him turn.

Liam strode down the central aisle, seeing the frown on the man's craggy features as he struggled to identify his visitor. But as Liam drew nearer and stepped into a shaft of light, the eyes softened.

Father O'Keefe clasped his hands together and a benign smile danced over his thin lips. The years had not been kind to either of them, booze and saintly devotion having left their mark on both men's health, but it was reassuring that each still recognized the other.

Father O'Keefe stepped forward as though to take both of Liam's hands in his, but then he saw Liam's ruddy cheeks and his watery and bloodshot eyes, smelled the brandy on his breath. He hesitated.

"What brings you back to our humble little church after all this time, young man?"

Liam licked his lips, remembering how Father O'Keefe had helped him once before and he fervently hoped the clergyman's loyalties remained steadfast. He'd taken a huge gamble by coming here but had little choice. Wanted in England and Ulster, on the run, where else could he turn to except the Church?

He opened his mouth to speak, but before the words even passed his lips, Father O'Keefe interjected, his astuteness remarkable.

"You need help again, don't you? Yes, in more ways than one, I suspect."

O'Keefe frowned.

"Ours is a peaceful parish, these days. Untouched by the violence ripping apart our lands. Mostly, that is. I trust that your sudden arrival will not change the tranquillity of Templepatrick?"

Liam shook his head. "I'm finished with that life, Father," he said, the words echoing what he had once told his friend, Francis Bailey.

O'Keefe smiled knowingly, for Liam's promise meant little in this part of the world. They both knew that the past had a habit of catching up with you.

"Still," the clergyman went on, "the Church has always been a place of sanctuary for those in need."

He spread his hands apart, adding, "Welcome."

Liam breathed a sigh of relief, feeling the tension drain from his body.

"There is one condition, however, that is non-negotiable if you wish to stay here."

Liam raised his eyebrows.

Father O'Keefe held out one hand and made a grasping motion with his fingers.

"A total abstinence from alcohol and drugs is the first step to forgiveness, Sayeth the Lord. Hand the bottle over, young man."

Liam hesitated. The weight of a bottle in one's coat pocket was a constant and reassuring presence to a drunkard, and he was disinclined to part with it. He even entertained the idea of quickly swallowing the last dregs of brandy before turning it over.

He looked again at Father O'Keefe's hand.

He made a decision.

Mark Hobson
January – August 2022

Acknowledgements

This book would not have been possible without the support of a great many people. Rather than thank them all individually, I would instead prefer to say a huge thank you to this wonderful group as a whole. Their knowledge is vast and their enthusiasm always tremendously addictive.

However, there are a few that I'd like to single out.

Dr Joyce Peterson for her invaluable insights into the psychological makeup of murderers.

David Maseby, retired pathologist, for help with the trickier aspects of post-mortem procedure and the anatomy of human cadavers, as well as his wealth of knowledge on fly larvae gestation cycles.

Neil Gardiner (not his real name), former prison officer at HMP Wakefield.

To my good pal, Paul McGleenan, a friend of 27 years, as well as the late Bruce Trinh, who is never far from my thoughts. Our nights out became legendary and they inspired certain elements of the plot of *A Murmuration of Starlings.*

I also owe a deep debt to my editorial team at Harcourt Publishers, husband and wife Martin and Valerie Crofts, for their consistently high standard of copyediting prowess.

Thank you all from the bottom of my heart.

ABOUT THE AUTHOR

MARK HOBSON IS A WRITER AND HISTORIAN. HIS WORKS
SPAN NUMEROUS GENRES, FROM MILITARY HISTORY TO
CRIME THRILLERS AND SUPERNATURAL HORROR. HE HAS ALSO
WRITTEN NON-FICTION HISTORY BOOKS.

HE LIVES AT HOME IN YORKSHIRE WITH HIS 3 CATS.

facebook.com/yorkshirescribbler

BOOKS BY MARK HOBSON

WORLD QUAKE
GREY STONES
A MURMURATION OF STARLINGS

THE AMSTERDAM OCCULT SERIES
BOOK ONE – WOLF ANGEL
BOOK TWO – A STATE OF SIN

NOW MAY MEN WEEP – ISANDLWANA: A STORY FROM THE
ZULU WAR

NTOMBE 1879 (NON-FICTION)
ISANDLWANA – A MILITARY ENIGMA (NON-FICTION)

HARCOURT
PUBLISHERS

Mark Hobson

WORLD QUAKE

It was a day like any other. People setting out on the commute to work or taking the kids to school or chatting to their friends in the park. Normal. Routine. Nothing to mark it apart.

By lunchtime, everything they had ever known, every aspect of their lives, would be changed forever – marked by the most catastrophic series of global disasters to strike the planet in over 6000 years.

MANKIND STANDS AT THE GATES OF EXTINCTION

The world is being ripped apart by a great geological cataclysm. Cities crumble and entire continents disappear beneath the sea as earthquakes and mega-tsunamis lay waste to the land. For the human race there is no escape and nowhere to flee. Millions perish.

From the rubble, a disparate group of survivors emerge.

A school teacher hell-bent on finding his pregnant wife.

A scientist with the fate of the world in his hands.

The workforce of a power plant who fight to prevent a nuclear meltdown that would poison a nation for millennia.

While the politicians hide in their bunkers beneath London and Washington, these ordinary people will have to fight to stay alive in this new world, an existence blighted with violence, cruelty and death as they journey across a devastated landscape.

They must ask themselves profound questions about their own morality while humanity descends into chaos.

A new epoch in Earth's history is underway.

THIS IS THE AGE OF DEATH

AVAILABLE ON AMAZON ISBN: 9798795916309

GREY STONES

Carter Middleton returns to his childhood home in Yorkshire to bury his father and to reconnect with his estranged family. Yet, after fifteen years away, he quickly learns that the old bitterness and feuding that first drove him to leave is still as deeply rooted as ever. Others in Stansfield Bridge make it clear they want him gone too. His arrival stirs memories from the past, of events best forgotten, of secrets they would prefer kept hidden.

Jessica Bates has also come home. Years earlier, her mother left their caravan one evening and never returned. Her whereabouts remain a mystery to this day. Now Jessica is determined to get to the truth, whatever the consequences.

An act of brutal violence brings Carter and Jessica together. With steely resolve, they set out to investigate, soon unearthing terrible decades-old sins and revealing a darkness at the very heart of the community.

They soon discover that everything comes at a cost. Life is cheap in the countryside.

Set against the hard and unforgiving landscape of northern England, **GREY STONES** is a shocking tale of betrayal, revenge, loyalty and grief.

A SMOULDERING BUILD-UP TO A DRAMATIC AND TERRIFYING ENDING.
THIS IS A RARE BOOK. THE FLOW OF THE STORY KEPT ME ADDICTED.
NOT A RUN-OF-THE-MILL MURDER MYSTERY... I FOUND IT A GREAT READ.
WOW! WHAT AN AMAZING STORY.
AVAILABLE FROM AMAZON ISBN: 9798548418586

Mark Hobson

WOLF ANGEL
AMSTERDAM OCCULT SERIES
BOOK ONE

The City of Amsterdam is gripped with fear.
A series of brutal murders have left homicide detectives baffled.
With no motive or clues to work with, they find themselves probing
blindly through the city's dark and violent underworld.
But Inspector Pieter Van Dijk is not convinced this is the work of
one lone psychopath.
Drawn deeper and deeper into the shadowy heart of the case, he
unearths a terrifying history of family madness and occult conspiracy
echoing across the decades.

BRILLIANT... GRIPPING... A WELL-THOUGHT-OUT AND WELL-
WRITTEN BOOK.
A DARK STORY WITH LOTS OF ACTION.
THIS ISN'T JACKANORY.
THIS IS SIMPLY A GREAT READ WITH ALL THE ELEMENTS TO KEEP YOU
TURNING THE PAGE.
GRITTY DRAMA... WITH THE SUPERNATURAL ELEMENTS CLEVERLY
WOVEN IN.
INTRIGUE SOAKS OUT OF THE BRICKWORK OF AMSTERDAM'S
ALLEYWAYS.
AVAILABLE FROM AMAZON ISBN: 9798696036946
**For more info and news on upcoming releases please visit
www.occultseries.co.uk**

A STATE OF SIN
AMSTERDAM OCCULT SERIES
BOOK TWO

Three psychopaths are haunting the streets of Amsterdam this winter.
A doctor, who leaves his patients horribly disfigured.
A hunter from South Africa, determined to add to his collection of human trophies.
A kidnapper, who keeps his victim locked away in a small metal cage.
When Dutch cop Pieter Van Dijk answers what he thinks will be a routine call to investigate a case of arson, little does he realize the chain of terrifying events that are about to grip the city with icy fear.
Fresh back from a break of rest and recuperation, and trying hard to deal with the aftermath of a brutal case, he soon finds himself plunged deep into a new nightmare. What links the three crimes? Just who is behind them? And why does he feel that this time the answers hinge on his own past?
From the snowy alleyways of Amsterdam to the frigid shores of the North Sea, the hunt to put a stop to the rampage of murder and bloodshed soon becomes a race against time. Because one thing he has learned over the years is that Amsterdam is a city of shadows, hiding the worst in human nature.

THERE ARE SEVERAL HIGHLY DISTURBING SCENES THAT GAVE ME CHILLS.
VERY HIGHLY RESEARCHED AND WOVEN TOGETHER WITH LAYERS OF HISTORY... A GRIPPING CRIME DRAMA.
AVAILABLE FROM AMAZON ISBN: 9798724812566
For more info and news on upcoming releases please visit www.occultseries.co.uk

Mark Hobson

NOW MAY MEN WEEP
ISANDLWANA
A STORY FROM THE ZULU WAR

JANUARY 1879 – ZULULAND

Lord Chelmsford, commander of British forces in South Africa, leads an invasion into Zululand. At the head of his main spearhead column, he expects a quick and decisive campaign against a poorly armed, ill-disciplined force of tribesmen. To achieve this aim he has with him the veteran soldiers from the 24th Regiment, 'Old Sweats, as they are referred to, men with years of campaigning behind them. Just days into the invasion Chelmsford's force sets up camp beside a strangely-shaped crag, barely a few miles from the safety of the British Colony of Natal.
The battle that develops in the shadow of that mountain, with British redcoats fighting hand-to-hand with their Zulu foe, will become the stuff of legend.
It is a story punctuated with acts of incredible courage and heroism and moving sacrifice, a human drama that will shock the world.
ISANDLWANA!

I FEEL LIKE I'M PRESENT AT THE BATTLE OF ISANDLWANA.
PAGE-TURNING EXCITEMENT... RIPPING YARNS 21ST CENTURY STYLE!
CAPTURES THE TERROR... GRIPPING MOMENTS OF ACTION.
AVAILABLE FROM AMAZON ISBN: 9798666828472
Please follow my author's Facebook page at
facebook.com/yorkshirescribbler

A Murmuration of Starlings

WHAT READERS ARE SAYING ABOUT MARK HOBSON'S BOOKS

I COULDN'T PUT GREY STONES DOWN... A GREAT READ – **GREY STONES**

THIS IS A GREAT STORY AND SERVES AS A GREAT SETUP FOR THE SERIES
WOLF ANGEL (AMSTERDAM OCCULT SERIES BOOK 1)

MARK HOBSON BUILDS UP THE TENSION NICELY WITH RARELY A DULL
MOMENT – **WOLF ANGEL (AMSTERDAM OCCULT SERIES BOOK 1)**

YOU HAVE THE INGREDIENTS FOR AN EXCITING THRILLER... GREAT
READING – **A STATE OF SIN (AMSTERDAM OCCULT SERIES BOOK 2)**

HAD ME GRIPPED FROM THE VERY START, I HIGHLY RECOMMEND THIS
BOOK – **A STATE OF SIN (AMSTERDAM OCCULT SERIES BOOK 2)**

I COULD NOT PUT THE BOOK DOWN. IT IS A REAL PAGE-TURNER THAT IS
FOR SURE – **NOW MAY MEN WEEP**

YOU FEEL YOU ARE THERE WITH THE SOLDIERS, FEELING THEIR FEAR AND
PAIN... ABSOLUTELY BRILLIANT – **NOW MAY MEN WEEP**

WELL WRITTEN AND VERY FRIGHTENING... WELL-DEVELOPED
CHARACTERS AND A GREAT STORYLINE – **WORLD QUAKE**

A REAL PAGE-TURNER OR FINGER-SWIPER – **WORLD QUAKE**

LOVED THIS DISASTER NOVEL, WELL RESEARCHED WITH LOTS OF ACTION
WORLD QUAKE

Printed in Great Britain
by Amazon

84497569R00192